A LITTLE ADO ABOUT LOVE

EMILY CHILDS

A LITTLE ADO ABOUT LOVE

Emily Childs

CHAPTER 1

"*Think about this, Elle," Auntie Kathy said, my keys in her hand, well out of reach. She wasn't my aunt, but everyone in the department called the director of nursing, Auntie. "Really think about this, sweetie."*

I made a swipe for the keys, but the woman was six foot; it was a hard miss.

"Give me my keys."

Kathy shook her head. "No, not unless you promise me you're using them to drive away, and not to carve some cuss word on the side of his car door, sugar."

"Fine, I'll write tool, or jerk-off . . . or—hic—bald . . . baldness," I sobbed.

"Baldness? That's creative."

Swiping salty rivers from my face, I offered a guttural attempt at a laugh, but it set off a gush of more tears. "You . . . know he's afraid o-o-of . . ." My face pinched as I covered my eyes with my hand and the final words escaped as a wail. "Of receding hairlines!"

I know Kathy didn't want to laugh, and there were a few grunts made to try and stop the sound, but her pleasant chuckle came anyway. "Oh, Elle, take a breath, sugar plum."

"I can't! Let me do this, Kath, please give me this last thing."

Kathy curled her fingers around my keys, and tightened her dark lips into an aunt-worthy frown. "You're better than this. I know this is tough, but I went to bat for you. I've got y'all set up. Don't ruin those chances on some whim and a misdemeanor!"

Burning tears squeezed from the corners of my eyes as I puffed a few times to keep the sob buried inside. "I don't understand why I can't . . . stay."

Kathy wrapped me in her thick arms. Her touch was like smooth cocoa on Christmas morning. "Oh, sugar plum, I know it's not fair. Not one bit, but the dog is an exec, and . . . well, I tried."

Running my hand under my nose, I nodded and pulled away. Plus, I liked that she called him a dog. "I know you did, Kath."

She cupped my chin and smiled so her dark complexion gleamed in the sunlight. "You've got this, girl. You hear me?"

"I feel like I'm being run out of my home," I admitted.

"Pumpkin, home is where your heart is, and you're going to find that again."

I offered a watery laugh. "I don't think Lindström is where my heart is."

"You never know. I'm a believer of things happening for a reason. Besides, you know that girl, karma, she's a . . . well, you know what she is."

I wiped the sticky run from my nose again and laughed. Kathy was the quintessential cusser, to the point her husband had a bet she couldn't go an entire week without letting one slip. She was on day four.

"Oh, come here." She wrapped me up again. "Don't lower yourself now. Don't you dare."

"How do I do this, Kath?"

"With your head held high, sugar. With your head held high."

I nodded, but didn't feel the same confidence. The phone call would be the hardest. I could already hear the silence on the other end as I asked—gulp— my parents in Lindström, Minnesota if I could move back home.

Pulling out my scratched phone, my fingers trembled as I tapped the numbers.

Here goes nothing.

* * *

TEN YEARS. That's how long I've had my driver's license, so you can imagine it is more than a little embarrassing having my mother drop me off by the curb.

"We're going out with Maya and Graham tonight," she says without looking at me.

"Oh, what time?"

"You'll still be at work, I'm sure."

My mouth tightens, but I keep my voice light. "Those blasted twelve-hour shifts."

Folding the driver seat mirror, her attention locks on me like a missile. For two seconds she fusses with my long braid and tsks. "You didn't dry your hair?"

"I didn't have time. I'm not here to impress anyone with my hair."

Mom shrugs and taps the steering wheel. "I know that sort of thing hasn't ever been a priority for you; I just thought it being your first day and all . . ."

With a sigh, I close my eyes and smack my head on the headrest. "Mom, can we not?"

"What?" she asks innocently, even adding a dramatic shoulder shrug for good measure. "I'm just saying, I think you'll feel better about things if you . . . spruce up a bit sometimes. Maya says you could have as much time in the salon as you wanted."

I steal a stick of chewing gum from her open purse and shake my head. "Curling, dyeing, or extending my hair isn't going to solve this. I better go. Wish me luck."

"I doubt you'll need luck," she says with a scoff. "You've been working in the exact setting for the last six years."

I roll my eyes. Call me immature, but the ten-minute drive has worn me down so much that my inner teenager can't resist. Adjusting the woolen satchel Auntie Kathy gave me over my shoulder, I open the passenger door and practically leap out. "It's just an expression, Mom. Thanks for the ride; I'll see you later." *Have fun with my successful sister and her perfect husband without me.* That's what I should have said.

Mom offers a wave that I meekly return before squaring toward the towering building. A natural smile tugs at my lips and it seems easier to breathe now that I'm out of the car and on the sidewalk. The start to a new chapter is about to begin, wet braid and all.

A pungent wall of antiseptic, latex gloves, and a touch of greasy fried chicken accosts my nose as the north doors slide open. Golden sun paints gilded ribbons on the floor tiles, and although each busy bee bustling about hardly acknowledges anyone else, it feels like the heavens welcome me to my new beginning. I utter a silent thanks to Kathy. I won't spoil her efforts to help me out.

Closing my eyes, I take a moment to embrace the new opportunity. Maybe I release my breath too dramatically because when I crack one eye, I meet the stare of a squirrely woman seated at the front desk whose granola bar is paused halfway to her mouth. Certain my cheeks are as pink as cherries, I realize my mini meditation has blocked traffic through the doors. In front of me, a quizzical nursing assistant grips a wheelchair with a woman clutching her newborn. Even the baby hushes, adding to the thick awkwardness. I smile and step to the left, only to smash against a man gripping blue balloons, a stuffed diaper bag, and a novel of hospital paperwork.

"Whoops, sorry," I say as I step back toward the outside walk.

"Watch it," says a supplier pushing a towering cart of metal oxygen tanks.

"Sorry."

I jump to the side and bounce back and forth like a fly against a glass window as I try to clear the path. My satchel slips off one shoulder and succumbs to the weight of the moving wheelchair. Slats from the rubber mat create indentations in the chevron pattern, as the wheels squish overtop, along with a nice streak of dirt from some muddy shoe.

"Oh, sorry," says the assistant, but she doesn't stop her errand of freeing the new parents into the wild.

I wave her off. What else can I do before the earth swallows me whole? After an eternity of my clumsy dance I'm able to stand straight. Okay, so the new beginning had a rocky start. It's only eight in the morning; all it will take is trying again.

With a shrug, I secure the braided strap of my bag and take my first, successful step over the threshold. Clearly, I've mistaken my celestial welcome to North Lindström General Hospital. The bustle catches hold of me as I drift into the lobby, and I immediately become nothing more than a piece of the hive. True, one person might be a small part of the hive, but I can play my part—and I am determined to play it well.

"Hi there," I say with a grin to my squirrely front desk friend. Living in North Carolina for the last ten years gave me the right to claim the sort of accent southern mamas dream of for their little ones. It suits, since growing up I sounded too much like our Canadian neighbors for dear old Dad, and too Western for Mom. If I can't be a proper Minnesotan, then I'll be southern. "I'm looking for Orthopedics. It's my first day."

The woman offers a nod, never saying a word about the front entrance debacle. She spins her chair and returns with a blue lanyard. The plastic card on the end is unremarkable, with the simple word *visitor* printed on one side. "Head to the second floor, and just after the therapy gym on your left, you'll see the front desk. They'll make sure to set you up."

"Great." I guess I have too much chirp because the woman lifts a brow again. I don't know what to say, so I blurt out, "I'm a nurse."

"I can see that," she says; her eyes scan my new charcoal scrubs. I think they look shiny and professional. She doesn't seem too impressed. "Well, welcome. Hope you enjoy working with Lindström General."

Don't sound too thrilled. I determine her lethargic tone doesn't matter; even the waltz with the maternity ward isn't going to ruin this for me. This is a new day and I take to the elevators with an extra skip to my step.

After ten years, I'm back home, if I even know what that word means. Truth told, I left for a reason, you know, to spread my wings. I figured a decade offered plenty of time to forget a face. So, maybe I'm starting anew in someplace old, but I have serious doubts anyone will recognize me. I count that on my list of positives.

Standing in the elevator as it buzzes though the walls, I inspect my overgrown roots in the shiny aluminum. Maybe I ought to take my sister up on her offer to visit her salon. She always says I can't let dark hair fade, especially since I have the stormy blue eyes. I guess that adds to my washed-out look that drives her insane. Those eyes aren't so starry-eyed now. Not like they once were. Since leaving Lindström, life has taught me a thing or two.

Maybe I'm not the beauty queen like Maya, with her high cheekbones, perfect brows, and hips that will make an hourglass jealous. But I don't need the endless reminders on how I need to fix me, you know?

I inherited the round face, with a smile that always crinkles my nose and reveals my top gums. My hips . . . well, my hands always have a place to rest without a problem. Late night study sessions in nursing school around pizza boxes developed into a lifestyle. I'm a jogger and carbs are a way of life for runners. Even cheesy carbs.

The elevator doors ding and open. I can't help smiling as I step onto the quieter floor. If anything is home, it is this hallway. Surrounded by wide corridors with beautiful canvas paintings of the city on the walls, I am promptly reminded of where I truly belong.

As I round a large potted plant, I hear laughter and faint music from across the hallway. What would an orthopedic wing in a hospital be without the cheerful therapy staff to work those broken bones and joints? I stop to enjoy the scene in the gym for a few breaths—I have seven minutes until the start of my shift, and the front desk is only ten feet away. There is time.

Patients with bandages on knees, hips, shoulders—anywhere you can imagine—lift weights, struggle up boxy stairs built specifically for treatment, or shed tears as therapists torture with smiles on their faces. I've always been a little envious of the relaxed environment on the therapeutic side; especially days when I'll dart between room calls and medications and skin checks. My shoulders slump simply thinking of the unavoidable rush.

"Whoa, hold up, Lou. Excuse us, coming through."

You know those voices that just sound handsome? The excuser

behind me has one of those voices.

I back out of the doorway with a smile, and turn to find a therapist facing his patient; a tall man with two thick bandages lining twin scars over his kneecaps. The patient grins at me before he leans onto a silver walker and winces with each step.

"Doing great," I say and back up, so the therapist can squeeze past.

The guy flashes me a white smile and my lungs topple out the soles of my feet. By the way his eyes widen, and he chuckles, I imagine he feels much the same.

"Are you kidding me? Elle, is that you?" He pauses and turns to his patient. "Take a rest, Lou—yeah, in the chair, buddy."

The older patient obeys and plops into a narrow chair against the wall with a grateful sigh. My heart stomps in my chest like a toddler having a tantrum. What a romantic notion that no one from my 'back then' would recognize me. But why does it have to be him?

"Axel Olsen," I say after the frog leaps out of my throat. "Wow, it's been a long time. You look . . . the same."

Lies! All lies. Axel Olsen isn't the same lanky teenager I'd known. No, since the fates of Lindström have a vendetta against me, he's transformed into a man, all tone, and sinew, and woodsy aftershave.

"Really?" Axel says with a raised brow as he surveys his biceps. "I don't know, I think I've changed a little."

Allow me to shed some light on Axel: my high school heartthrob, turned heartbreaker. Swallowing the bitter pill after scanning his chiseled face, I am forced to admit that handsome no longer belongs only to his voice.

He tilts his head so the sunlight brightens those pale blue eyes that have always taken my breath away. The sun announces my arrival on the first floor, now the heavens betray me by casting such a delightful glow on such a delightful face. To make matters worse, the man still has the same alluring smile I forgot existed.

Don't think of his lips, Elle.

Any woman with eyes would have sudden dry mouth too; it isn't just me. He smiles, knowing he's won whatever competition starts to brew between us. I should have stomped my heel on his toes for causing my pulse to bruise my skull from its beat. Don't let that face of utter perfection fool you, Axel isn't a one girl sort of guy. I'd thought—in my naïve seventeen-year-old mind—that we were different during those months of high school love. Pathetic, I know. But I'm not seventeen anymore and I can practically smell what sort of guy Axel still is with his smirk; even the way he leans against the wall. Put bluntly, he isn't the sort I plan to suffer raging heartrates over.

"Right, well I've got to get going."

Axel glances at the nurses' station. He takes in my new scrubs and white tennis shoes. "Wait, are you working here? I thought you lived in Tennessee or something."

"North Carolina," I say and take my first steps in the opposite direction. "I moved home, and yes, I'm starting work. Good to see you, but I'd hate to be late on the first day."

Axel nods and his fierce eyes drill a hole to my soul as if he is reading every secret thought. "Okay." He helps Lou the patient stand from the chair, so I get one final glimpse of those arms, and inches toward the gym. "See you around, Elle."

"Maybe," I say over my shoulder, trying to sound as off limits as possible.

"Oh, I'll see you around," he says again.

Is that a challenge or a promise? Either way, he has some nerve. The fog in my head distracts me enough that I strike my hip against the corner of the nurses' station. I'm not sure, but it sounds like Axel chuckles before he disappears into the gym with Lou grumbling at his side.

Resting my open palm on the nurses' desk, I force down the truth that I will be stuck working next door to another man who pulverized my heart. For months I've practiced positivity, maybe balancing the line of hippie a little too closely, but I'm starting to think this day is doomed.

Hoping for one last shot at epic coworkers, I drum my fingers until a nurse with spiky hair lifts her gaze.

"Hi, I'm Elle," I say. "I'm supposed to start today."

She smiles, and my mother would call her grin gummy, just like she calls mine. I happen to like her smile.

"Perfect!" She shoves away from the desk and hurries to the outside before I know what's happening. Taking my hands in hers she bounces on her toes. I mimic because who doesn't enjoy a dance party in the hallway? "I'm so excited you're here." She bends at her knees to emphasize each word.

"Me, too." Finally. A person who lifts the weight of returning home rather than adding to the load.

"Come on." She leads me through a door toward the back office. "I'll show you around and introduce you. I'm Viv, by the way. You've gone through orientation, right?"

"Yep, finished last weekend."

"Great. You'll be following me around, just to get the hang of the wing. I'm sure you'll be great on your own by the end of shift. It's the documentation system that's a little tricky."

Viv chatters as she introduces me to each nurse, assistant, and a few surgeons wandering the halls. Two hours in, I feel at ease doing what I love again. Viv is friendly and open—probably telling me more about her boyfriend's habits than I need to know—but she helps me feel right at home.

Home. The hard truth is, it wasn't my choice to return to Lindström. Life is funny that way. When one door closes, isn't another one supposed to open? Well, in my case, the back of U-Haul opened. With my tail between my legs, three suitcases, and more than one *I told you so*, I came home.

The sun is set by the time I leave the orthopedic wing. I stretch my neck and offer a swift glance at the therapy gym, which is now locked. Taking a long guzzle of water from my bottle, I pretend I didn't look, hoping to catch a glimpse at one annoyingly tempting therapist.

In my cynical opinion, home is a place that warms your heart, only to crumble at the first gust of fierce wind. I'm not about to let another house crumble. This time I'll be cautious.

No matter how attractive blasts from the past might be, allowing anyone to mess with my clean slate simply isn't worth the risk.

CHAPTER 2

*B*us exhaust blows in my face as I hurry down the steps. I cough and wave away the rank air. Even with the smells and bubblegum stuck to my scrubs from my seat, the bus seems the least dramatic way to get to work. Until I can get a car, that is. My fingers twitch in anticipation with thoughts of the weekend. My brother-in-law already assured me he'll play the part of my chauffeur and take me to Minneapolis to hit as many dealerships as we can before the day's end. After the car, I'll be on the hunt for an apartment. For that, I can't wait.

Lindström main is getting ready to close shop for the night. I've always loved window shopping in the little Scandinavian stores. Each is part of the spirit that made up the city. I mean, we Webers are German, but no one needs to know that.

The air has a bite to it. Tugging the thin jacket from my bag, I take in the changes to my hometown. I haven't been home in almost four years. Some things have changed; a few shops boast different names, fancier streetlamps, even a few new buildings that stick out against the older shops. Savory smells waft from *Snyder's Bistro* and I have half a mind to enjoy a late-night Reuben. Maybe tomorrow. Besides, there is a delectable whiff of caramelized sugar and dough. And that can only be my favorite bakery. *Clara's Chokola*—wait? I tilt my head—*Clara's* isn't there anymore.

Taking an about-face, I search for the rival bakery, *Hanna's*. Staring back at me is a large sign that reads *Scandinavian Market*, and has a rainbow of different Scandinavian flags behind the text.

What happened to the Olsen's bakery? Yes, as in Axel Olsen. I'm not specifically looking for Axel—I just happen to enjoy his family's heavenly treats. The bakery once was my favorite stop on the way to school, and now it's gone.

I've been gawking too long because I don't even notice the lights flicker off in the new market, or the side door jingle as it opens.

Laughter catches my attention and I consider it might be time to take a hard look at my dozing sessions in public. When the couple leaving the market rounds the corner of the building, at first glance I see Axel laughing with an attractive brunette on his arm. My heart cramps, but when I take a closer, rather tentative second look, it isn't Axel.

Close enough, since the man with the same shape to his face is his twin.

Jonas Olsen meets my eye, his brow furrows, then he smiles shyly. If I remember right, Jonas isn't the outgoing half of the pair, so I take the initiative and wave. "Hi, Jonas."

"Elle!" It isn't Jonas who squeals my name, but from his lady friend.

"Brita? Oh, my gosh," I say.

She prances over and hugs me briefly. When she slips her fingers into Jonas's, I'm a little embarrassed that my mouth drops like a trout.

Brita doesn't seem to mind, or even notice. "It's been so long." She beams at me.

"Yeah, it's been a while. But what's up with—" I wag my finger between them, "all this? I never thought I'd see this day where a Jacobson and Olsen could walk down the street together."

Brita laughs, and Jonas smiles, though his cheeks flush. In Lindström, it's no secret that Brita's family and the Olsens aren't friendly, well, at least last I checked. I considered Brita a casual friend in high school, she'd been a grade younger, but we'd played softball together and I remember her many bouts of frustration in the dugout over the feud.

Clearly, going dark on social media really did mean you miss out on major changes, like Brita Jacobson snuggling up with Jonas Olsen, and the disappearance of two major bakeries.

"Water under the bridge now," Brita tells me. "Are you in town long? We should meet up and I'll fill you in. I'd love to hear about living down south."

"I actually moved back, but I'd love to catch up." My eyes drift to the diamond on her finger. I'm pretty sure my eyes bug out of my head. "Wait, you two are . . . when did this happen?"

"We just had our second anniversary," Jonas says, wrapping an arm around Brita's shoulders.

"You're kidding?" I grin, curious how wedding bells came from such a warzone. "Congratulations two years late."

Brita beams and nuzzles closer to Jonas. "Thanks. So, what brings you back home?"

I open my mouth to answer with my practiced response, but words are lost in my throat when the door jingles again.

"Grandpa, it isn't a big deal. Just let me help a bit. You'll feel better."

"You think I don't know my own knees?" a thick Danish accent follows.

"I didn't say that."

"Let it go, Viggo," another voice in broken English adds. "You move slower than a *sköldpadda*. Let the boy look at you."

"Well, you hunch and trudge slower than—"

"Alright, easy you two." How I wish I ran when I had the chance. Axel rounds the corner—still dressed in his therapy polo and nametag —followed by two old men leaning on identical canes. Axel's brilliant pale eyes lock on me in another heartbeat, and that same toe-curling smile curls the corner of his mouth. "Are you following me, Elle?"

One of the old men tries to smack the back of Axel's head, but Axel stands tall and out of reach.

I scoff, tightening my grip on the strap of my bag until my palm starts to sweat. "Please, I can find better things to do with my time."

Axel's smile doesn't fade, but my palms grow wetter. "I was heading home and ran into Jonas and Brita."

"Right," Axel says, shoving his hands in his pockets. "Watch out for these two, they never stop touching."

"Stop," Brita laughs, and she swats his arm.

"It's true."

Shrugging, Brita rests her head on Jonas's shoulder. "Maybe a little. When did you and Axel meet up?"

"We didn't meet up," I reply too quickly. "I . . . we ran into each other at the hospital."

"Elle's a new nurse in my wing," Axel says with a touch of smugness. Still the same cocky guy I knew before.

Brita winces and pats my arm. "You have to work with Ax? I'm sorry."

"Hey, watch it." Axel flicks her ponytail.

"I'm teasing, but I think that's great." Brita glimpses over her shoulder at the taller of the two old men. "Farfar, why are you and Viggo even still here? I'm warning you both, you need to stay out of the shop tomorrow."

"Ack," says one of the old men. "It's our shop."

"I know, and none of us are afraid of locking either of you outside."

Brita's grandfather mutters in Swedish under his breath, but he pats her cheek, then Jonas's, even Axel earns a pinch from the man before he mutters all the way into the house attached to the bakery.

"Come on, grandpa," Jonas says. "We'll walk you home."

"I can walk."

"That's not what Axel says."

Brita muffles a laugh behind her hand when Viggo shoots his cane in the air and curses the stars for such pesky grandsons.

"It's good to see you, Elle. I'm serious about lunch," she says before they cross the street.

"Let's do it."

I've always liked Brita, and most of my friends have moved on, had families, or careers. I've lost touch with everyone. Yes, everyone. So, having girl talk outside my own family sounds amazing.

The fuzzy feeling disappears once I realize Axel is standing two feet away. And we're alone.

I rock on my heels, offer a tight smile, before clapping my hands together because this can't get any more awkward. "Well," I say. "I better get going."

"Want a ride?" he asks, nodding to a silver Honda.

"No, I'm fine. It's just down the road."

"I know."

Prickling heat tickles around my neck. Of course, Axel would know my parents' house. "It's okay."

"Alright, well then I'm walking with you. It's ten thirty; you're not walking alone."

I snort. "You aren't serious."

"Dead serious," he says, and points his car key toward the Honda. "So, car . . . walk . . . you choose."

Play it cool. I don't even remember how to be myself sometimes.

"Uh . . . walk, I guess."

"Good choice. It's going to start getting cold at night; we might as well enjoy it while we can."

Axel locks his car and shoves his hands in his pockets again, then joins me on the sidewalk. We keep quiet until the next block. The slap of our feet on the pavement stacks the tension. I ought to say something, right?

"So, what happened to the bakery?" A good opener. Neutral. What any common acquaintances might talk about. I swallow past a lump in my throat. Overthinking one sentence—I feel like life has turned me into something less than human. I hardly can interact with people. Or maybe just people like Axel. Either way, I can't get my brain to stop reeling.

Axel turns to meet my eye, before glancing over his shoulder at the shop. "Oh, you mean when did they combine?"

I nod. Better not risk dissecting another comment.

"I guess a little over three years ago. It took some time getting the plans made and additions to the Jacobson's building to accommodate our bakery, but it's worked out well."

14

"I thought your families hated each other."

Axel smirks. "Thank Jonas and Brita for fixing that. The new market has gotten busy enough that—get ready for this—they've even hired help from outside the families."

I can't keep my laugh in. Knowing what I do from my time dating Axel and tossing softballs with Brita, the two patriarchs are about the stubbornest bulls on the block. "I never thought I'd see the day. So, what is it that Brita is going to lock them out for then?"

"Oh, they're both turning eighty this year. Brita is coming in to make some of the party desserts and doesn't want them to see. I have a feeling they'll both find a way to sneak in."

I laugh again and wish I didn't feel so comfortable. I need to be on my guard. "Sounds fun."

Silence settles naturally.

Two houses from mine, Axel clears his throat. I might be losing my mind, but it's like some of the smug I'm-every-woman's-wildest-fantasy tone has left his voice. "So, what made you pick nursing? I didn't know you worked in healthcare." Axel faces me, walking backward. "I think it's a good choice for you."

"What makes you say that?"

He turns right again, and ushers me to cross the road first when my house comes into view. "Didn't you take some early college classes? I just have this memory of you checking my blood pressure. I don't know, you were good at helping people, so I think nursing is a solid choice."

Life has taught me to keep my heart close and never trust another with its care, so instead of brimming with all the swoons, I frown. "I didn't think you'd noticed much about me back then."

His brows knit together, but his eyes only brighten, like a clear, blue lake. "I noticed things. That was called a compliment, by the way."

I stop in front of the white, wooden gate surrounding my parents' front yard and try to play nice. "Thanks, I guess. I am happy as a nurse, but to be honest, I didn't expect to see you as a physical therapist."

"Why is that?"

"Oh, I always imagined you as some hot-shot sales guy, sweet-talking, and driving a Mercedes or something."

He laughs easily, but Axel has always been a tease and quick to smile. "Sales? No thank you, I'd claw my eyes out. I wanted to be a therapist when we were together, now who's the one not noticing?"

My throat feels like a knot in a straw. The first acknowledgement that we've been together once—but admitting the past only reminds me of why we aren't together. "Sorry, it was a full-time job keeping up with all the other girls you were trying to date to focus on what you wanted to major in."

Axel clutches his chest, but one corner of his mouth twists in a sly grin. "Ouch. Still witty as ever, Ellie."

I drag in a sharp breath through my nose, so the air whistles. Nose whistles are worse than snorting. No one, and I mean no one, calls me Ellie—not since Axel. A shudder runs down my spine, and I can't even find the gumption to correct the folly. Maybe because I'm angry, or maybe because I like it.

"I'm going to go inside." How elegantly stated. My voice is mousy next to Axel, all soft and wrong.

"Okay. Are you on tomorrow?"

I unlock the gate and hustle behind its safety. "Yep."

"I guess, I'll see you then."

"Okay."

Axel is still smiling. What can he possibly smile about? Surely, he noticed how uncomfortable this was.

He steps away from the gate. "Sleep well, Elle."

I shoot a glare over my shoulder. He laughs at me. The man has some nerve—repeating our stupid little rhyme, a decade old. He thinks our past is nothing but a joke, well the joke is on him because . . . well, just because I'm not going to fall for his charm, or wit, or ultra-attractive eyes. Turning my back on all that makes Axel Olsen . . . Axel. I wave without turning around and swiftly unlock my front door, slamming my back to the wall once I am safely tucked inside. I close my eyes.

Oh, I really don't like Axel. Not because he is rude, or he broke my teenage heart, no I don't like him because he is a threat to each wall I've strategically placed around my heart. And I don't know why.

When I left North Carolina, I promised myself life would be happily lived on my own; men could keep a solid distance. Axel is a fluke, a shudder-causing, stomach-twirling fluke. In truth, I haven't thought of him in years, but here he is, still chiseled and charming and . . . *gah!*

For goodness sake, I don't even know if he is single! I didn't see a ring, but that means nothing. Tonight, walking me home could have simply been a gentlemanly gesture. For all I know, he was on his way back to his wife and kids by now.

I hope not, because he looked at me that way—you know—the way that makes your heart flutter like a caged bird?

No. I definitely do not like Axel Olsen.

CHAPTER 3

Somehow the hot water is already spent at six in the morning. Goosebumps dot every inch of my body as I briskly shampoo my hair. Forget conditioner, I can live with a little frizz. I shiver as I wrap a chunky towel in place. Leaning over the counter, I groan and poke the fresh, puffy bags pillowing beneath my eyes.

After surviving the walk home with Axel, I'd tried to calm my racing mind by reading. With the intent to read one chapter, time wound up with me wide awake at one in the morning, gnawing my thumbnail to see if the tormented hero got the girl in the end. He does.

Half-dressed, I hurry back into my room, but shriek and clutch my sopping towel against my body when my door swings open without warning.

"Maya!" My sister casually strolls toward my window and pulls open the blinds. "What are you doing? I'm not dressed."

I rush to return the blinds to properly closed.

"Good morning," she says, drawing out the word so she almost moos. "Really, Elle, I've seen you in a bra. You don't need to be so shy."

"Oh, you know, I just thought a little thing called privacy was still

18

socially acceptable," I snap and tug my scrub top over my head, my hair drenching the collar straightaway.

How is it that Maya is catwalk ready so early? Her plum lips are, well, plumped; her auburn hair is styled and tucked behind one ear, and the cutesy sweater hanging off one shoulder looks too amazing to be properly appreciated when the sun isn't even certain it wants to rise yet.

Maya flutters her long lashes. "You're so dramatic sometimes, Elle."

"What do you need? In fact, why are you here?"

"I came to help Mom pick out her new carpet. You know I'm good with colors."

"Right," I say as I slip on my tennis shoes and rush back into the bathroom down the hallway. My childhood home isn't large, making it simple to shout into my bedroom from my place at the mirror. "I didn't know carpet picking started at the crack of dawn."

I hear Maya scoff. "We're going to a new coffee shop and running a few errands before." She saunters down the hallway; her ballerina flats hardly making a sound, she's so graceful. Leaning against the door frame she watches me sloppily draw on eyeliner. "I wish you could come."

I flash a quick smile, wrapping my hair in a messy bun at the base of my neck. My sister doesn't try to hide her disapproval. "That's okay," I say. "You know it's not really my thing."

"I know, I just . . ." she steeples her fingers over her lips and pauses. Great, a lecture is coming. "I would love to see you get back out there, Elle. You spend all your time alone in your room."

I slip on one tennis shoe, bouncing on one leg back into my room; the stubborn shoelace hardly budges. "Not true. I was at your house four days ago. Want me to drop in all the time?"

"Not out there with family, but with other people," Maya says, following.

"I'm about to spend the next twelve and a half hours with a lot of people." I bustle around, gathering snack bars into my satchel, because lunch isn't always certain in the nursing world.

"You're purposefully avoiding what I'm trying to say," Maya says.

She loses a bit of her charm when she rolls her eyes. "Fine, I get it. But just remember we want the best for you and you're going to wind up making the same mistakes if you keep doing what you're doing."

"Doing what? I've only been here for—" I shoot a look at the cat calendar my mom hangs in my room each year, even if the room is empty—"Okay, for six weeks." The pitch in my voice is aiming for critical levels. I take some deep breaths, drawing my thudding pulse back to normal. Getting emotional wouldn't do any good.

"My point exactly. What have you done in that time?"

"Um, gotten a job, tried to clean up a mess left behind . . ."

"I know, but how many times do I need to invite you to the salon? Or to go with me and my friends. You don't even seem grateful for what we've done."

Deep breaths. "Maya, I'm grateful. I've been focused on getting back to work and finding a place, that's all."

My sister sighs, but gives me one of her motherly smiles, clapping her hands on top of my shoulders. I'll be fifty years-old and Maya will still look at me like I'm some little bird that fell from the nest. "Don't be defensive when we try to help, Elle. Okay?"

I smile, but add a deliberate crinkle to my face so mother hen will know my special touch of sarcasm is just for her. "I'll sure try."

Maya tosses her hands in the air. "See, this is exactly what I'm talking about."

"Okay, what can I do?" I ask, stomping back to the bathroom to brush my teeth. "What would make you happy?"

Maya doesn't spout off the typical answer of 'whatever makes you happy', no, she takes a moment to think about her response. "Double with me and Graham. A guy from his office is out of town, but coming home in a little over a week; we could go then."

"Thanks, but no," I mumble through a mouthful of toothpaste.

"I swear to stop bugging you if you come."

Gurgle. Spit. "Who is it, Maya. I'm not going out with some stranger."

She grins as if I've already said yes. Knowing Maya, she likely assumes I have. "He knows Graham, Elle. That's got to be good enough, right? Oh, you'll love him. I think you'll hit it off."

"Have you already arranged it?"

She shrugs. "I might have mentioned you a few times. Come on, you'll have a great time."

"Really? What makes you think we're a match made in heaven?"

"Well, you've both been through similar things. He's older than you, and he's taller."

"Fabulous, everything I need in a man," I say.

"Can you ever *not* be sarcastic?"

"I'm sorry, but it hasn't been that long, and I'd rather make sure I'm settled before getting out there again." I'm not going to get out there again, but I appease my sister so she'll leave my space.

"One date, Elle. That's all I'm asking."

I bite my bottom lip as I sling my jacket over my shoulders. "Then you'll stop pestering me and let me live my grown-up life all on my own."

She holds up a palm and covers her heart. "I swear."

I free a kind of growling noise because I have a flare for dramatics, but nod. "Fine, one date. That's all, Maya."

Maya squeals and her feet dance a bit before she flings her arms around me and squeals again. "Thank you! Okay, but you need to come to the salon. Seriously, Elle. How long has it been since you had a trim?"

I shirk her off, snickering. "I agreed to a date, not a makeover."

"Yeah, I don't care, I'm going to put Stacy on your case. She's excellent with damaged hair."

I lead the way down the stairs, with Maya hot on my tail. "My case? I'm not a crime zone."

"The fact that you've let your hair go this long is a crime."

Don't get the wrong idea about my older sister, she says the last part with a smile and flick to my ear. Maya is simply passionate—about a lot of things. Hair, style, and beauty among those passions.

We slip into the kitchen shoulder to shoulder, neither of us willing to let the other go first. Why my family opts to rise before their alarms is beyond me. Mom hurries around with a plate of turkey bacon. Public service announcement: turkey bacon is not bacon.

"Hiya, Dad," Maya says and presses a kiss to my father's balding head.

"Morning," he grumbles, flicking the newspaper.

The scene reminds me of an old 1950s sitcom. Mom hands my dad a mug of steaming joe, my father's eyeglasses slide halfway down his nose as he catches up on current events. The two obedient daughters sit down to a hot breakfast. All we need is the cheery housekeeper and some puffy skirts.

"How are you feeling today, Dad?" I ask, and snatch a low-carb English muffin. Not delicious, but who am I to complain, living rent-free in my parents' home?

He tips his dark eyes over the edge of the paper, before offering his half grin and shaking his head. "You going to ask me every day?"

"Until you die, yes."

"Elle, don't say it like that," Mom says as she pours a mug for herself.

"Don't drink too much, Mom," Maya whines. "We're going to try those new pink lattes, remember?"

"I'll save room."

Dad waves the comments away and looks at me with less grumble, and more gleam to his expression. "I'm fine, E."

"Good." I spread something that isn't really butter and coat the cardboard muffin. "You understand that I'll know if you aren't following the doctor's orders."

"I have three pushy women in my life, girl, do you think there's any chance I'd get away with not following orders?"

I laugh and nudge his elbow. He gives me his famous half-grin and returns to reading. Dad is gruff and expects a great deal from his daughters, even now that we've both flown the nest—sort of. One came back, I guess. He might be strict, but the man will always be the voice in my head telling me I can be better, to keep trying. Mom wants what's best for us, too—I know that—although, sometimes I'd take her love with a little less criticism. My family isn't perfect, but as nosy and irritating as they can be, they've taken my broken pieces and taped me up again. Perhaps some jabs in their healing techniques, but at least they're trying. I can give them credit where it's due.

"So, Elle agreed to a date," Maya says through a tiny nibble of not-bacon.

I kick her beneath the table. She snorts out some of her bacon.

"Really?" Mom says, her interest locked and loaded. "With whom?"

"Edgar, one of the brokers Graham works with."

"Edgar!" I gag on my tasteless muffin. "Exactly how much older is he?"

Maya tilts her head and gives me another mother hen look. "He's only thirty-seven."

"Elle, don't be so hasty to judge," Mom directs. "We know what happened last time you rushed into something."

"Ugh, yes we do, Mother," I mutter and flick the rim of my plate.

"You don't need to get snippy," she says. "I just hope you'll take your time to look for real qualities. An established man might be exactly who you want, and he'd take care of you. That's all I'm saying."

"Yeah, established and money didn't help me before. And I don't need to be taken care of."

Mom widens her eyes as she sips from her mug, voice low, but loud enough to be heard. "Based on past results, I'd beg to differ."

I drum the table and stand abruptly. "Alright, and with that, I'm going to go to work."

"I can drive you, dear. It's not a problem."

"I'm good. The bus works," I say, and take a snide remark by the shoulders and give it a swift shake before it rears its head. "Thank you for the offer."

"I'm scheduling your appointment for Monday, Elle!" Maya calls after me.

I wave without turning around, and disappear down the narrow entryway to the front door. Outside the whisper of chill in the air chases away the taste of waxy, fake butter, and guilt that my life has taken a tumble in the ditch. No—I can't think like that; positive thoughts and head held high. Gulping another breath, I trudge toward the bus stop. Lindström has a magical glow that kisses the sidewalks and streets at this time of morning. Sunlight creates rivers of gold and yellows that add a unique peace I admit I've missed living away.

A few shops are awake; grates clang as owners unlock their livelihood for the day. The scent of coffee, chai tea, and vegan bagels come from the newest hip café on the corner. I take time to wave at old Mr. Carlsson, the man who's managed his late wife's antique store for the last thirty years. Talk about true love—the poor guy hasn't had the heart to let the shop go. That is the sort of love everyone deserves.

I wish it still existed.

Out of habit I glance across the street to tempt myself with *Clara's Chokolade Café,* but of course it isn't there. At least the new *Quik Hardware* is tidy and not a sore spot, but not the same as the pleasant Danish bakery. I'll get used the change, eventually.

I trace my finger over the painted words along the window of the Scandinavian Market. The Olsens and Jacobsons have created a transformative setting that'll whisk customers to cities across the Baltic Sea. Inside, plush chairs and round tables are painted white, with hints of blue and red and yellow. Nordic symbols are embossed around the borders in gold, with blossoms painted in the corners of each window. Clean, tidy, like both bakeries always were.

The door opens and I step back as Brita aims for a parked SUV. She rushes past without seeing me, before she dips inside the back seat and returns with two twenty-pound bags of chocolate chips. Why did I go into nursing again when she gets to work with those all day?

Slamming the door with her foot, she catches my eye and smiles. "Hi again! Heading to work?"

Giving a quick scan to my scrubs, I nod. "Yep. Here let me help."

She gratefully hands over one of the sacks.

Slinging it over my shoulder, I follow close behind her. "Everything smells amazing inside. You must have gotten here early."

"Oh yeah, if I hadn't my grandpa would've snuck inside and taken over. But he's being entertained by Agnes, my cousin. Farfar can't resist Agnes."

"I don't think I've met her," I admit, scanning my memories for the name.

"Yeah, I didn't think you had," Brita says. "She was born right when you graduated high school. But at least Oscar is on break for Labor Day, and of course I've forced him to come help."

I peer through the window again and notice more than the quaint Viking-esqe décor. I quickly recognize Brita's aunt sliding trays inside the display cabinet, and there towering over is her cousin. "Whoa, that's Oscar?"

Brita follows my gaze and laughs. "Yep, he's only two feet taller than me now."

"Last time I saw him he was just a scrawny kid."

"I know. Now, he thinks he's something else because he plays basketball for Minnesota State."

"Wow, I suddenly feel really old."

"Right there with you," Brita says in a sort of lament. "Why don't you come inside, and we can put these bags down—if you've got time."

I steal a glimpse at my watch. "Yeah, the bus isn't coming for a few minutes."

"Great, I'm glad I ran into you; I need your number so we can meet for lunch."

"I'm off tomorrow."

"Uh, perfect! I only work until one tomorrow." She plops her bag behind the small counter and reaches for mine. "Inez, Oscar, do you guys remember Elle Weber?"

The woman stacking Swedish tarts pauses and studies my face. Oscar, all man and muscle now, stops sweeping to look.

Inez wipes her hands on her apron and dimples pucker her cheeks. "Oh, sure. Angela and Reed's girl."

"Good to see you," I say with a smile. "I love what you've done combining the bakeries."

Inez rests her hands on her plump hips; a clear flash of pride on her features. "Thank you, we're pretty proud of it all. Should have been done years ago."

The door to the shop dings, and a desperate voice breaks the ambiance. "Brita!"

Everyone turns toward the front door. A younger Axel rushes into the room dressed in baggy shorts with tousled hair. Face flushed, he sinks back toward the door when he realizes there is a crowd. Again, I feel older than I am. He's easily recognized as the third Olsen brother, but still I haven't seen Bastien since he was missing his front teeth.

"Hey, Bass," Brita replies. "What's wrong?"

"Oh, uh . . ." Bastian clears his throat, and leans coolly against the wall. "My car . . . it isn't starting and, uh, there's open gym with the team. Jonas said you might be able to drive me."

"What about when Ax goes to work, could he take you?"

I keep my face schooled in neutral indifference, but truth told, I'm interested.

"Like always, he never answers he stupid texts," he groans. "Please."

"Too cool for the bus," Oscar scoffs.

Bastien grins. "Is that even a question?" He turns back to his sister-in-law. "So, what do you think?"

"You're coming to help after school, right?"

He grunts, but Brita pinches her mouth, so he quickly nods. "You know it. Come on, I wouldn't let you down."

"Oh, I don't know, Bastien," Inez says, sliding a new tray of chocolate mousse cups into the display case. "Your mom wasn't too pleased with your reasons for missing your shifts last week."

Bastien's cheeks redden. "That was embarrassing."

"What happened?" Oscar asks.

"Nothing," Bastien says, desperately.

Inez coughs with intention and Brita seems ready to burst from a pent laugh.

Mini-Axel glances at me and offers a quick, friendly smile before trying to leave, but Oscar isn't finished. "Wait, dude, what happened?"

The two boys rush out of the bakery, Oscar pestering Bastien until the first bellows a laugh—obviously, Bastien caved.

"Sigrid caught Bass behind the school last week after he kept saying he'd be too late to work," Brita whispers to fill me in. "Let's just say the windows of his old clunker were a little too foggy and both front seats were occupied."

I snicker with the other two ladies, but with a screech and hiss, the bus pulls up with no warning. I suck in a breath and dart outside in a desperate dash to catch the ride before the driver pulls away. Too late.

I curse my bad luck. First a blind date set up by Maya, now I'll be late on my second day.

"Hey, hop in," Brita chirps. She wiggles a set of keys. "I'll drop you off."

"You don't have to do that."

"I absolutely do, you were helping me and missed the bus. Now, come on. My chauffer service comes with pastries and Swedish tea."

"Sold," I say as I adjust my bag over my shoulder again.

Bastien doesn't grumble being pushed to the back seat, and by the time I find my place, the teen is buried in his cell phone.

Brita glances in the back. "I thought your mom took that away."

"Pretty sure she got sick of not being able to text me a hundred times a day. So, that lasted about two days."

Brita shakes her head. "Well, I'm taking Elle to the hospital first, because work comes before basketball."

"You watch your filthy mouth, Brit," Bastian says with a grin. "But fine, I'm just along for the ride."

Brita pulls into traffic as she hands me a to-go cup filled with fragrant tea and a cream filled bread of some kind. I take a sip and my tongue dances with unique spices and just a hint of smooth silk to finish it off.

"How are you doing being back home?" Brita asks after a few more sips.

"Oh, it's been interesting."

I'm grateful she doesn't ask the hardest question: *Why did you move home?*

"I get it," she goes on. "It was always hard to move home between semesters during school."

"Where do you guys live now?"

"Well, we just moved back last year ourselves. Jonas, graduated law school in Ohio. I thought for a second we'd be moving in with his parents, but we found a little house about three miles away and snatched that up." She pauses for another sip and a laugh. "But I'm sure you can guess we're always around."

We chat about law school adventures, my favorite southern foods, living close to family, and old softball musings. No pauses, nothing but genuine conversation. All my years away, I suppose I almost forgot how it feels to speak without someone without them analyzing every piece me.

The hospital comes too quickly, but before I close the door, Brita says, "I sent you a text, so you've got my number." She waves her cell phone with a grin. "Let's plan on tomorrow."

"For sure. Thanks for the ride," I say. "Bye, Bastien."

He salutes. "See ya. Hey, if you see Axel, tell him he sucks and should answer his brother's emergency messages."

"If I see him, I'll make sure I give the message verbatim."

I wave once more feeling a kin connection to the Olsen family—yes, Brita is an Olsen now in my mind. I shouldn't feel these things since my willpower around Axel's annoying charms are pathetically weak after speaking with him twice. Poor Bass, but I won't deliver his message, because frankly, I'm not going to see Axel.

At least I'll try to avoid him.

Maybe.

CHAPTER 4

"So," Viv drawls as she shimmies her shoulders. "How is the second day going?"

If fairies existed, they'd have Viv's face, hair, and sing-song voice. Somehow, she manages to gossip and blab with everyone, while still making all her rounds at just the right times. Viv is the sort of nurse I aspire to be.

Crunching a slightly wilted celery stick between my teeth, I gaze at the bustle of staff, patients, and visitors drifting past the cafeteria. "It's been nice. Not too busy, but not exactly slow."

"Oh, you wait until right before the holidays," Viv says with a snort before she takes a swig of water. "The surgeons all try and get their scheduled surgeries finished so they can take weeks off during the winter. It's going to get wild, but then Christmastime will slow down again. It's always, up and down, up and down."

I laugh softly. "Sounds about right."

"Looks like I won't see you until Tuesday, though. Bummer, I have Saturday this weekend."

"Don't worry, I've got next week."

She slurps tomato soup and leans back in her seat. "It's not so bad, and pretty quiet. Usually the therapists that are scheduled on the weekend will bring some sort of treat for the wing because they're amazing," she says. "It's like some big bonding breakfast."

"You know a lot of the therapists?" I probe because I can't resist.

"Oh sure. The Director of Rehab is my uncle, girl. He's the one who got me the job. Everyone is great. You've probably noticed we all sort of revolve around each other's schedules, mutual respect for separate disciplines and all that jazz—it goes far in cultivating loving working relationships."

"Yeah, I haven't seen too many of the therapists actually. Whenever I go in a patient's room, a therapist is either bringing them back or they haven't gone for their session yet." The truth, and a blessing. It allows me to adjust to my new life as Nurse Elle at Lindström General without irritating blue eyes slapping me in the face every time I turn around.

"Well, you should get to know them, so they share their pastries. Especially because one of them has a family bakery. Word of advice, when he's working the weekend, make sure you're working."

"Noted."

My stomach does a summersault. *Ridiculous, Elle.* I don't want Axel; I don't like Axel. Smug, arrogant womanizers aren't my type, and he certainly won't take the dump truck of baggage I brought to a table. Not that I want him to. I close my eyes, digging myself into a pit of thoughts I can't shut off.

I remember how the man kisses. Oh, heaven help me, I do. Unfortunately, even young love leaves a permanent stamp on the heart.

Viv nudges my arm after a few quiet bites. "Now, tell me if I'm too nosy—Spence says I'm too pushy sometimes—but I don't see a ring. Do you have anyone special? Looking? What's your love story?"

I laugh sincerely. "You only want to know about my love life?"

"Of course," she says, resting her chin in her palms. "We'll get to the other friend-stuff later. Spill all the gooey, dirty, personal details."

I've concluded it is impossible not to like Viv. "I'm . . . single. But I'm not really looking. I just got out of a pretty serious relationship."

"Oh, you poor thing. Break ups are the pits, like . . . The. Pits." She taps her hands on the table for emphasis. After a brief pause, she shoots me with her fingers. "Hey, Spence has a few single friends. I could set you up whenever you're interested."

"Thanks, but my sister already set me up against my will, so I think I'll skip the blind date department."

Viv dips her head. "Girl, I hear you. Just know, if you give the word, I've got you covered."

"Thanks."

Viv seems pleased with her offer and crumbles a few crackers into her soup. Lifting her spoon, she starts to slurp, but stops midway, forcing a napkin over her chin to stop the drip. "Oh, oh there he is."

I glance around. "Who?"

"Axel, the therapist with the bakery. Get on his good side and he'll hook you up."

A pout forms on my lips when Axel stalks into the cafeteria with a therapist with beautiful brown skin and dark hair that could pass for satin. Another meaty therapist trails behind as the third wheel. Clearly, number three realizes his role and keeps his eyes locked on his cell phone he incessantly scrolls through. Axel folds his arms and leans closer to gorgeous therapist, says something, and she giggles— of course she giggles like a goddess. When I giggle, I sound like a goat.

Now, I'm monologuing like a jealous person. I close my eyes to pep-talk my traitorous thoughts into taking a chill in a big way.

"Hey, Mack," Viv calls. "Mack . . . Mack . . . *Mackerel!*"

Cell phone therapist glances up, catches sight of Viv's wild waving, and smiles as he grabs a sandwich wrapped in cellophane.

"That's good old Mackerel, a name I came up with, it's really just Mack," Viv whispers. "Probably the nicest guy you'll ever meet. I'm pretty sure we're like third cousins, or something. Anyway, he hasn't been sleeping. The wife just had baby number two and their oldest isn't even two yet. Nuts, right?"

"Hey, Viv," Mack says, scrubbing one side of his face. He does look tired. "Did you bring me something awesome?"

"Gotcha covered, my friend. I've got the good stuff," she says with a squeak as she crinkles her nose and dips into her purse. She pulls out a small bottle with *energy* spelled out in big block letters on the label. "Here you go."

He sighs. "You're the best. My stash is sitting on the kitchen counter. I was so tired this morning I walked right by."

Viv narrows her eyes and juts out her chin, changing her accent to sound a bit like the mafia would—at least what I imagine. "No worries, my man." She pinches her fingers together and kisses the tips. "What's mine is yours. Don't worry about it."

Mack pulls up a chair and skips straight to chugging his miracle caffeine awakening before peeling back the plastic wrap on his turkey club. "Hi," he says, finally noticing me. "Sorry, I don't think I've slept in two years. I'm Mack."

"Elle." I shake his hand. "Viv filled me in, congratulations. That's exciting."

Mack smiles. "It is, unexpected, but she's already got me wrapped around her little finger. Guys, over here."

My stomach tightens. Who else could he be waving to, but Axel and goddess?

"Hi, Vivie," the girl says and takes a seat with her salad. My eyes drift to my white bread sandwich that pales in comparison. "Haven't seen you down here in a while."

Viv relaxes in her chair. "I know, amazing the day nurses get a full lunch break, right? Hey, you," she glances over my head, and I know Axel must stand right behind me. "Come meet my friend, Elle. I was just raving about your bakery treats we get spoiled with when we share weekends. She just went through a break-up, so I bet she—" Viv claps her hands over her mouth when my eyes widen. "Oops, I'm sorry that slipped out."

"Oh, hey," Goddess says, tapping my arm. I look at her nametag— Abby. It fits her. "Don't worry, we've all been there."

The chair slides out from beneath the table and echoes through my head like a bell tower announcing the hour. Maybe it isn't that loud to everyone else, but to me, I suddenly have a headache.

"Really? Well, if Ellie asks, I'd bring anything she needed."

Great Gatsby, if he says that name again I'll swallow my tongue—or kiss him—one of the two.

"Axel," I say, hardly looking at him; a weak attempt to avoid drowning in his eyes. "Thanks for the offer, but I'm good now."

"You two already know each other? Why the heck didn't you say anything?" Viv tosses a piece of her roll at my head.

"I didn't know you were talking about him," I lie.

"Honest mistake," Axel says. "There are tons of PTs that have family bakeries in Lindström."

I glare at him; he seems extra pleased with himself as he chomps a fry and flicks his brows. Great he has a whisper of scruff on his face, as if he knows I'm a sucker for a bit of facial hair. A delightful rumble fills my stomach and I want it to stop.

"How do you two know each other?" Viv asks.

"Ellie and I went to high school together," Axel says, rolling another fry between his fingers.

He stares at me when I finally look up, like he's challenging me in a way. Straightening my shoulders, I'll meet his challenge with my own. He thinks he is some sort of devilishly handsome king that can control the awkwardness to stand in his favor—well . . . well . . .

"Actually, we dated, too," I say with forced confidence. "Until Axel ditched me for someone else."

Viv gags on her water, and Abby's mouth forms an 'O' when Axel's confident smile falters—yes, the king was wounded.

"What? Axel, you dirtbag," Abby snaps, smacking his shoulder.

"Wait a second, Ellie, isn't remembering things clearly," Axel says, his confident smirk in place.

You know what, not today. I've felt out of control in my life for too long, and I need something to reel under my power. "Huh, please refresh my memory."

"I didn't break up with you for anyone else, let's make that clear right now," Axel says, until his coworkers smile, and his spell placates them into docile followers again. "Let's put this into context; Mack help me out, remember what it was like being seventeen? I was *imma-*

ture and could hardly focus long enough to make it through a school day. I dated around."

"Oh, that's what you call it?" I say, hoping my grin is light and hiding the nerves rattling inside. What am I thinking bringing this up?

"Yeah," he says lightly. "That's what I call it. Immature."

"Excuses," Abby says through a bite of her salad. I'm still trying to gauge if anything more than coworker is between her and Axel. Stay tuned.

Axel rests his palm over his heart with his coming vow. "No, it's the truth. Trust me if I'd have known Elle was—"

My heart jolts and my head spins. Where will he take this? I've heard more than a few descriptors to what I am: emotional, demanding, nosy, paranoid, lazy. To name a few. I hold my breath waiting for Axel's opinion.

". . . still this gorgeous, I'd slap my teenage self."

Abby swoons and pats his cheek. Viv agrees saying, "Yeah, you missed out buckaroo."

It takes two breaths before I narrow my eyes, watching him with all the suspicion I can muster. He stares right back, chomping another fry before grinning and looking away when Viv compliments his chivalry.

"Come on, Elle," Viv turns on me. "What do you say to that?"

I'd rather be anywhere else than sitting at the table. Forcing a smug grin, I flick one of Axel's droopy fries. "I think . . . Axel knows how to sweet talk to cover up the truth. Don't worry, it's all in the past, but it doesn't change the fact that you dumped me two weeks before prom."

Mack bellows a catcall and Axel buries his face with his hands. I laugh to prove it's all in good fun.

"Fine, you win Elle. I was a teenage dirtbag. Good thing people change, right?"

My smile weakens as I swallow a touch of pride and dare meet his gaze. He isn't smiling. Everyone at the table keeps chatting as the lunch hour wanes, but they fade into white noise. There is a moment where Axel's words mean a thousand things.

Shaking away my newly developed nerves, I slide my chair out and gather my things. "Sometimes people change, but according to your younger brother, you haven't. He told me to tell you that you suck."

Axel laughs softly and I'm forced to admit each time he flashes those straight, white teeth my legs turn to jelly. Jerk.

"When did you see Bass? Or did you talk to Jonas? He is a little bitter that I'm older."

"I was lucky enough to catch a ride with Brita and Bastien this morning. You should check your phone, then you'll know why you suck."

Axel immediately pulls out his cell and scans through his messages, his smile widening the longer he reads. "What a little pansy. He could've taken the bus."

"Well, I promised to relay the message. Guess it's time to get back to it. Coming Viv?"

"Yes," she says and bounces to my side after tossing the rest of her lunch.

I wave to the therapists as a whole, wishing I resisted the temptation to look once more at Axel. He's watching me, smiling, but I swear it's dimmed a little.

"You two need some time to hash out some unfinished business. And by hash out I mean make out," Viv says at the elevator.

"What are you talking about?"

She gripped the ends of her short hair. "You can't be that blind. Come on, *good thing people change . . .*" she says in her best Axel impression.

"He's putting on a good face for his therapist friend."

Viv chortles, like a hen, at least three times before explaining. "Abby? Girl, she's engaged. *To someone else.* But I get it, you were scoping out the competition."

"I was not."

"Mmmm-k." Viv folds her arms. "Do as you please, but I think you'll feel a whole lot better if you dig up those heartbreak issues in the sexiest ways. Then maybe you can move on and double date with me and Spence."

"I don't need to move on from Axel."

"Oh, I understand. Stupid high school romance, you think nothing is there, right? Maybe so, but I have a sixth sense when it comes to this sort of stuff. My solution—kiss that guy smack on the mouth and get it out of your system."

I scoff, but can't stop the heat from rising in my face. "Well, you keep your advice, because there isn't anything there. And there definitely will be no kissing Axel, at least not by me."

And that is the truth. Cross my heart.

CHAPTER 5

*F*riday breaks with storm clouds and rain dusting the streets. I love it, and am huddled in my gabled window with a chunky, knit blanket, and cup of much too expensive cocoa Auntie Kathy gave me before I left. The opportunity to stay in my pajamas well beyond six in the morning is a new life goal.

A knock stirs me from my bliss, and I shoot my dad a cheeky grin when he steps inside.

"Vegging out, E?"

"Of course," I say. "Why are you all spiffed up?" Then I frown. "Dad, are you sure you want to go to work? That's five days this week. I thought you were sticking to three and half."

He waves me away, a classic Reed Weber move. "Between you and your mother, one would think a man keeping his job was a crime. I'm doing just fine, and yes, there's an important board meeting today. I need to be there."

I huff and sip more of my liquid gold before flipping my legs off the side of the window seat. Dad works as a busy accountant among three different banks. Money never rests. "At least promise you'll come home after the meeting if you—"

"Excuse me," he says with a chuckle.

Good at least he's still teasing. If I push too hard, stone-faced dad will come out.

"When did you become the bossy parent and me the child?" he asks.

I smile, but my voice comes with fierce sincerity. "When your heart tried to kill you. Call it natural to worry."

"Touché," he says and leans one shoulder against the wall. "Anyway, do you have plans today?"

"Actually, I'm meeting a friend for lunch." I confirmed with Brita and we're on for one thirty at Snyder's. I'm probably overly excited for a simple lunch, but only Kathy texts me occasionally. Sometimes I wonder if I've been blacklisted from my friends in North Carolina. Not that I'd blame them, who knows what threats were leveled against them, but it doesn't make it any less lonely. "Need me to do any errands or chores while I'm off."

"You read my mind," he says, fiddling with a large envelope in his hands. "I hate to ask, but I still have a hard time reaching over my head—"

"Well, you shouldn't be for one thing."

". . . there's some build up in the rain gutters on the side of the house. The news said tomorrow is supposed to be a downpour," Dad goes on, ignoring my interjections. "Water could block up and puddle on the roof. I'd ask your mom, but . . ."

We both share a grin at the idea of my mother reaching her manicured nails into grimy gutters. That isn't a jab, some ladies just have a thing about their nails. My mother and sister are two of those ladies; nothing wrong with it, but by the state of my stubbled nails—not a worry for me.

"I can get it done," I say.

"No rush this morning; looks like it's clearing up out there right now, but before tomorrow would be great. Thanks, E."

"No problem. Excited for the weekend?"

Dad shrugs. "Oh, it will be nice to go see your aunt and uncle. Usually when your mom and Aunt Tina get together, though, Bill and

I are dragged all over the place to tiny little stores that have price tags that will give me another heart attack."

I laugh, understanding completely. "Still, it's been awhile since you guys have gone to Connecticut. Should be fun."

"Should be. Well, I'd better get going so I can come home and pack. Your mom thinks I've already finished, so don't tell her I haven't even started."

I snort and lean my head against the cool window. "Dad, do you think she really doesn't know?"

"You're probably right. Hey, this, uh, came for you." Dad shifts and seems hesitant to hand over the envelope.

The smile I found on this most pleasant blustery day falls as I scan the return address and name. I feel like the superior cocoa in my stomach turns to acid, eating through my insides.

"Thanks," I whisper.

"E, you going to be okay?"

"Yeah, I'll be fine."

Dad taps my chin, so I lift my gaze. "Listen to me, you're better off. No tears, okay. You're above all that, remember?"

I nod stiffly, and tuck the envelope under my hip. I'll open it when my dad isn't around. I may have a brave face now, but I can only fake it for so long. My parents seem to demand it of me. I know they're only trying to help, but it seems on days like today that a savage storm is waiting to burst in the center of my chest the more I try to wear one.

"Alright," he says. "See you later. Thanks again, for the gutters."

"No problem, Dad."

After he leaves, I stare at the crinkled envelope. Lumpy and flimsy, I can only guess what's inside, and truth told, I've no energy to look. After lunch, then I'll peek. Today I simply want to forget, and maybe see a glimmer of light at the end of this bleak tunnel.

* * *

"This is fun," Brita says, after a large bite of pasta. "I haven't had a good girl's day since Ohio. And then with my job, well, I think I'm quite a homebody."

She's filled me in on the joys and pitfalls of freelance editing, but from what it sounds like, Brita has quite the steady workload and she manages herself like a solid business with working hours and all that. I'm impressed. If I worked at home, I have no trouble imagining how I'd spend all day reading and watching cheesy romance movies.

The restaurant swells with high school kids. With Labor Day weekend starting tomorrow, I guess they've all gotten out early for the holiday. "It is fun," I say, watching a group of kids wearing football jerseys sit two tables away. "So, do you stay in touch with anyone from high school?"

She tilts her head back and forth. "A few people, but we never see each other. I keep in touch with more people from college. My old roommate and I used to meet a few times a year when she still worked in Pittsburgh, but now she's on the west coast so it's mostly phone calls at this point. Although, she's pretty serious with a guy out there; I made Jonas promise if there's a beach wedding in the near future, we're there."

I laugh. "I'd do the same. I miss the beach. It was one of my favorite parts of North Carolina."

"Oh, I guarantee it would be mine, too. I feel bad you and I lost touch. You were on social media for a bit, but then—"

"Oh, yeah." I wave my hand. "I got off the sites, you know, being on too much, they sort of took over my time."

"Gotcha. Well, I'm glad your back now."

"Yeah, it's been different, but I'm car shopping tomorrow and then I'll be on the hunt for an apartment. I can't wait."

In another breath she claps one hand on the table. I practically see the light bulb flash over her head. "You should check out those new condos by the highway. Axel bought one, and it's cheaper than rent. But they lease a few of them, too. They're really nice, but won't break the bank, you know?"

"Really?" I take a nervous drink of my soda. "Yeah, I'll need to check them out."

Brita leans over the table, a villainous smirk on her face. "Speaking of Axel, tell me honestly—is it weird to see each other again?"

"Why?" I swallow the scratch in my throat.

Brita scoffs. "I didn't forget, Elle. You guys were hot and heavy for a bit in high school. My junior year, Axel never missed any of our games."

That's true. He might have had his faults, but I remember the time could've been set by Axel's prompt attendance to the softball fields.

When I try to laugh, it's all wrong, quivery, and breathless. "It's fine. We dated so long ago and it's not like we dated long term. It was only a few months."

"I guess," Brita concedes. "He wasn't exactly the steady type back then."

"Or now," I mutter as I stare out the window."

"Oh, I don't know. I think Axel wouldn't mind settling down."

"He's not seeing anyone?" I force my voice to be casual as possible. "I imagined he'd have a few choices."

Success. Brita takes my indifference for my word and sips her lemonade without raising a brow. "He was like that for a while—I mean—even *I* went out with Axel for two seconds."

I bark a laugh. "What! But you married his brother?"

"Oh, girl, it's a whole story, but that's how Jonas and I ended up together. Still, the last few years—I don't know this could just be me—but it seems like Axel is done with causal stuff. He'd never admit it to anyone else, but he's said a few things to Jonas. And let's face it, I'm Jonas's wife—I have brother-in-law snooping privileges, and Jonas spills the goods."

Axel confessing his fatigue in bachelor life has its appeal; dangerous ground for me in one breath, but thrilling in another. My heart is on the rebound, that's all this is, a desperate search to make a new connection. Yet, seeing Axel again shook loose something a smidge deeper, and I don't like it. I'll also never admit it to anyone.

The main reason for my silence being: how lame was it to still have a crush on your high school boyfriend? The lamest.

He brought the same deeper something at seventeen, and wouldn't you know it, at twenty-six I've slipped right back there again.

Thankfully, we change subjects and talk about other things. By the time we pay and leave the bistro, I feel lighter than I have in months. Time hasn't changed my friendship with Brita, and that can be a bright spot, I suppose. Outside, it's still gloomy, but a few sunbeams work hard to dry the puddles from the early morning rain. I love the chill, the rain, the scent of an approaching autumn.

"So, what about you, Elle?" Brita asks as we walked toward the bakery. Why pay for dessert when an array of the sweetest sweets in Lindström are at our fingertips. "Are you dating anyone?"

It's such a common question between girlfriends, I know I can't escape it forever. With Brita though, I don't pause my answer. Strange. "Actually, that's why I left North Carolina."

Her eyes go wide, not with sympathy, but genuine curiosity, like she cares. "Really? Bad break up?"

"The worst. I caught him cheating," I admit as we walk into the side of the bakery.

I'm not sure, but I think Brita might have just growled like a she-wolf. "What a loser."

"Pretty much," I say. "The worst part of it all, he didn't even have any repercussions—at least in my mind."

"He lost you," she says, digging through a fridge stocked with desserts not available to the public yet.

I snort and take a tasty-looking chocolate regret. A hardened outer shell that when broken spills out a gooey custard filling inside. Brita must have a sixth sense that this story requires the hard stuff.

"I'm not sure losing me was a repercussion to him," I say through an enormous bite. "After he was caught, he turned everything on me. I lost my job, my house, so I turned tail and came home."

"How in the world did you lose your job?"

I tap the top of my chocolate shell and pause for a moment. "He's the business marketing executive for the entire hospital chain, the one

Lindström General is part of, but since the hospital in North Carolina serves as the headquarters, his office is there. He spun things so it would create a hostile working environment for my coworkers—and him—if I stayed."

"Executives." Brita snaps her own bite off her spoon with fire in her eyes. "Okay, loser isn't the word I want to use, but—" she nods toward the door opening as her aunt, a young girl with a limp, and Axel's grandfather step into the shop. "Children are present."

"It's okay." I smile and lower my voice. "To be honest, you're the first person I've talked to about this since coming back. I mean, my family knows, but we don't talk about it too much."

"Well, you can vent about the dirty cheat any time you want," she whispers, before turning to her family. "Agnes!" The thin girl struggles to rush, but seems desperate to get to Brita's side. Brita squeezes her cousin before directing her attention to me. "Aggie, meet my friend Elle."

"Hi," the girl says shyly.

"How was therapy?" Brita asks.

Agnes pops out a rainbow lollipop as big as her hand. "Uncle Axel said I earned it."

"Funny, he always says that."

Brita turns to me once Agnes has limped toward the refrigerator with her mother. "She insists Axel and Bastien are her uncles. Axel works with her once a week and he must have a magic touch because she used to wear braces, but not anymore."

"CP?" I ask. I completed one of my clinical rotations with children diagnosed with Cerebral Palsy and take a guess.

"Yeah." Brita's gaze follows Viggo who's settled in a chair. "How are you feeling, Viggo?"

I understand why Brita asks the question with a hitch of concern in her voice. His breaths are haggard, and his sides kind of pit with each draw of air. The old man smirks and rubs his knees.

"Fine, fine," he grumbles. "The boy must think I'm fifty the way he worked me."

"Oh, Viggo, it wasn't so bad," Inez calls from a back kitchen.

Viggo waves her away, but Brita hasn't lost her focus on the old man. Nor have I. In fact, my nurse sense kicks in.

"You seem tired," Brita says.

Viggo leans forward on his knees. I'm already on my feet and soon crouched at his side, my fingers on his wrist, as I check the thud of his pulse. The old man doesn't protest and slumps a little more.

"Elle . . . what's wrong?" Brita jumps from her seat and rustles enough that Inez pokes her head out of the kitchen.

"Viggo?" Inez hurries to join us.

I keep my attention on the faint *thwomp, thwomp* coming weaker than it should. "Mr. Olsen," I say. "Do you feel like you can't breathe well?"

He nods and closes his eyes. I whip around. "Brita, will you get in my bag, I have an oximeter in the side pocket. Yeah, it looks like a clip thing."

Brita doesn't hesitate and tosses me the oxygen reader. I curse in my head when it takes too long to read on his finger, and spend a few moments trying to warm his hands. When the reading finally comes through, my pulse makes up for what Viggo's does not. "He needs to go to the hospital."

"What?" Inez says.

"His oxygen and heart rate are way too low."

"Should we call an ambulance?" Brita asks.

I keep running my hands over Viggo's shoulders to keep him awake and nod. "I would."

The next ten minutes are a bustle. The bakery fills with Axel's mother, Brita's grandfather and uncle. Brita tearfully calls Jonas, as I stick with Viggo who keeps fluttering his eyelids until the ambulance crew has him nestled safely in the back. Axel's mother rides with him, and I am stuffed behind the steering wheel in Brita's SUV, driving her and her grandfather toward the Lindström General.

The man is eighty; I understand he has more life behind him than ahead of him, but still I can't help but pray for the Olsens that they won't say goodbye today. All the Olsens, but most of all, Axel.

CHAPTER 6

*V*iggo curses in Danish. I don't speak the language, but it doesn't take much to guess that the words aren't gentle as they settle him in the emergency department. To me, a little passion comes as a good sign.

Both Axel's parents are now here, leaving Brita, me, and her grandfather to sit in the waiting area. Jonas has the task of picking up Bastien from school, so I shouldn't have been surprised when the sliding doors open, and Axel is the first grandson to arrive.

He frantically glances around for a second before spotting Brita and darting to her seat. "What happened?"

I don't think he knows I'm here.

"I don't know." She wipes her eyes. "He got home and seemed so tired. Elle checked his oxygen and we called an ambulance. From what your mom was told they think he might be sick, so his lungs aren't working well, but I don't know."

Now, Axel finds me. His playful blue eyes aren't playful, but shadowed. I don't remember a time I've seen him so unsettled.

"I don't get it, he was fine when he left the gym," he mutters. "I checked his stats constantly."

"It's not your fault, Axel," Brita insists.

Apart for ten years, but I know how to recognize the look of guilt —even in Axel Olsen.

"It's not your fault," I reaffirm. He takes to pacing, but he locks eyes with mine and listens. Scooting the edge of my seat, I hope he'll believe me. "They think he might have the flu and that compromised his lungs. You know sometimes these things just hit. It could also be that he's over-working himself, we don't know yet, but it's not anything you did, okay?"

He shakes his head and rakes his fingers through his hair. "I should be able to recognize when an eighty-year-old man is sick."

I shoot to my feet, and before I come to my senses, my hand is on his arm, urging him to stop pacing. Axel does pause. First his gaze drops to my hand, next he meets my stare.

"Hey, I'm sorry this happened," I say gently, "but it's not going to help your grandpa if you're out here blaming yourself. The exercise could have stirred things up a bit, but that might've happened by walking up a flight of stairs, or manning the shop."

I release his arm, heat tingles in my fingertips, but I simply offer an encouraging smile.

"Sit down, boy," Philip Jacobson tells him. "It's not on you. Now, come worry with us."

Jonas and Bastien couldn't have arrived at a more perfect time. With the encouragement of Philip, and the arrival of his brothers, Axel finally sits with his family.

I step back when Brita nestles against Jonas's arm and fills him and Bass in on what happened. Time for me to go; I'm not part of this.

Turning away, I creep toward the doors but stop at my name.

"Elle, wait." Axel chases the space between us. "Thank you, for what you did."

"It wasn't anything."

"It was. You know . . . you know how close my family is, so thank you for being there."

I smile and tuck a lock of hair behind my ear. "Brita has my number; will you guys keep me updated?"

"You're leaving?"

I nod slowly, maybe a little reluctantly. "I better go, but I mean it, please keep me updated."

"Okay." Axel shifts on his feet like he wants to come closer, but in the end decides against it. "Thanks again."

I leave worried, but more hopeful Viggo will recover, and with my fingers still tingling from the memory of Axel's skin.

* * *

"GROSS," I grumble as rotted leaves, grass, and gunk that somehow worked its way into the rain gutters squishes through my fingers. The mess in my gloved hands reeks in something sickly-sweet, and I struggle getting the wet leaves off my fingers. A soft rain drizzles, and I can't put off the clean-out any longer.

"Need some help?"

I've never swallowed my tongue, but I can sympathize with the feeling. I forget how to breathe, and my voice catches as I turn over my shoulder, looking down the ladder.

Axel stands on my driveway, his eyes brighter than when I left him, but his grin is still missing. Brita and Jonas are behind him, a similar somberness on their faces, but Brita clutches a handful of candy bars and offers a small wave.

"No." I tug off the gloves and make the shaky descent to the ground. "Thanks, but I'm almost finished."

"Here," Brita says, shoving the candy into my arms. "I should've brought you something from the shop, but . . . well, I made a stop at the vending machines. We wanted to say thank you."

"You didn't need to—"

"It's not worth arguing with her," Axel says, a twist in the corner of his mouth. Jonas nods.

"How is he?" I meant the question for each of them, but look at Axel.

"Stable, good, frustrated, and bossing the nurses around," Axel said with a laugh. "He has buildup in his lungs, so it's a bug that hit hard; that's what they think."

"The doctor said it could've been a lot worse if his oxygen dropped any further. You might not think it was anything huge the way you jumped in, but to us it means a lot," Jonas adds.

My voice is rough, and I hope they take it as exertion and not emotions. "I'm glad he's doing better."

"We're also returning the favor." Axel drifts toward the ladder. "Jonas, take off that fancy suit coat and help me."

Jonas loosens his tie, slips it over his head, and hands the tie and jacket to Brita.

I wave my hands in protest. "You guys don't. Really . . . I . . ."

"Might as well not argue with them," Brita repeats the same admonition and nudges my shoulder.

I sigh, but wave a peanut butter cup in front of her face. We sit together on the porch swing, watching leaves, dirt, and what I think is an old bird's nest tumble over the edge of the house for the next thirty minutes.

"You sure you're okay?" I ask, as the guys start stuffing the mess into black trash bags.

"I'm okay." Her jaw pulses. "I'm not oblivious to the fact that both Viggo and my grandpa are aging, it's just . . . imagining running things without them someday, it hurts. Axel is beating himself up, don't let that cocky grin fool you."

I click my tongue and pick at a tin foil wrapper. "Why? He's not irresponsible."

"You can imagine—I mean, think of your family—if you treated them and then something happened . . . it's hard not to cast blame."

I understand exactly how such a feeling can eat at a heart. "Yeah, that would be hard."

Biting into a chocolate bar, I watch Axel shove Jonas in the shoulder, leaving a dirty handprint on his white button-down shirt. I like the way Axel laughs. I'll admit that.

Brita clears her throat and breaks my studious gaze.

"What?"

"I've said your name like three times." Her knowing eyes bounce to me, then Axel, then back to me.

"What's that look?"

Brita shrugs.

"Hey, don't you be thinking crazy things."

"I try to think crazy at least once a week," she says, scooting against my side so Jonas can plop next to her. Axel rests one hip on the white railing surrounding the porch. Both a little dirtier, a little sweatier, and one staring at me unashamed.

"What's crazy?" Jonas asks, sliding his fingers into hers, then wiping the grime on her arm when she protests.

Brita laughs, shoving him away. "Nothing," she says, finally relenting and leaning against his shoulder. "I thought I saw something for a second, but I guess . . . I didn't."

Brita waggles her eyebrows at me, and my cheeks grow hot as I stare at the half-eaten chocolate bar in my lap.

Time to redirect. I point to the gutters. "Thank you for cleaning that nastiness out."

"Not a problem," Axel says.

Jonas glances at his phone. "We should probably get back. We're supposed to hang out with Agnes so the rest of your family can go to the hospital."

Brita nods and stretches as she stands. "Should we just have her sleep over at our house?"

"Might as well, we've been promising for a week." Jonas takes Brita's hand again, but looks to me. "Thanks, Elle. Plan on getting more pastries and junk food than you can handle over the next few days. Saying the word *thank you* is never enough for our family."

I grin, imagining my mother's horror at the idea of saturated fats in the house. Brita waves and promises we'll get together again without the ambulance finish. Axel is still at my side, but I don't have the guts to look just yet.

He clears his throat and steps down one stair, so he's in front of me. "I wanted to let you know, I still would like to repay the favor."

I close my eyes for half a breath. "Axel, you don't need to do anything. I'm a nurse. You work in healthcare, too, and would've done the same thing."

A burst of moisture soaks my mouth as the muscles in his jaw tighten and pulse. "I know, but this was personal for me. I can read the notes, Elle. He could've died. You didn't tell my family that his oxygen got down to sixty-seven percent."

I chip some old paint off the banister knowing how dangerous Viggo's oxygen levels had been. "Still, it isn't a favor that needs to be repaid, it's what I do."

"Well, I'm grateful. And maybe I can't make it up, but I'm going to try. I can be stubborn when I want to be."

"You know what I want?"

"No, what?" he asks, stopping halfway down the porch steps. Axel studies me—really sees me. This little revival of an old crush creates a warzone in my head.

"I want you to stop blaming yourself. You do that, and the debt is repaid, alright?"

He rolls his eyes. "Easier said than done."

My voice comes in a burdened whisper. "I know. I really do." Releasing a nervous breath, I smile through sad memories. "A few months ago, my dad had a heart attack."

He climbs up to the top step again. "I didn't know that."

"I know, he and my mom don't like to talk about it. I'm not sure if he's embarrassed or if it scared them enough that they don't want to bring it up, but it happened. He'd been training for a half marathon coming up in the spring. I talked to him on the phone the night before it happened. My mom said something in the background that caught my attention, and he admitted he'd been having 'indigestion' pains. You know what I told him? Take some Tums the next time he went running.

"On his run the next morning he dropped . . . Tums and all. Looking back, he'd actually described the classic symptoms, but all I heard were indigestion pains. I missed the signs, then encouraged him to push harder during his run to train his body out of an upset stomach."

"Elle . . ." Axel says.

But I quickly shake my head. "It's fine, but I understand what it feels like to think you did something wrong, and have the shoulda, woulda, couldas. Don't do it, okay."

He smirks, and I'm starting to suspect that sly grin finds its place when Axel feels uncomfortable. Very psychoanalytic, I know.

"I'll try, how about that?"

"Good enough, for now," I say.

Axel leaves the stairs, and walks backward for a few paces. "It still doesn't change the fact that I'll make it up to you."

I make a little *humph* sound and shake my head. "It's impossible. You can't make up for my awesomeness."

"Finally, you admit it," he says with a laugh. "But, don't underestimate me, Elle. I'll find a way to beat your own epic awesomeness."

"You know, you've always been too sure of yourself."

"Thank you," he says easily before opening the door to the car. "I thought that was always clear."

"Ugh, go away."

He laughs and slips into the back seat. Brita waves out the window as they pull away. I look to the clean gutters. A frightening afternoon and I'm exhausted. With the house to myself, I plan to eat too much and waste away in front of the TV for a few hours. I think of everything as I try to shut my mind down. Viggo, the Olsens, Axel, heart attack symptoms. Axel.

Hours later, when my mind is about to slip into the numb, binge-watching oblivion I wanted, my phone lights up. Rubbing my eyes from the strain of mindless screen gazing, I squint at the text message.

Unknown Number: *Hey, this is Axel. I forced Brita to give me your number. Now, when you're ready to cash in on that favor you know how to get in touch.*

My stomach flips, and I laugh, but this laugh is real. Easy, unforced. Such a sound has been lost to me for too long. I've been burned, and lost in cynicism that the laugh isn't only a noise to me, but the first hints of a heart opening to new possibilities.

I have no business opening my heart, especially to a guy who once had it and gave it back. But I smile the entire time I reply.

Very sneaky

My short response would have to suffice for the night. Curling a pillow in a strategic fashion so it cushions my head, chest, and the top of my stomach, I fall asleep with the grin still on my face.

CHAPTER 7

$\mathcal{M}$y heart sinks into the deepest pit of my gut as I read the text message. No, not from Axel, from Maya. My bright, happy plans of car shopping need to be put on hold. My sister insists Graham—my chauffer—must help her paint the chipping doorframes in the salon; a matter of complete urgency, but I don't feel the same. At least she apologizes, sort of. Maya's apologies sometimes sound more like a challenge to get upset with her, because it will most certainly end with me (or whomever dares rise to the challenge) being in the wrong.

Quiet blankets the house. My parents left before five this morning to catch their flight. Their single vehicle is nestled in the Park n' Jet for the next four days. Maya and Graham are crossed out; I consider Brita, but vaguely remember her mentioning at lunch that Jonas has been working Saturdays lately, and he finally has a weekend off. No chance I'll disturb whatever schmoozing is happening over there. Plus, Agnes might be at their house.

By all accounts, my dream of jumping into debt and car payments will go on hold for another week, or so. Unless . . .

I trap my bottom lip between my teeth and shake my head as if responding to the back and forth in my own brain. No, a ridiculous thought, crazy even. Why would he? Then again, he said he wanted to repay the non-favor.

No, I stand by my statement there is nothing owed. But I really want a car . . .

I let out a little *eek* as I rapidly shoot off the text, complete with one typo, and toss my phone to the center of the table. Tugging my knee against my chest, I press a fist against my mouth and stare at the dark phone, waiting.

Picture this: a twenty-six-year-old, college educated woman sitting in knots; an old heirloom grandfather clock ticking the minutes by, and her insides tumbling like a sweet sixteen waiting to learn if her secret crush has feelings for her, too. Ridiculous. Yet, I nearly split my skin when the screen brightens after five minutes.

Axel: *A trip to Minneapolis? Are you kidding? I've been sitting here all morning hoping you'd ask that exact question.*

My face goes flushed, and my stomach cramps in a good way as I write back.

So . . .???

Three blinking dots stare at me for too long until finally: *Be there in 20.*

I spring into action. My hair still looks like a bird's nest, my teeth aren't clean, and a shower would be wise. I glance at my watch—quick rinse, messy bun while I brush my teeth, cute new leggings and sweater Maya bought me as a welcome home gift—

Heart stop. Why am I spiffing up—my version of spiffing up—for the first time in weeks, and for Axel Olsen? Rolling my eyes, I know the answer and refuse to think it. My false explanation: I'm spiffing up for the car dealer, of course. I need to look like a serious buyer, ready to get down to business.

The man is prompt. Twenty minutes later, I zip up ankle boots and bounce on one foot toward the front door. Brushing a piece of hair that frizzed out over my brow, I adjust my sweater and crack two knuckles before opening the door.

Oh, goodness, something about a black T-shirt and faded jeans on Axel Olsen forces my eyes to do a complete scan of his entire six-foot two frame. I don't think he notices because he is half-turned around when I answer.

"Hey," he says beaming his perfect smile. "You look nice."

I snatch my satchel hanging on a hook by the door and flash a quick smile. "Thanks." *Oh, by the way you look amazing and I can't keep my eyes off you.* "You sure you're up for this?"

He doesn't hesitate for a second. "Yep. I don't want to brag, but I know how to score deals on cars."

"Yeah, we'll see," I say and lock the front door. "I'm thinking you might be all talk."

"Oh, you'll be impressed, I promise." He holds open the passenger door. A simple gesture, but I can't remember the last time it was done for me. Axel moves on instinct and not to impress anyone. The inside of his car smells like pine trees after a rainstorm; it takes some effort not to breathe in the smell of him inside the car.

Once he slips into the driver's seat, I tap the console. "Well, even if I'm not impressed, I do appreciate you doing this. My brother-in-law ditched me last minute. In his defense though, my sister rules her fix-it needs with an iron fist."

Axel laughs. "From what I remember of Maya, I could see that. It's not a problem, Elle. You made my choice on what to do today easy."

"What were the other options?"

"Laundry, that's pretty much it, and I would rather stick a pin in my eye."

"What? Laundry is my favorite job."

"Stop it," he snaps, but with a smirk. "It is not."

"It is too." I can't keep my smile away. "Fresh clothes smell so good when they're all dried, and you can do it while you watch a show or something. It's cathartic."

"Okay, great I'll expect you around eight tomorrow. You can get your Zen on."

Resting my head back against the headrest I snicker and watch the buildings of Main Street pass by. "Sorry bud, you can wash your own underwear."

Axel pretends to be offended as he pulls up in front of the shop. "Come on, road trips require good drinks and something to eat."

I step outside and we face off over the roof. "You want me to have a Danish in your squeaky-clean car?"

He leans over the top, but dips his head so I earn a glimpse of the mischief in his smile. "Well, I can get a plastic bib some parents use for their kids if you want. I mean I thought you could handle a pastry."

I glare at him and turn toward the front door. "Never trust me with a pastry, sir."

The front of the shop was already busy with breakfast goers and happy chatter. Inez, Oscar, Bastien, and a kid who looks like one of the out-of-family hires busies about to keep the shelves stocked. Axel waves and instantly drifts behind the counter.

"What do you want to drink?" he calls over his shoulder.

"Do you have the Swedish tea? Brita gave me some the other day; it was amazing."

"Did she put some cream in it?"

"No."

"Well then she failed you." He dances around his family who hardly care about the extra body snatching food, and soon hands me a steaming to-go cup. "What sounds good?"

"You know if you guys keep giving me food, you'll be rolling me out of here," I tease, but still point out my flaky, creamy choice without much of a pause.

Axel bags up the treats, takes his own cup and waves to the others. We're nearly out the door when a little voice calls his name.

"Wait, Uncle Axel!"

Agnes hurries as fast as she can with a piece of paper in her hand. "Aggie, how was the sleepover?" he asks.

"So good," she chirps. "Jonas let me eat two big cookies before I ate dinner."

Agnes sticks out her hand and Axel reacts in turn. I watch as he twiddles fingers, snaps, claps, and fist bumps in a rhythmic, preplanned handshake with the kid. Agnes doesn't bat an eyelash, nor

Axel, when it's over. The ritual seems like a daily occurrence, and I bask in the sweetness a little too much.

"I drew this for Grandpa Viggo," she says and holds up the picture of rainbows.

Axel smiles. "He'll love it."

"Are you going to see him?"

"Probably not until tomorrow."

Her shoulders slump. "Oh. Me neither. I wanted him to have it today."

"You know what," I interject. "Axel and I can stop in and visit him on our way home. Then he'll get it tonight."

"Really?'

I nod, even without seeing if my designated driver agrees. He studies me a little strangely, but I take his expression as yes. "Sure, it's so pretty, he needs to see it today."

Agnes is satisfied and hands her creation to Axel for safe keeping. We offer a final wave before heading back to the car. I sip the tea and he's right, Brita failed me by skimping on the cream.

"So, where are we heading first?" Axel asks, finishing the final bite of a churro-like pastry once we're on the freeway.

I tick off the three dealerships I've been scoping out, and subtly keep checking for any irritation in his expressions. His eyes are hidden by sunglasses—as much as I love his eyes, Axel in aviators earns two thumbs up—but he's relaxed. I stopped worrying.

I gather the wrappings from our treats into the original paper sack. "I've got to say. I was wrong when I said you were the same. You're different in a lot of ways."

He glances over at me, one brow raised. "I can't decide if you think that's a good thing or not."

I rest my head against the seat. "It's good. For example, with Brita's cousin, you guys are so cute I about turned into a puddle back there."

"Don't do that." He gives me the type of smile stirs my insides. "Ag is basically Brita's little sister, and once she and Jonas were married, we got close, too."

"It's not only that." I feel heat rise up my neck. My big mouth—I wish I hadn't said anything.

"What else is so different?"

"I don't know. You're just . . . different."

He grips the steering wheel tighter. "You're different, too. In a good way."

I'm not so sure I've changed for the better, but I ignore the urge to contradict him. Surface talk fills the rest of the drive. He tells me about living in Wisconsin, how he imagined living somewhere along the east coast, but Minnesota called him back home after therapy school. I skim through living in North Carolina. Part of me doesn't mind the idea of taking things a level deeper, but I can't. Like a plug blocks anything that might dive below the surface, I can't find a way to go there.

The drive is over before I finish describing my first encounter with a jellyfish, and we pull into the first car lot with high hopes.

The search for 'the one' takes just over three hours. Axel, seems to revel in his role as passenger for the test runs, offering a few observations time and again. He helps haggle, but when it matters, he steps back with a nudge to my waning confidence that I can, in fact, take the reins and seal the final deal. The second lot on the list is the golden child and an hour after the test drive, I am the new, financed owner of a silver Toyota with leather seats.

I splay over the hood and sigh, stroking my new pet.

Axel laughs softly "Happy?"

"Very," I say. "Thank you for getting me here."

"Well, now that it's done . . ." Did he shuffle his feet? Must have been a trick of the eye because when I look again, he leans confidently against my baby. "Want to get something to eat?"

I grin, and nod. "Yes, I'm starving. You picked the smallest . . . what was it called again?"

"*Semla*," he says with a touch of accent he's probably known since childhood. "And I did not. I picked the one with the most whipped cream."

"Agree to disagree; bottom line, I can definitely eat."

"I'll follow you then."

He waits until I settle into my new car before hurrying to his own.

I beam as my fingers trace the shiny steering wheel and the smooth black leather, as I breathe in the new car smell. I was nineteen when I last made an independent purchase—my first room in an apartment in North Carolina. And it feels amazing, empowering even. The fact that Axel Olsen is part of this new memory and chapter— well, that is a bonus. I'm in such a cheery mood as I pull out of the car lot, I don't even mind that I've admitted Axel is another bright spot.

In fact, having him there laughing and teasing, leaves me hoping I might surface from the muck and sludge after all.

CHAPTER 8

The sky deepens into gray blue by the time I follow the red taillights into the hospital parking lot. I can't remember laughing so hard over nothing than I did during a lunch of greasy hamburgers. We talked about funny stories from high school and college, with enough material to split my sides and draw tears to my eyes.

Snuggling in an open spot one space away from Axel's car, I wipe a bit of smudged eyeliner from the corners of my eyes, and replace the wisps of hair free of my elastic before stepping into the brisk evening.

"You don't need to come inside," Axel says, finishing the job of opening my door, but he steps back as if he knows I'm coming anyway.

"Tired of seeing my face?"

He scoffs—wait a darn minute—I think I just made Axel blush.

"No, time flies when you have fun, Ellie, but ask me in a few minutes. Things could change."

I shove his shoulder, but at this point it's easy to fall into the back and forth without overthinking every pulse beat, or every flirty grin.

"Don't forget the picture." I note his hands are empty.

"Good call." He dips into his car and carefully handles Agnes's masterpiece.

Aroma of Hospital is my new perfume, and after working in it, the colliding smells don't faze me. A quiet evening with relaxed hallways, not like the mornings, could've been a fluke, but I gather a little envy for the night shift.

Five minutes and an elevator ride later, Axel knocks gently on the door before slipping inside. Muffled sounds of the evening news and chatter are met with silence as Viggo and Elias Olsen, Axel's dad, glance to the door. It's like looking into a crystal ball to see how well the Olsen brothers will age

"Hey grandpa," Axel says, offering Viggo a quick squeeze to his shoulder before clapping his dad on the back. "We come delivering works of art."

I smile when Viggo's lips curl over Agnes's picture. "That girl," Viggo says. "She's called twice, you know." Viggo slaps Axel's hip, since his grandson has been sucked into a report on a football game. "Who've you brought."

I drift from the doorway so the old man can catch me in his line of sight. Elias taps Viggo's leg. "Elle Weber, Dad," he says. "She's the one who made sure you took your foot out of the grave."

I brush the accolade away, hoping my face isn't bright red. "I'm glad you're feeling better, Mr. Olsen."

"Ack, call me Viggo," he says, while urging me to come forward. Viggo reaches for my hand and pats it. "Quick thinking on your part; I might be old, but wasn't quite ready to go."

"Not for a long time yet," I agree.

"How are your folks doing, Elle?" Elias asks. "I haven't seen your dad on the course for a while."

I'd forgotten my dad and Elias Olsen were basically friends. Both finance men, living within a mile of each other, it isn't hard to make connections in Lindström. But still, my dad toes the line of hermit at times, so a friendship—acquaintance-ship—whatever you call, it is a big deal for Reed Weber.

"They're doing well," I say. "They took off to visit my aunt and uncle for a few days, but keeping busy."

I take a seat on a stiff chair to answer more questions about my family, new job, and the purpose of our joint visit. Viggo quizzes Axel on his bartering skills to ensure I received the best deal on my new car. Once satisfied that I had, Axel takes the chair next to me; my palms go sweaty when his hand rests an inch away from mine on his armrest.

When the game returns to the TV, I settle back, even whoop for a good play.

Axel stares at me like he's seeing me for the first time. "You're watching football?"

"Surprise you?" I nudge his arm. "Come on, you've forgotten how I used to watch with my dad?"

He grins and sat a little closer. "Ah, that's right. I forgot one of your qualities that made you the perfect woman."

I bark a laugh. "I'm so obviously perfect, how could you forget?"

Axel is teasing, but I shudder when he pins me in a look that causes my mouth to go dry.

My team wins, and Axel's lost. All in all, I'd say the visit has gone perfectly. Elias leaves with us, and thanks me personally for my part in helping Viggo before going to his car. Both bridges of my cheeks ache from smiling more than I have in months by the time we stop at the two silver cars.

"I think my grandpa likes you more than me," Axel says.

"I'm glad you noticed, too."

"I had fun today, Ellie." His tone is chipper and light, but sincere enough the sound shoots a hole through the center of my chest. "I guess it's too late, but I should probably ask if you mind that I call you Ellie."

I snort. "Yeah, it's a little late. It was your nickname to begin with. I don't mind."

"Good."

Axel fiddles with his car keys for what feels like a thousand heartbeats.

"Well," I say, breaking the silence before something dangerous happens. Like me saying we should do this again. "I really appreciate you helping me out today. Do you have a cash app—I'll send you some gas money."

"Seriously? Don't be weird. I'm glad you asked me to go."

More sincerity in his tone. Okay, I shouldn't panic, but I define the word. This isn't how the fresh start was supposed to go; flutters in my heart, fog in my brain. Nope, this isn't part of the plan. I'm not ready, as much as I want to be. Besides, Axel likely isn't sharing anything like sweaty palms, or racing hearts around me.

I open my car door and slip into the driver seat. "I still appreciate it. Are we finally equal with the paybacks, though?"

"Definitely not," he says, pointing his key at me as he rounds his car.

"You're not going to turn into an annoying guy that feels a lifelong indebtedness, right?"

"Probably. It will be less annoying if you just accept it."

I tilt my head. "We're even."

"That's what you think." He smiles over the hood of his car.

"Ugh. I'm leaving. Goodnight, Axel." Hiding the desire to hear him say something else, or ask me to stay, is easier inside my car. Not standing outside, close enough so I can smell his skin.

He waits until my door is nearly shut before saying softly, "Goodnight, Ellie."

I enjoy the solace and quiet of the house when I get home. It gives me time to process the day. One thing is certain, charmers were my weakness. Axel seems genuine, and in a way, he is a genuinely nice guy. But he's never been serious with anyone—at least as far as I know. He dated his sister-in-law for crying out loud.

Lindström serves one purpose, helping me wipe my slate free of silly distractions like handsome, charismatic men. Caution seems the only way to recover, and a crush on another lack-of-commitment sort isn't the mindset a rational, adult woman needs. Not at all.

* * *

Despite my best efforts, a shift has taken place inside my heart. Almost as though a fault line drove through my center, and the ability to stand on my own over the weekend shakes the two halves and shifts the broken pieces nearer to the grave.

I don't even grumble that much when Maya drags me to the salon on Monday morning. I sit in the chair for two hours while Stacy, her employee, jabbers about her dad's new wife and the outdated way the woman colors and styles her hair.

At the end, Maya stands, beaming, behind my chair. "Like it?"

My hair dances just above my shoulders; lazy ponytails will be shorter, but I nod. "I do. I like the colors she put in." The sun catches the bursts of caramel and red.

Maya claps and squeezes my arms. "I knew you'd like it. Now, if you'll commit to every six weeks it will always look amazing."

"We'll see."

"Don't forget we're going out Friday night!" Maya shouts as I leave the salon—because I have my own car and can now do such adult things, like leaving a hair salon when I feel good and ready.

I groan. Her diabolical blind date had slipped my mind. Oh well. I'll entertain my sister's know-best attitude as a thank you for dishing out hours of free hair time. It's Maya's way of helping me feel better, and even if all I need is a book or a brisk run, I appreciate her attempts.

I feel like Joan of Arc slaying dragons through the week. Even when a patient takes a roaring turn for the worst, when a clot dislodged from a wound, I approach without a glint of trepidation. I'm pleased to say, he's recovering well.

My smile rarely fades, and I don't roll my eyes once when my mom tells me to wear more eyeshadow. Clearly, I should've purchased a car a long time ago.

Of course, my sunny disposition is added upon by lunch breaks with Viv . . . and others.

Axel and I enter a strange friendship with real laughter, reminiscing, even admitting a few future plans now and then. He's been tearing up all the floors in his condo and has agreed to run with

Bastien and Jonas in the same marathon my dad had to drop. I tell him that finding my own place is a top priority, and like Brita, he mentions the for-lease condos in his complex. To my satisfaction and pleasure, Axel never asks for the reasons I've plopped back into the Lindström borders. Through the week, I'm lulled into a sense of security that backstory will never come up.

Of course, the dump truck filled with baggage still follows me around, but no one needs to peek inside. I plan to simply enjoy these new witty comments, and bubbles of excitement whenever I see a certain therapist. Those easy moments will end if he sees beneath the surface. Better to keep our past apart in the past.

Axel, still the playful, impishly delightful tease. Even if he shocks my system with those baby blues, remaining cautious friends who've kissed as teenagers seems a good option.

The tapping of fingers over the massive nurses' desk draws my attention from my documentation at the end of the day on Friday.

"Hello, Mr. Olsen," I say, adding my cheekiest grin. "What brings you here to bother me today?"

Axel leans on his elbows and smiles so tiny fireworks explode in my head. "Mr. Borrows is asking for some Tylenol."

I pull up my medication dose schedule. "Torturing today, I see."

"Every day, Elle."

"He's good to take some. I'll bring it to his room."

"Thanks." Axel turns, but wheels back with another tap on the top of the desk. "One more question."

"No, you can't have any of the blood sugar smoothies. I know you love them, but you need to leave them for the patients."

"But why?" He doesn't skip a beat. I laugh; he laughs. Sparklers in my head. "Actually, I wanted to see if you're busy tonight."

Now sparklers are full-on aerial bursts of fire powder and color. Until a downpour fizzles the lot. "Unfortunately, my sister has set me up on a blind date. I promised I'd go. Why, what did you have in mind?"

His smile hasn't dropped, but Axel takes the smallest step back. Without paying attention, I might've missed the retreat into a safer zone. "It's nothing huge. Now that my grandpa is home and feeling better, we're finally doing that eightieth birthday party for him and Philip tomorrow. All the grandkids are doing late-night prep and trying a few recipes tonight. It's basically a junk food binger. Brita thought you might want to come since you seem to love our stuff as much as we do."

Brita thought I might want to come. Not him. "That sounds a thousand times more fun. I wish I could."

"No big deal," he says as he pats the top of the desk again. "Have fun on your date, and thanks for bringing the Tylenol. I'd better go. We've got a new therapist and I'm the lucky one to show her around."

"That is lucky." I smile like friends do. And that's . . . well, that's that.

CHAPTER 9

$\mathcal{H}$e smells the same as the mint dust left behind in a tin. The awkward place that isn't quite the sweetness of peppermint, not yet the refinement of cinnamon, and more like menthol. Edgar Greeves shifts in his seat, so I gain a blast of air carrying his scent.

Maya jabbers on; Graham smiles like the dutiful husband; Edgar offers the occasional chuckle. I sip my water and watch the flurry of pianist's fingers tickling the grand piano in the corner. The restaurant is nice, and I feel underdressed in my mustard corduroys and sweater.

"So, Edgar," Maya says. "Graham says you have quite the library in your office. One of Elle's favorite things to do is read."

Bless my sister's heart, she's trying to resurrect the awkwardness of the evening. But the night died an hour ago. I knew from the moment Edgar inspected me like a tick embedded in his arm. Edgar is average, I suppose. His face dignified, his hair receding, but that doesn't bother me. What bothers me into uncomfortable chit-chat is the way he looks down his nose at me.

Edgar slurps some of his gourmet drink, though I don't know what it is, and looks to me. "You enjoy reading?"

I smile and nod. "I love it."

He chuckles. Okay, maybe we're breaking through those first date jitters.

"What sort of books do you read? Supermarket Harlequins?"

My water glass stops midway to my lips. Maya shakes her head—good the other woman on the table didn't miss his tone.

I tip my head to one side, and take my voice to a higher valley-girl pitch. "You don't? They are like amazing, and like, I pity the person who doesn't."

He laughs, condescending in a way, as if he's won something I don't see. "Figures. Most women tend to drift to the mindless fluff. To your point, Maya, my collection is filled with biographies and non-fiction written by some of the most brilliant minds in the country." He glances to me. "Not the lazy sort of reading."

"How do you find the time to read such intellectual books at your terribly busy job?" I cradle my chin in my palms, leaning over the table on my elbows.

Maya pinches her lips, but I have Edgar's attention now.

"I keep a precise schedule," he says earnestly. "I can show you how much value can be added to your success in life and career by planning your days—even down to the fifteen-minute mark. Life changing. It wouldn't be hard for you to have a disciplined schedule, especially since you only work three days a week."

Edgar sips his water, looking at Graham—I guess for validation to his superiority. My brother-in-law doesn't bite.

"Well, my shifts are twelve hours," I add. I'm in an all-too familiar place. My heart tightens and the old sense of withdrawing robes my shoulders like an old foe has found me again.

"Right." He scoffs as he winds up for round two. "So, Elle, what was the cause of your divorce?"

I choke on a chip of ice. Even Maya gapes at the man.

"That's a little personal," Graham says. I give my brother-in-law a grateful smile.

Graham is kind, but not outspoken. I assume that will be the only wall of defense I'll get from the man, but still I'm thankful.

"I don't think so," Edgar says. "It's a perfectly reasonable question when we both come from divorce. Better to get the skeletons out of the closet before it goes any farther."

I might be wrong, but I think Maya mutters *idiot* under her breath before guzzling her lemon water.

Blinking several times to make sure no tears will suddenly burst forth, I stare at the man who most certainly will not be getting a second date. "I suppose I could ask you the same."

"Easy," he says. "She couldn't handle the duties of marriage and all that comes with being a wife. Our ambitions and goals were clearly out of balance. When she started pressing for children, that was the final straw."

"You don't want kids?"

"Of course, but not until I know my partner is capable of rearing them. She wasn't, and refused to take any strides to get to that place. I couldn't see pursuing the relationship any longer. See, nothing so terrible explaining why a marriage failed. And yours?"

"You don't need to answer, Elle," Maya says.

But I do; Edgar is a jerk, but I let it spill out anyway. "My husband was seeing someone else behind my back."

"Infidelity," Edgar says so matter of fact, it takes me back to that moment in the cruelest ways. He points a finger at me. "Have you ever queried as to his reasons for being unsatisfied?"

"What is that supposed to mean?" I snap.

Edgar sniffs, and takes another step. "If a man is content at home, he won't step out of the marriage."

My mouth drops. "Hold on. Are you suggesting it was all my fault?"

Edgar lifts a brow. "The choice was his, but I can't fault him if he wasn't having needs met at home."

"Oh really." I'm on my feet now. Maya has her face covered, but Graham gives me a thumbs-up. "Please, tell me what sort of needs a man requires before he's justified in betrayal."

"I can see this is tender for you," Edgar says without a glimmer of remorse in his tone. "But think of it as an opportunity to learn how to improve yourself so it doesn't happen again. Were you keeping a tidy house, showing enough affection, asking about his interests?"

"You know, it's been a pleasure meeting you, really, a treat," I say, gathering the borrowed purse Maya offered for the night. "But I'm so exhausted from all my personal wifely studies and my only-three days of work, I better head home."

"Elle, don't go," Maya says, but her tone tells me she understands.

"See you later, Maya."

"So easily offended," Edgar chuckles. "Emotional; I'd suspect that would be one reason for a failed marriage, too."

"Would you shut up, you know nothing," Maya snaps. The woman is composed, beautiful, charming—but too much scratching and Maya will snap with the best of them.

"Good night," I say and beeline it toward the door.

"Let me drive you, Elle," Graham says.

"No, thanks. Walking sounds perfect."

I wave without turning around and once I'm out on the street, I let the first tear fall.

* * *

LINDSTRÖM MAIN. My new place to find some sort of peace. It's late since I took a few detours during my rant-tear-filled stroll back home. Shops are closed for the night, but a soft back light glows inside the Scandinavian Market. I smile, peeking through the window as Brita sweeps behind the counter. The woman never stops. I check what I can see of the front room, and thankfully, it seems as if the grandkid baking party has wrapped up—apart from Brita.

I swallow some pride and tap on the window until she glances my way. With a tiny wave through the window, I catch her attention. She beams and quiets her broom against the wall. Five seconds later, she greets me at the front door.

"Hey there." Her smile falls in another breath. "Elle, have you been crying?"

"What?" I prod my cheeks. Great. I was too hasty, and my face is still puffy. There isn't a reason to lie. My shoulders slump. "Maybe a bit. Would it be annoying if I bought some afterhours chocolatey sweetness before I head home?"

She tugs on my elbow and pulls me inside. "Oh, I can supply the chocolatey stuff, but you keep your wallet and come spill."

I help Brita pick three bittersweet chocolate scones for each of us. She artfully sprinkles a dust of sugar over the top and we dip our treats in double chocolate cocoa. The tears come again the moment I open about the disastrous tale of my latest dating calamity. Yes, the story comes along with admitting the terrible break-up I mentioned is, in fact, a divorce.

"Elle," Brita says, tilting her head as I swipe the last of my tears away. "I didn't know you'd gotten married."

"Yeah. My parents never got on with him, so we only visited as a couple once and I doubt they bragged about their son-in-law much. Looking back, I can see my mistakes. I think him being fifteen years older had me infatuated with his position in life, you know."

"And since he's a hot shot in Eastern Medical, you still get to deal with him."

I braid the shorter ends of my hair. "Yep. That's how my nursing director spun things, so I wasn't jobless. After he'd been caught, my ex started doing anything to get me out of the picture and his girlfriend moved into my place. Things cooled off during the divorce process, but then about four or five months after we'd finalized, I must've done something to irritate him, and he tried to get me fired. Kathy, she's the nursing director, suggested instead of being let go, the board transfer me to Lindström. She knew I'm from here.

"I'm sure he put up a fuss so he could win, but the other board members couldn't find a valid reason to fire me. But a transfer, sure. He assured them if I wasn't booted out, I'd create a hostile working environment."

"But he was the one who—" Brita begins, but stops when I nod angrily.

"I know. I'm sure I wasn't perfect—well, I know I wasn't, but I would never have betrayed him. I'm dumb for thinking someone like him would want to stick with me, but when we met, this sounds ridiculous, I convinced myself that I *needed* to be with him. He's intelligent, speaks three languages; he's traveled the world, he had so much to offer . . ."

"Elle, don't you think you do, too?"

"Nursing school debt, youth, and inexperience is what I brought." Brita shakes her head, but allows me to return to my rant. "Anyway, we were married nine months after we met. I moved into an amazing home, had clout at work, the only problem was my parents weren't thrilled. My mom even warned me I was arm candy to the man. I figured in time they'd just come around.

"After a while I stopped visiting home because I didn't want to hear the criticism, but mostly because my family was right. Things changed quickly. He started working later, pointing out everything I did wrong. I guess, I got to the point where I felt like I couldn't even chew right, and stopped doing anything that would make him think less of me. That included friends he didn't like, hobbies, anything immature in his eyes. I worked hard at the hospital, tried to do and be everything for him—"

"And the payoff was you lost yourself," Brita says without judgment.

I'm not sure it was such a thing to lose. "Tonight, that guy brought out all those old resentments again."

"Because he's a nightmare," she says with great deliberateness.

"My ex said the same things, Brit. He wasn't happy, that's why he looked somewhere else. Or I didn't make the house comfortable, wasn't attentive enough, too curvy. I was too tired all the time, or I stayed up and read too much. After a while you start to believe things like that. Everything dumb Edgar said, wasn't news to me. I'd heard it before."

Brita opens her mouth to reply, but we're both stopped by the rumble of a deep voice, dripping in frustration. "Because they are both morons."

I whip around to the back of the bakery and it takes all my gumption to keep a new wave of tears from spilling out. Not out of sadness, but sheer embarrassment.

Axel stands in the door frame; a look painted on his face I'd never seen before. His forehead is furrowed, and his soft blue eyes are sharp, pointed, and borderline dangerous.

"I thought . . . I thought you guys were cleaning up out back," Brita says. She must have seen my entire face color purple from holding my sob inside. She offers me a sympathetic look.

"We're finished," Axel grumbles and sure enough, Jonas follows close behind.

I start gathering napkins, mugs, and crumbs, desperate to keep my face hidden behind a curtain of my hair. "I should go."

My heart thuds so painfully I worry it might snap a rib when Axel stomps over to me.

"You think all that?" His voice seems stuck in the dark rumble. With a stretched look, Brita steps to the side, so Axel takes her place in front of me.

Tears well in my eyes, but I keep my attention on the table.

"Elle," he says again. "You really think that what he did is your fault?"

"No," I insist, meeting his eyes. Straightening my shoulders, I blink through the blur in my eyes. "I don't know, maybe part of the reason."

He hardly takes a breath. "You're wrong."

"You don't know that," I whisper. Brita slowly drifts with Jonas to the kitchen, holding the mugs and plates. Now, it is me, Axel, and the stare between us. "You can't know, because you weren't there."

"Maybe not, but that doesn't change the fact that I know it's not your fault. It's on him, Elle."

Desperation to lighten the mood takes over as I inch toward the door. I force a shaky laugh and smile. "You can't tell, but I might be awful. I could be whiny, or needy, or bad at kissing; the worst person in a relationship."

Axel covers ground in three paces, his chest against me. A raging, delightful chaos fills my system. Axel doesn't smell like menthol Edgar, but of spice and a hint of chocolate.

"You forget, Elle," Axel whispers. *Oh, Mylanta his lips are so close.* "I was with you before him, and I can promise that you're not awful. And . . ." –one inch closer– "you're absolutely not bad at kissing."

My throat bobs like I've swallowed a grapefruit and I can't keep my eyes focused on any clear spot. My knees feel close to buckling. Overwhelming doesn't cover what the collision of despair, affection, fear, and hope feels like. I only know breaking down in front of Axel Olsen is the last thing on my docket of life goals.

"As you said a couple days ago," I whisper in return, slapping my hand around the door until I find the knob. "People change."

He simply shakes his head and takes a step backward.

Half of Brita's face peeks around the kitchen frame. I smile and wave. "Thanks, Brit. I'll see you later." My eyes blink back to Axel. "See you at work."

For the first time in my memories, Axel doesn't offer a witty retort, he doesn't smile, not even close. His jaw tightens as if he keeps a thousand words locked inside. I force a smile for us both, and practically jump out onto the street. Axel has walked me home at night once, but I take to a jog in case he opts to be chivalrous again. Since running into the blast from the past, vulnerabilities I don't want to see keep creeping to the surface.

I don't know what to make of the fracture in my mind; a battle between opening to Axel, who keeps finding a way to catch me in needy moments, or keeping my comfort and safety behind the walls.

When I reach home, I plop onto the porch swing. I've missed four calls between Maya and Graham, but I'll call them in the morning. Right now, I need to grapple with the truth tumbling about in my mind. As I stare into the dark, I knew those safety walls are cracking and it is all Axel Olsen's fault.

CHAPTER 10

*R*olling out of bed takes all my will power on Saturday morning. Duty calls. The sun isn't up yet as I slurp a thermos of herbal tea to ease the new scratch in my throat. I refuse to get sick. I'll drink the bitter tea all day long if it means the sniffles and coughs stay far, far away.

Maya texted me late last night to inform me of her disgust for Edgar's behavior. She must have felt guilty for setting up the date, even after I explained it was going in the books of funny stories to tell the grandkids someday, because my sister came over after eleven with a sappy romance and asked to have a sisters' late night; something we haven't done since I was sixteen.

This morning, I tear up thinking of Maya and her confessions over her fertility struggle. My sister puts on a strong face ninety-nine percent of the time, but last night she let me in on some of the hurt she's endured the last three years of negative tests, no answers, and dimming hope. Maybe, just maybe, coming back home isn't the terrible, no-good situation I thought it might be. If it strengthens a sisterly bond, that is worth it, right?

The hospital is sleepy when I stride inside with a yawn. Settling down at the desk, I take inventory and greet a few of the other nurses who exclusively work the weekend shifts. Rubbing the sleep out of my makeup free eyes (who has time for that at five in the morning?) for the tenth time, I begin the day.

Two hours later, I slump back into the seat at my desk. Morning medication is out, and I have a minute to breathe. There is something different about my desk. With a grin, I peek into the opened box decorated in Scandinavian flags. Already some of the sweet goods are missing, and I promptly help myself to a cream-filled piece of heaven. Yep, no question, I need to take a jog in the morning.

With breakfast being served to rooms, and a good fifteen minutes before I can give anyone any pain medication, I meander to the therapy gym. Only a few lights are on, and no patients were being battered yet. Still, the sound of rapid typing at a computer tucked in the alcove near the back offices, draws me inside.

I study the back of Axel's head for a second. He has earbuds tucked in his ears, and one foot taps to a beat I can't hear.

"You know," I say, loud enough he should hear. "I would've moved back sooner if I'd known there would be free bakery goods basically every day."

He wheels around in the office chair, and pulls out an ear bud. Smiling is Axel's superpower. The sight can melt, stun, and kill in one whack.

"Hey, I didn't know you were working today."

"That I am." I waggle my sugary pastry and grin. "And I think I found the highlight of the day."

Axel leans back in his chair, earning me a glimpse at the tone in his arms; a silver watch adds to the chiseled look. Hurriedly, I school my attention back to the pastry before he catches me staring.

"Well, I'm glad I could be part of the highlight." His smile fades a little bit and that stern look in his eye returns.

"So, how's the party going to go tonight?" I ask, picking a piece of the flaky crust and popping it onto my tongue.

His expression doesn't change, except his eyes brighten. "The same as everything. Imagine two men who used to be sworn enemies sharing a birthday party that serves as a homage to their accomplishments."

"Competitive?"

He nods. "Very."

"Sounds like you and Jonas. If I remember right, you two always try to outdo the other."

Axel snorts. "Oh, we're still competitive, but my grandpa will scrutinize all Philip's accomplishments, spout off a few times how superior the Danes are. I'll give you a warning, don't ever say Lindström is nicknamed Little Sweden."

"Sounds like they aren't always fun."

With a shake of his head he chuckles. "No, it's fun. That's how they are all the time. By the end they both will probably get emotional and go on about how they're proud of their families and all that. It's fun. Personally, I think they need to take a comedy tour on the road or something. They don't even try, but their grumpiness and rivalry provides the comedic relief in my life."

"It'll be awesome then."

"Next Olsen-Jacobson party you'll need to come."

"Well, I guess I'd need an invitation," I say, flirting without knowing—and not very well.

"Noted. Want to come tonight?"

My voice sticks in my throat. "Uh, well . . ."

"Got a blind date?"

I groan. "Definitely not."

"Okay, well?"

"Would your parents be okay with it?"

Axel rolls a pen between his fingers. "Are you kidding. You're the one who saved grandpa; you'd be the guest of honor."

My stomach flutters and my cheeks feel hot. "Um . . . okay. That sounds fun."

"Great." He pauses for a moment. "So, how are you doing?"

"Wait, what are we talking about? Are you asking how I'm doing because I'm about to gorge on butter, sugar, and regret? Or how am I doing because my big, nasty divorce secret spilled?"

He scratches one side of his stubbled face. "I knew you were divorced, Elle."

"What?" Inside feels like a fist has gone through my insides.

Axel pushes off his knees and folds his arms—*geez Louise*—he even has the vein bulge in his forearms and hands. "I knew you were divorced."

"But you . . . never said anything."

"It's not something I thought was my business, really."

"But how did you know, and not Brita?"

"I found out by accident. Maya cuts my mom's hair, and a few months ago her car was getting fixed, so I picked her up from the salon, and she let it slip. Maybe I'm wrong, but I didn't think it was something I should go tell everyone about when I hadn't seen you in years."

"No," I say through a gasp. "No, I appreciate that it's just . . . I thought you would've said something to me or tried to tease—"

"Really?" he interrupts. "You think I'd tease you about getting divorced? Wow, you must really think little of me."

"Sorry, that's not what I meant. I haven't had . . . many positive comments. Naturally, I assume something uncomfortable will happen. I'm surprised I admitted it to Brita, but I was so upset it all spilled out."

Axel steps closer; I can almost taste his spicy body wash and soap.

"I can understand why you were upset," he says. "I was, too. As insensitive as this might sound, I'm glad you got divorced. Your ex sounds like piece of work, and that's putting it mildly because I'm on the clock."

I pick at the flaky crust of the pastry. "Well, thank you, but I still wish it wouldn't have happened."

"I can imagine. I don't think most people set out to get divorced. It doesn't make you those things that he said, though. It was *his* mistake, Elle, and his alone. Trust me, it was a big mistake too."

My breath catches in my throat. What is that supposed to mean?

Anything, really depending on how I want to read into the words. Any way I view it though, my pulse still thuds in my ears.

"Why do you keep saying things like that?"

"Because the girl I knew wouldn't let some jerk stomp her down like this. I'm surprised he's able to walk without a limp." Axel leans in, my back pressing against a gray filing cabinet. "There was a part of that break-up before prom situation you conveniently left out."

"I don't know what you're talking about," I say, urging my smile to stay hidden.

"Do you know how long it took to get the scent of rotting rodent out of my car? It took Jonas and me two weeks to find that mouse under the seat."

My mouth drops. "Axel, I continue to deny any involvement in such sinister things. Now, if you were to ask if Malorie Hamblin found said decaying rodent and was supplied the idea . . . that is a different story."

Both our smiles are gone; in a moment when we ought to be laughing, we suddenly aren't. We stare unblinking at each other, his lips slightly parted, but the cataclysm between us shatters when the therapy door opens, and a tall redhead strolls in with perfect freckles sprinkled over her thin nose and two coffee cups in her hand.

Axel takes three steps back, and I try to hide the up and down of my chest as my lungs grapple to recover from the moment I could have easily kissed Axel. He could have kissed me. I dare to think that he might have wanted to.

"Hi Beth," he says, voice rough.

The therapist is one I've not met, but I do remember Axel mentioning a new hire. She smiles, all innocently gorgeous. Her hair falls straight and reminds me of cinnamon. Therapist Beth glances my way, but quickly turns all focus to Axel after a polite smile at the out of place nurse.

"Hi. Brought you something," she says handing over one of the cups. "Just cream, right?"

He nods and takes a sip. "You got it. Thanks."

No reason for jealousy; I have no claim on Axel, and I don't want one.

Beth asks Axel to show her again how to sign into the documentation program. Using the moment of distraction, I leave, glad to fall back into the hustle of the day. I force myself to think clearly. My heart isn't ready for another fracture.

As sweet as he is, we're friends. Clearly, nothing more. And that is fine with me.

Perfectly . . . fine.

"WHERE DID you run off to earlier?" Axel says, guiding a patient past the nurses' desk. His patient seemed to have a steady gait, but still Axel grips tight to a thick belt around the man's waist.

"Oh, you were busy, and I needed to get back to work."

"I wasn't busy."

"You had to help your . . . coworker."

He lifts one brow and I'm not sure how I feel that the patient asks to rest in the chair by my desk. I admit the way Beth looked at Axel itched wrong, and I don't want him to know that.

"Why did you say it like that?"

"Like what?"

Axel helps his patient stand. "You're not going to get awkward because of the other night, are you?"

My forehead furrows in the center and my eyes narrow so I could see my lashes. "What if I do? I don't need you or anyone telling me how I should react to the situation."

Axel chuckles, maybe a little nervously. "Whoa, okay. I was going to tell you not to worry about it. React however you want. Maybe cuss a few times. I'd pay to see that."

"Sorry, I'm undercaffeinated and I don't know if you noticed, I'm a little defensive on the subject."

"I get it . . . well, I don't, but don't be awkward. That's what I'm trying to say."

"Maybe I like making you feel uncomfortable."

"You do," he says. "I really think you do. So, be there tonight at seven!"

He says something else, or maybe he doesn't, I can't tell since he disappears behind the wall. I smile and turn back to my computer, yawning and stretching as I type up reports for the morning. I must have dozed a bit because I shriek out loud when she taps me on the shoulder.

"Yikes, sorry. Didn't mean to sneak up on you," Beth and her freckles have joined me.

"No, it's fine. I need to wake up a bit."

She points to the stacks of patient files. "Mind if I take a look at Room 401 that just showed up today?"

"Sure." I spin around and hand the binder stacked in surgery notes and treatment plans.

She studies the file as I type, feeling more foolish for caring who Axel is friendly with in the first place. Beth seems nice.

"Thanks," she says after a few minutes, handing the file back over.

"No problem." I glance over the top of the monitor with a small smile. "How are you liking the job?"

"Oh, it's great. I only graduated last May and finally found a good set up," she says. "Everyone is really nice."

"Yeah, the therapists are great."

"I've gotten to know Axel the best since he's training me, but that's fine with me."

"Yeah." My voice croaks. "He's a nice guy and a good therapist."

Professional. Unassuming. Neutral.

"Not bad to look at either," she says, biting her lower lip. "Not that I'd cross the line or anything . . ."

That's what I want to hear. *Stop it, Elle.*

". . . well, maybe I'd break my rule just once."

Not what I want to hear. Beth giggles like we've been friends for years, waggles her fingers in a wave as she walks away, oblivious to the storm toiling inside my chest. Biting the inside of my cheek bitterly, I'm not typing anymore, more like smashing the keys.

Why did I have to see Axel Olsen again? He messed up all my

plans. Friendship: line crossed. Attraction: line crossed, at least on my part. Dating: out of the question. Beth the therapist is proof Axel isn't looking to pull himself off the ogling market; he thrives there.

I just wish I'd convince myself to ignore the natural pull toward the man. Without a doubt, if I go there, it will crash and burn.

CHAPTER 11

*H*ere's the thing. Despite my frustration at myself for allowing Axel to hit my radar, I won't break an invitation. I forced myself not to overly glamorize, simply to prove Axel is a rekindled friendship and nothing more

Then Maya saw me.

She and Graham don't have a TV currently, and sometimes come over to catch up on their favorite crime show. She insisted on helping with my hair, telling me I need to learn how to style the sort of cut I have, then when I wasn't looking accosted me with a matte lip color.

Feeling too fancy, I pause at the bottom of the steps leading into the bakery. At least five people have time to stroll past me on the sidewalk before I finally knock on the door.

Bastien is the one to open, and he beams at me. "Hey, Elle." He turns toward the open space that connects Philip's house to the bakery. "Mom, she's here."

I hang up my coat at the door as Sigrid Olsen rounds the corner, her smile much like her son's, white and beautiful. "Elle, hi. I'm so glad you made it. I wanted to say hello before everyone else snagged you away."

My eyes pop when she pulls me into a tight hug. "Thanks for having me."

Sigrid ushers me toward the house side. "Are you kidding? Everyone was thrilled when Ax told us he'd asked you. You're our VIP."

I feel more at ease as she pulls me into the front room. Brita finds me instantly and leads me around the room, reminding her side of the family who I am; everyone promptly reminds her they already know.

Against my will, my breath catches in my throat when Axel comes down from upstairs. The tight blue T-shirt shows him off too well, and my palms start to sweat.

"Hey, you made it."

"I did."

Axel opens his arm so I'll step in front of him, deeper into the room. Brita sits on the seat I planned to take, leaving me in the middle of the couch, and my left side open. Jonas stands behind Axel; he sees the spot, then the recliner on Brita's other side, and takes the chair. Axel sits next to me, and of course his hand settles half an inch from mine. I fold my arms over my chest, because that hand is tempting. Problem solved.

"Want a drink?" he asks after a few moments.

"Sure."

He hands me a clear plastic cup with a reddish liquid. "It's juice. We keep things mild with the little ones around." He tousles Bastien's hair as the youngest Olsen brother takes my other side on the couch.

Bastien smooths his hair. "Dude, I'm going to Amy's after this."

"Yeah? Well, you look better now."

"Shut up, or I'll make Jonas sue you."

Jonas rolls his eyes. "Doesn't work like that, Bass."

Axel laughs, speaking loud enough Jonas will hear. "Besides, Jonas never leaves his desk. He doesn't know how to sue people."

Jonas whips his head our way. "Keep going and let's find out."

I snicker, leaning forward to look at Jonas. "I wouldn't do court-rooms either if I was a lawyer."

Jonas grins, shier than Axel, but when they are side to side, clearly anyone can see they are twins. "See, Elle gets it."

"Don't worry," Brita says. "I think Ax is still struggling with his Jonas jealousy. Your job is awesome, and you've got a perfect wife."

"Jonas, what? Jealous? Brit, do you really want to get this started? I know you love my little brother—"

"Three minutes, man, three minutes," Jonas says.

"As I said, my *little* brother, but you know I'll win if you get this going. You know it."

"Nope," she says. "I don't want to get it going right now because we're getting started." She hops off the couch and stands in the front of the room.

"You two, simmer," I say with a laugh when Jonas and Axel keep tossing underhanded comments at the other, even Bastien joins in, alternating which older brother he sides with.

"Okay, now that everyone is eating, I thought we'd say a few things," Brita tells the room.

Sigrid hands me a plate filled with meatballs smothered in gravy with a unique flat bread I've never tried before. Delicious, and worth sitting between a twin battle.

"Happy birthday, Grandpas," Brita says brightly.

Everyone mumbles their birthday wishes and Viggo and Philip puff up a bit in their separate reclining chairs.

"I'll take a few thoughts on my Farfar, because . . . well, because I called dibs," Brita says.

Axel leans into me. "Get ready for the fact checking."

"What?"

He grins and nods at the two older men. "Just watch."

Brita tenses a bit, as if readying for an attack, when she goes into the life and legacy of Philip Jacobson. Likely a paragraph in, Viggo has his first comment.

"Now, I'd like to say, I was the one who encouraged, dear Hanna to marry this sod."

Philip huffs. "Hanna didn't need your help. It was love at first sight, although she did convince Clara to take pity on you, give you a chance. Told me so herself, and are you going to disagree with her, rest her soul."

Viggo narrows his eyes and pinches his lips.

"Oh, point for Philip," Axel says. "Grandpa won't argue with anyone who's dead."

"I didn't know I got a personal commentary." I nudge his side.

"It's a full service we offer, helps explain things to people."

"No, älskling," Philip says after Brita describes opening the bakeries. "It was my idea at first."

"*Wrong*," Viggo snaps. "You know I wrote the initial business plan."

"Okay and on that note, your turn, Sig." Brita slumps next to Jonas in his chair, rolling her eyes as her grandfather keeps arguing with Viggo.

When Axel's mom takes over, Philip has just as many corrections as Viggo gave.

"I told you," Axel says after nearly choking on his drink when Philip and Viggo face off over whether a certain sweet bread originated in Sweden or Denmark.

"They're sort of adorable," I admit.

Bastien rolls his eyes. "Yeah, they're kittens."

It doesn't take long before Viggo and Philip cool, and start to praise their families, grandchildren, and their love of the heritage living on through the shop. I think Viggo gets teary, and everything about this scene blooms warmth through my chest.

Then Viggo pauses, turning to me. "You, love, you are Danish, yes?"

"She looks Swedish," Philip says.

"Maybe she's Norwegian," Brita's dad offers with a bit of irony.

I smile, and stare at my plate. "Um, we're . . . German."

Philip and Viggo, and basically everyone groans dramatically.

"That's okay, it's okay," Viggo insists after a moment. "We will make her Danish, keep bringing her food."

The night continues much the same, apart from a few German jokes tossed my way. By the end of the evening anytime someone says something off, or a hitch happens, the joke becomes: *It's because Elle is German.*

I help Brita, Elias, and Sigrid take plates into the bakery kitchen when the dong of the antique clock announces ten o'clock.

"Thanks," Brita says, taking the plates.

"I think it's hilarious watching your families together now," I say through a yawn.

She chuckles. "I know. They're nuts."

Searching the front room, I don't see Axel. He invited me, so I ought to say goodbye to him at least.

"Hey, can I ask a favor," Brita says, interrupting my search.

"Sure, what's up?"

"Well, Jonas and his brothers are running that spring marathon."

"Yeah, Axel mentioned they were, that's awesome."

She smiles. "Yeah, except Jonas hates running. I promised him I'd run with him, and I know you're into running—"

"Want me to run with your husband?"

She laughs. "No, with me. He has a few things to do at work tomorrow morning, I thought we could go, and I'd start getting into shape. Then I can force him to go with me."

"I was planning on a run tomorrow at the park. You're welcome to come with me."

"Okay, but it's a judgment free zone, right? I'm not a runner."

I make a *pfft* sound, and wave my hand. "No judgment, I haven't been running for two weeks. I'll be puffing right along with you."

Brita squeals, adding a little dip to her knees. "Thank you. If I can get Jonas to come in even one minute faster than Axel, you will have saved me endless twin battles."

I can see the scene perfectly in my head. One night spent with the Olsen family again, and all my memories of the brotherly dynamics rush back. Even though Jonas was shy in high school, outside, in his element, I heard him get a few jabs in on Axel.

"I'll just meet you at the fountain in the park," I say. Sound good?"

"Yes. You'll have a partner for sure."

Axel and Jonas came around the corner, carrying more plates. Axel looks my way, setting a tray on top of the glass display case. "You leaving?"

"Yeah, I better get going. Thanks for inviting me, I had a lot of fun."

He shoves his hands in his pockets, and rocks on his heels, subtle enough I doubt anyone but me notices. "I can walk you home."

I smile nervously, and hope *he* doesn't notice. "No, that's okay. I was extra lazy today and drove the two blocks."

He opens the door for me. "Well, then I'll walk you out."

With a final wave to his family, the door jingles as Axel closes it behind us. We're shoulder to shoulder, close enough his knuckles brush mine as we walk down the stairs. I draw in a sharp breath and hide my discontent behind a grin. "I forgot how great your family is."

"Yeah, I'll keep them."

I unlock my car door, then turn to say goodbye. I must've miscalculated how near we'd stood because we're nearly nose to nose. My mouth waters, forcing me to swallow three times. Axel smells like the morning after rain—so good. I blink through the fog in my head.

"I'm glad you came, Elle, really. You're . . ."

"What?" I press, though I don't know how much I want him to finish the thought.

"You're easy to be around. Everyone relaxes, me included."

My heart skips; my voice is raw. "I wouldn't say you're uptight."

He shakes his head. "No, but . . . when I am, well, I'm glad you're easy to be around."

I tilt my head when he shoves his hands in his pockets. A cue, I've discovered, Axel uses when he feels uncomfortable or vulnerable. "Axel Olsen, are you saying you can be yourself around me?"

"Alright, no one asked you to embarrass me," he says, and glances at the ground, adorably vulnerable.

"Oh, I kind of like making you blush a little."

His eyes are like sapphires in the dark when he looks up. "Okay, that's the last time I'm ever complimenting you."

I lose my mind and squeeze his forearm as if touching the man is an everyday thing. I'll admit this once, that sometimes the idea of one Axel touch a day doesn't seem like such a bad idea.

The dark might play a part, but I think his smile fades a bit, in a good way, like my touch surprises him, too.

I hurry into the car before I do something insane like hug him. "Well, thanks again for the invite. See you at work."

He nods, clearing his throat. "Thanks for coming, Elle."

"Anytime."

He follows and closes my door for me, with a little slap to the top of my car as he backs away. I drive the whole minute home, my body tingling from the laughter, but also from the way Axel has hooked into a piece of my soul. I'm not ready.

But the funny thing is I want to be.

CHAPTER 12

*M*y muscles burn as I stretch my heel to my rear. Brilliant sunbeams cast golden ribbons over the park. I don't want to wait too much longer to start the jog, but Brita has yet to show. Turning to my phone to give her a call, I notice a missed text.

Brita: *Girl, I'm so sorry. I caught a bug . . . it's not pretty. But, don't worry I didn't leave you partnerless. Honestly, I think he was glad to go . . . if you catch my drift.*

Smiling, I shoot back a reply with feel better vibes and several question marks because I have no clue what she means, until I hear the familiar voice that starts to curl my toes.

"Elle?" Axel comes up behind me, holding his phone, too. In my opinion there aren't many people who can pull off a dignified look in sweatpants, but Axel has the gift.

I stare at Brita's message in a flash. She'd sent Axel, and he . . . wants to go?

"Hi," I say. "So, Brita forced you to take her place, huh?"

Axel lifts one brow, glancing at his phone when it dings. He laughs. "Well, if I'm replacing Brita—who doesn't run, by the way—then you're replacing Jonas. Again, who doesn't run."

I tilt my head, and tap my chin. "So, your scheduled running partner ditched, too? I smell a fish."

"Maybe, or husband and wife are both sick . . . at the same time."

"Fishy. But whatever, I'm going to get started. The trail gets crowded after eight. Good to see you." I start plugging in my earbuds, but stumble slightly when Axel grips my arm.

"You're ditching me?".

I sneer playfully at him. "Oh, you couldn't keep up."

And just like that Axel's superpower smile melts my kneecaps. "We'll see. Loser buys lunch next time we work together."

Turning up the volume on my playlist, I shake his hand, then settle into a lunge. "You're on."

I HAD a patient tell me once that he'd take up running the moment he saw a runner with a smile on their face. If only he saw me now. I double over on the grass at the end of the loop, laughing. Not two seconds later, Axel drops by my side, gasping, sweaty, and grinning.

"You . . . cheated . . ." he says through deep breaths.

I guzzle some of my water, shaking my head. Although the air is getting chilly, my forehead is soaked in sweat. "No, I . . . warned you . . . that you couldn't keep up."

Axel shoves my shoulder, causing me to laugh harder as I rest against the grass. My pulse races, and the run invigorates every sense in all the right ways. Axel lies back, a hand over his chest, and he turns his face to me.

"I maintain my loss was unfair, but I'm a man of my word. When do you work next?"

"Tuesday."

"Tuesday it is. The best food a hospital cafeteria can make is yours."

I sit up and hug my legs against my chest as I study him. It's a carefree morning, but now, as quiet settles between us, the same tingle I always get around him shivers up my arms. "You've got lunch, but how about I supply a drink. My house is closer."

He shoots me with his fingers and flashes his white teeth. "Deal.

You might need to carry me to my car."

"Oh, come on, you drove?"

"Yes," he says, curling onto his knees. "Because I'm not a lunatic like you, who runs to the place where she's going to go *running*."

"Amateur," I say, staggering toward the parking lot.

"Or smart. It really depends how you look at things."

"I'm going to sweat all over your car." I offer him one last chance to change his mind.

With playful waggle to his brows, Axel opens the door and is too close for comfort—who am I kidding, he can get a bit closer—as I slip inside. "Nothing is better than sweat residue."

"You're officially disgusting."

"I live to please, Ellie."

My parents' car sits in the garage when we pull up the driveway. They'd gotten home early this morning—a day earlier than expected —but apparently there'd been an emergency involving my uncle's mother. From what my dad said, things didn't sound good. My aunt and uncle skedaddled to Portland and my parents hopped on the next flight home. I make a mental note to give my uncle a call and check in as soon as Axel leaves.

"My parents are probably sleeping," I say with a sense of sneaki-ness. No reason to sneak Axel inside. The Olsens are friendly with my family, but it certainly makes things more fun. We whisper into the kitchen where I pour us both glasses of chocolate almond milk because—heart attack—then take us back to the porch swing.

"Are you glad you came back to Lindström?" Axel asks after a few silent sips.

"In some ways, now, but not at first." I tap his knee with mine. "What about you? I thought you wanted to get out of town and see the great, big world after high school."

He sighs and scrubs his face. "I did. You know I went to school in Wisconsin and had clinicals in New Jersey."

"Terribly far; you're right, practically different countries."

"Hey now," he says, finishing off the last of his milk. "I applied for jobs all over the east coast, but when this one opened up—I don't know, it felt like the right thing. My family is here, and now that I'm old and wise, I see the benefits of being close by."

"Don't say you're old. If you're old that means I'm old."

I settle against the back of the swing, enjoying the sound of morning birds, and the way Axel adjusts so our shoulders touch. Auntie Kathy would be proud because in the moment, I forget about the burdens of life and find true satisfaction simply being still.

Until the screech comes from inside the house.

"Elle Moira Weber!"

Axel and I both whip around as the storm door crashes open. My mother trembles, seething really, holding an opened package in her left hand and clenches the fist of her right.

"This . . . person can't . . . humiliate you like this," Mom spits through her teeth.

"Mom, what are you—" I finally survey the package. Oh no. I'd forgotten all about it. I look at my mother. "Did you open my mail?"

Perhaps she's too blind with rage, but my mom doesn't seem to know Axel is here. He's probably wishing he could teleport off my porch.

Mom shakes the package with vigor. "Have you read this?"

My body feels like ice and I can't see how the situation can be any more mortifying. "I didn't want to yet."

Mom isn't giving me the option. She tugs out a plastic zipper bag filled with jewelry—my jewelry—and tosses a second bag into my lap. I squeeze the milk glass between my thighs to catch all her zipper bag bombs. Some hold my family photos, rings, necklaces, makeup, even a birthday card I gave to my ex last year.

"Dear Elle," Mom starts reading.

"Mom, please . . ." At first, I thought Axel being here would be humiliating, but when he squeezes my shoulder and smiles at me, I feel better in a strange way. I mouth I'm sorry to him, but he only flattens his hand on my back; his touch is diverting and calming.

"Enclosed you will find odds and ends I've found as I've spent the week rearranging the house with Rebecca." Mom's eyes flash angrily. "He actually has the nerve to say her name. Her name!"

"Stop, then." She doesn't.

"I know you won't mind—he goes on," Mom snaps. "Since you didn't have the care to pack them, I allowed *Becky* to pick a few of the nicer items to keep for herself, should she want any. Among these was the pearl teardrop necklace I know you wore a total of one time." Mom bares her teeth and flames burst from her eyes. "I'm assuming the creep is talking about my mother's necklace! We have a certificate of authenticity for that necklace, Elle. It's an heirloom for my future grandchildren!" My mother loses every ounce of composure. As terrible as it looks, I know her rage isn't pointed at me, but at Rodney A. Mitchell, the sleezeball of North Carolina. Still, every word hurts.

Mom drags a deep breath through her nose, and tears burn my eyes. "And then this last part—"

"Elle," Axel interrupts, chipper, but louder than most would say a name. My mom tears her eyes off the letter, and for the first time since she'd barged onto the porch, she seems to realize we aren't alone. "Thanks for going running today since my brother couldn't hack it. I better get going."

With a watery smile I meet his eyes. I could kiss the man right now.

"Oh," Mom said under her breath. "Hello . . ."

"Axel," he says, and stands as he holds out his hand.

"Yes, of course, Axel. I know your name," Mom laughs nervously, giving his hand a pat. "I, uh, oh I apologize for all that. I didn't know . . ."

Axel dismisses the outburst with a wave. "Don't worry about it, Mrs. Weber, truly." He glances at me. "Elle, you forgot your jacket in my car."

My brow furrows. I didn't bring a jacket. He jerks his head toward his car, and it clicks. "Oh, right."

Mom bobs in the doorframe, looking sheepish, and I feel she deserves some of that. Axel waves, marvelously keeping the peace and tension from building any more. He opens the passenger door, and I hear the front door of the house close.

I hate the knot in my chest. I hate that I'm near crying in front of Axel.

"You okay?" he asks once we're alone.

"I'm so sorry you had to hear that. I got the envelope a couple weeks ago, but I guess I didn't want to read—"

I let out a small gasp, when Axel's strong hand curls around mine.

"Don't apologize, Elle." He sounds almost stern. "Please, don't apologize for that guy one more time. He's not a man. He's a coward, who wants to make sure he bullies you as much as he can until he turns on some other woman someday. He's not a man."

Each word draws him closer. A tear splashes onto my cheek, and for once I don't feel ashamed. I smile, giving his hand a tight squeeze.

"You know, as annoying as you are, sometimes you know the perfect things to say."

Axel laughs, and my insides turn to mush when he pulls me against his chest. I know Axel is strong, but I suppose until this up-close and personal opportunity I didn't realized how strong. My arms encircle his waist and I can't remember a time I've been embraced by a man other than my father with such sincerity, such tenderness. I don't even care that I'm desperately in need of a shower—or deodorant at the very least.

Pulling back when it hasn't been long enough, Axel grins slyly. "If I say such nice things, then when are you just going to start admitting I'm right about . . . everything."

I try to shove his shoulder, but he dodges, causing me to stumble. My cheek flattens against his chest, by accident, but he catches me with his arms around my waist. I'm inclined never to budge again. Slowly, my eyes peel to his. The tone of blue truly isn't ordinary. Sparks of green and gold mingle with the sky blue, with a bit of brown to deepen the hue depending on emotion. Axel's jaw pulses, and my tongue feels drier than a sand dune.

He clears his throat, and helps me stand straight. "I was wondering . . ." he begins, but doesn't go on.

"What?" I ask. He wants to go out—I can't be reading him wrong.

Ask! The word chants in my head like a crowd at an overtime basketball game and I don't care to stop it.

There is a moment when confident Axel Olsen is vulnerable, but only a moment. With a scoff, he leans back against his car and folds his arms as his charismatic, carefree side returns. "I was wondering how we're going to pay Brita and Jonas back for ditching us today."

Inside my stomach takes a plunge. "I don't know, it'll take some thought."

Axel shrugs, taps my shoulder the same way I used to do to my teammates. The time for tender embraces has flown the coop. "You sure you're good?"

"Yeah. I'm tougher than I look."

"I don't doubt it."

"Although, this mom reading my mail experience has convinced me I need to take my apartment hunt a little more seriously," I add.

Axel rounds to the driver side. "I told you there's still some condos for lease at my complex."

"They're more appealing than ever."

He laughs. "I think they're a decent size and fairly priced. I'm no house hunter, but if you want . . . I could help you out if you want to look over there . . . or something. I know one of the couples leasing their condo pretty well."

If I didn't know any better, I'd say Axel was a little nervous.

"You'd put in a good word for me, huh?"

He shrugs and pulls out the aviator sunglasses from the visor over the wheel. "Sure. If you're interested."

I bite my bottom lip, tasting the salt of my sweat. "That would be great. Thanks. First car shopping, now house shopping."

"I'm a man of many skills, Ellie. I'll text you when I hear from them."

"Sounds good."

Axel jokes a bit more about the run, and insists a final time that I cheated. He drives off with a wave, and I am left feeling light and relaxed. Thoughts of plastic bags filled with old memories and a crass, razor-sharp letter are a hundred miles from mind.

CHAPTER 13

$\mathcal{V}$iv clicks away on the computer across the command center, as we've come to call the cluster of desks at the nurses' station. Brita is pleading her case, and I'm loving every second.

"I'm serious, we both got sick."

Licking my thumb covered in cinnamon and sugar, I try to twist my grin into something smug. "So you think bringing me treats will make up for it?" I pinch off a chunk of muffin, fluffy and melt-in-your mouth.

"Personally," she says, taking back the small muffin box. "I have a feeling I delivered you a treat you really wanted by not showing up."

My eyes go wide, mouth open. I sort of shriek and toss a piece of muffin at her face. "What do you mean by that?"

"Oh, you know exactly what I mean."

And just like that, Viv's attention is snared. Spinning in her chair, she uses her heels to walk across the space to my side. "What are we talking about? Sounds saucy."

"Elle went on a sweaty, weekend run with Axel."

Viv bites her bottom lip, lashes fluttering. "Saucy, indeed. Tell me *everything*."

"Weren't you doing a note that you said needed to be finished by one?" I flick her ear.

"Are you kidding? I'm zoned now, no way I'll be able to focus."

Brita props her chin on her palms, grinning, as though she's defeated me. My own documentation serves as a way to hide the twitch in the corner of my lips. No sense letting them see how they've got me red in the face thinking of the more memorable moments of my day with Axel.

"Elle," Viv cries out. She whips me with her fingers. "Tell me. Now."

"Ouch," I say, rubbing the welt. "Sorry, but it was just a run. No gasping and passion like I think you're wanting."

Viv's shoulders slump. "I would've settled for a kiss at least."

Me too. The thought comes from nowhere, stirring a spark of heat down to my core. I blink as if through a fog, intent to hide how close we came to each other, how Axel's hands rested on the curve of my waist, my head on his chest. I rub the back of my neck, feeling feverish, and type the final paragraph of my patient update.

"When are you seeing him again?" Brita asks.

I fumble over my keyboard. "Um, we're not seeing each other."

"You could," Viv insists. She sighs and reclines in her chair, staring at the ceiling. "It would be a delicious romance. Mmmm, you need to do it. I've wrapped my head around the idea, and now it must be."

Brita's eyes squint behind her dark lashes. "Can't say I disagree. I think Axel might like you, Elle."

I take a drink of water, mostly to clear away the scratch in my throat. "He does not. We're friends again, and that's plenty."

"Listen, all I can do is speak as his sister-in-law; my gut tells me he likes you, but he might think you're not into him because you guys went out in high school."

"Oh, that doesn't matter," Viv answers for me. "Right, Elle? That doesn't matter."

I stand, staple a few sheets of paper together, then look to them again; Viv is practically drooling. "It wouldn't matter, but Axel had plenty of time on Sunday to do something if he liked me. Sorry kids"

Brita groans. "Saying we're just friends when your face is red is code for we're both dragging our feet in realizing our passionate love for each other."

Viv nods, wholly serious. I bark a laugh, but the sound comes out all wrong, pitchy and rough. "It is not, and I think you sort of like the idea of a friend dating your brother-in-law."

"Hey, my motives are pure. I call it like I see it, girl. And what I'm seeing is my brother-in-law liking you. But I get it, if the sparks aren't there, they aren't. No harm done. Oh, speak of the devil." Brita grins down the hallway; Viv and I both jump to attention and arch over the desk, craning for a peek.

Empty. With a laugh, Brita wags her finger of shame in my direction. "Huh, got a little excited, Elle. Maybe there is something there."

"Don't you have a job?" I turn my back to her.

"I do. I'm going to go, but I'll see you later, probably with Axel."

My face feels sticky; my pulse races.

Thankfully, after Brita leaves, Viv goes back to her paperwork and a rush of patients begging for pain relief keeps us from dredging up talk of Axel Olsen.

JUST AFTER NOON, the lunch club gathers in line at the cafeteria. Abby jabbers on with Mack about her upcoming Christmas wedding and Viv is forcing Beth's backstory, whether she likes it or not. Axel stands at my shoulder. Brita's loony ideas loom over me the closer we come together. Dressed in nice slacks and a gray polo, hands down, Axel is one of the most attractive men I've ever known; he's a little addicting, and I'm a little discomposed how quickly he unravels me. Even more, that he has no idea what he's doing.

"Alright, a bet is a bet," he says once we get to the menu options. "What am I buying?"

"Oh, I'm going to make it good today. Definitely something I shouldn't eat."

"I'd think less of you if you didn't."

"Hmmm, something greasy."

"Better."

"I think it's gotta be the cheeseburger."

His lips curl, and he gives a thoughtful look over the menu. "Now, the question is are you going to make it a western burger or bacon burger?"

"A western what?"

He's against me, his body brushing mine, one of his strong hands finds the small of my back as he points out the burger on the board. I hold my breath, every sense intensely alive; I'm acutely aware of the rumble of his voice, smell of his sweet and spicy cologne, the stubble on the sharp lines of his jaw, the gentle circles he draws on my spine. My tongue dances behind my teeth, as I unashamedly, lean a little closer.

"You can make it worth all the regret by adding onion rings and barbecue sauce."

"Yeah," I say, my voice weirdly soft, like a gasp. "Yeah, that sounds good."

He smiles, and his hand leaves my back. "That's more like it."

Axel takes the lead to order and pay for the two of us. I catch Viv's stare, and nearly burst out a laugh. Eyes wide, her mouth open, and her brows nearly to her hairline. I take it she saw the entire toe-curling moment. So did Beth. Maybe it was my imagination, but I don't think the therapist found it as endearing. Old insecurities slip into place, threatening to ruin the moment, until Axel calls my name and hands me a Styrofoam box filled with all the goods.

I drift on dangerous ground, and I know it. Heartbreak is a constant companion in my love life, and my heart has just stopped bleeding. But maybe, however small, there is a chance this burning compulsion might not end in pain and tears. I tried to convince myself that Axel is the same guy from my decimated prom, but . . . he isn't. It's as though the guy my teenage heart saw—the genuine, funny, compassionate man—has emerged.

"By the way, I talked to my neighbors," Axel says, after everyone was happily eating. "They're willing to show you the condo tomorrow night, if you're up for it."

"Yeah, that would be amazing." I take a sloppy bite. Axel scoffs, and hand me a napkin.

Funny enough, I'm not even embarrassed.

"What are you doing, Elle?" Beth asks.

"Apartment shopping."

"At Axel's place?" Viv says with a wink. I glare at her.

Axel is oblivious to the nurse stare down and goes on. "I told Elle there were a few condos that were up for rent, but come on, who wouldn't want to be my neighbor?"

"I think Elle does," Viv says. I kick her shin.

"I'll be there tomorrow then." I shoot Axel an easy smile that speaks nothing of the colliding emotions bunching in the center of my chest.

Axel grins and steals a fry off my plate before being roped into Abby's requests that her male coworkers not do anything embarrassing at her reception. There are rumors of an epic dance number, apparently, and the blushing bride-to-be is so adamant I wouldn't take the risk if I were them.

CHAPTER 14

"*Y*ou look nice," Maya says when I tromp down the steps into the kitchen.

My sister's compliments about my low-key style are few. Surveying my jeans, sweater, and flats, I don't think there is anything too remarkable about my look. "Thanks. What are you doing?"

"Graham had to do an overnight business trip, so I just stopped in to say hi on my way home. Where are you headed?"

Maya picks at a bowl of mixed nuts when I grab my bag off the counter.

"I'm going to look at that condo I mentioned, remember?"

"Oh, that's right." She peeks at our mother who dances around the kitchen, the house phone tucked under her ear, laughing with the other voice on the phone. Maya grins at me. "I hope it works out for you before you and mom kill each other."

I laugh when my mom slaps the counter and glares at Maya before returning to her gossip.

"It's not so bad, but I need to have my own space. So do Mom and Dad. They don't need their single daughter hanging out with them on date night." Glancing at my watch, I sling my satchel over my shoulder. "I better get going."

"Hey, if you end up renting the place, I get to help you with furniture."

"Nah," I say shaking my head.

"I'm serious, Elle. I'm better at coordinating décor than you."

She's right, but I like to irritate her. Call me easily pleased.

Driving across town, I embrace the thrill blooming through my chest. My own place. How quickly I've forgotten the satisfaction brought by my own independence. Married to Rodney I'd been given an allowance. Even though I made money, I believed him when he'd told me there was only 'our' money. Such an idea is well and good, my parents have joint accounts, but what Rodney really meant was: *our money is my money and I'll give you some.*

I see Axel the second I pull into the parking lot, leaning against the railing around the steps, checking his phone, looking perfect. He waves with that addicting smile when I park. The buildings are bright and new, with beautiful stonework and landscaping. The unit I hope to lease even has a side garden and a larger yard since it's on the end.

"Excited?" he asks as I lock my car.

"That's an understatement." Feeling rather bold, I saunter right up to him, a hairsbreadth of space between us. "You know, you've sort of become my official sidekick in all this adulting."

"Maybe I've finally found my calling in life."

I swallow the tantalizing rush to my stomach when he rests his hand, again, on the small of my back, urging me toward the door.

"These are really nice," I say, for once keeping my voice from going all shrill and weird, "but I'm still a little iffy about the neighbors."

Axel makes a face and knocks, pinching my side.

A few seconds later, the door swings open and we're greeted by a woman, no taller than five feet, bright red lips, and a baby bump ready to burst.

"Hiya!" she says cheerfully. "Come on in, now. Yep, getcha on in here. Excuse the mess and boxes, but we're heading out this weekend

with a load of our things. Call us crazy for packing up without a tenant."
We are both forced into the apartment when she pulls us by the arms.
The woman chuckles after everything she says, and even knowing her
for fifteen seconds, it's already impossible not to smile around her.

"Lucy, this is Elle," Axel says.

"Hiya." She sighs and rests her hands on her missing hips. "So,
you're interested in this place, are ya?"

I nod, classifying the woman as the epitome of Minnesota and
peer around the large front room. There's plenty of light, and French
doors open to the porch. The walls are pale yellow—not my choice—
but workable.

"Good. We love this place, but the husband got a promotion that
takes him to the heart of Minneapolis. We figure no better time to
move then now, you know. My guy sorta likes the idea of renting
out the place; an investment he calls it. Why dontcha go in the
kitchen."

Axel stays by my side during my inspection. The kitchen is enormous, larger than my parents' at least.

"When did you do these?" he asks, running a hand over the gray
granite counters.

"Oh, you know, a few weeks ago."

"Did Luke put them in?"

Lucy giggles as if it's the silliest idea. "Oh, now come on. He
wouldn't even know where to start. Poor guy's working late tonight,
so it's just me showing you around. But I think I know the place
pretty darn good."

Lucy drags us around the two bedrooms, the bathrooms. I fawn
over the walk-in closet, rough-cut wood floors, and the view of a
community park. Axel offers to trade since his unit overlooks the
parking lot.

"Well, whatcha think?" Lucy says once the tour wraps back around
to the kitchen. "Oh, and the fridge'll stay, did I say that?"

I tap the stainless-steel refrigerator, big enough to hold supplies
for a family of six. "It has everything I'd ever need. I can see why you
don't want to leave it."

"That's the truth. Everyone is so darn nice. At least we aren't going too far."

"Do you have an application I can fill out?"

Lucy hugs her bump and beams. "That I do, just hang on for a sec." The woman waddles down the hallway and I take the time to investigate the range, backsplash, and lighting they'd installed beneath the cabinets.

"You like it?" Axel asks again.

"It's perfect. Honestly, I don't know what to do with all this space and just me." I lean in closer to whisper. "They could probably charge more."

"Well now, we figure the utilities during the winter make up for the price of rent," Lucy says, popping around the corner. The woman must have the hearing of a bat. "Being on the end, sometimes that wind makes things pretty chilly. Here you go, although this guy's recommendation is better than any application," she snickers, patting his shoulder. "He's never complained when my guy texts him saying his crazy craving-filled wife needs one of those treats they make. Always follows through and brings a big box."

Axel's face colors a little as Lucy hands me the official application, and I tell her the bakery is Axel's secret weapon, and has been brainwashing me with treats for weeks.

After we leave, Axel stays with me, walking slowly back to the parking lot. He stares distantly at the sky, filled with rolling purple clouds. A storm is heading our way.

"I've got to admit when I moved back, I didn't expect to have you as my personal welcome wagon," I say.

Axel smiles, but doesn't show his teeth. He's almost somber, in his unique light-hearted-always sort of way. "I surprised myself. You know, I'd been thinking of moving."

"Why do you say that like some sort of dark confession."

"I never told anyone," he admits, walking with me to the driver's side of my car. "I love living close to family like I told you, but I sort of felt like I was missing something."

Wow. I can't recall a time when Axel had this tone—you know the type—a tone of voice that dips an octave because a typically invulnerable person is about to open the inner layers and be vulnerable.

"Anyway," he goes on. "I've had a good time the last few weeks, so helping out isn't a big deal."

Axel must have noticed his demeanor change and is quick to return to easy conversation. I have a sneaking suspicion Axel has walls of his own. He's crumbled a few of mine, so taking hypothetical wrecking ball, I strike, hoping for a peek behind the smiles and laughter. A peek at the deeper things Axel feels. "What made you decide to stay?"

He blows out a breath, like he's been sucker punched. "I don't know." He's standing close enough that I lean against my car to make room. "Staying seems like the better option lately."

I fiddle with my keys, biting my lower lip. My gaze flicks to his mouth, and part of me wants to throw caution to the wind and see if Axel's kisses still taste sweet. Those nights huddled on the bleachers at the football filed. The pitcher's mound in the rain—yes, we were rather romantic teenagers. Being close to his skin, I remember that buried beneath his pure masculine scent there is always the mouthwatering aroma of sugar and cinnamon. I blame—*no praise*—the life of being a bakery kid.

In all those memories, there is no recollection of the open blaze in his blue eyes like now. Almost as though Axel wants me to peek inside, but he doesn't know how to open without keeping the carefree persona. My mouth feels dry as sandpaper when I take a risk. Each throb of my pulse deafens my ears as I slip my trembling fingers around his hand. I lace our fingers together; his eyes drop to where we're touching. I take a brazen step closer, chest to chest. "I'm glad you stuck around."

His eyes pierce to my core when he looks at me; truly seeing me as Axel has always done. "Me, too."

For a moment I nearly lose my head, but old fears have an uncanny knack for tearing away the sweetest things. What was I doing? Slipping into some trance with my first heartbreak. I've had plenty of those, and if I let him in any more, if he sees all the broken pieces, I've no doubt Axel will be obliged to write this little tempting friendship off as a mistake. I swallow past the lump in my throat, and slowly release his hand.

"Elle . . ." Axel starts, keeping close.

"So," I interrupt, opening my car door. "If I get the place that doesn't mean you get to dump your laundry here. Just because you know I enjoy it, doesn't mean anything."

Axel tilts his head, that pensive expression returns. He studies me for a drawn breath before he returns to a cautious smile, and takes a safe step back. "I'm going to have Lucy add it to the rental agreement."

There. Phew. Back to easy friendship. We tease for a few more moments until Axel's phone blares and Bastien apparently summons him at their mother's request. Like a dutiful son, Axel makes me promise to let him know when they accept me—as if it is already set in stone—and he assures me the Olsen brothers will be there to help me move.

I sit in my car, watching him rush to his side of the lot, staying put until he leaves. Slapping my steering wheel, I bite against an unbidden burn of tears. As much as I wish it weren't so, those cracks in my barricades have invited feelings to form. I don't have a crush on Axel —I really, *really*, like Axel Olsen. And not as a friend.

The conundrum being, I can't see a way to get around the logic, the fear, and hesitation of taking the plunge into romance again.

I've become my own saboteur.

CHAPTER 15

$\mathcal{V}$iv slips her arms through her jean jacket as she gathers her things before leaving. "So, Spence and I will meet you at seven then?"

"That's really nice of you guys to come and help. I promise I'll supply pizza."

"Then that's all I need," she replies. "It's not a big deal. Sounds like you've got quite a crowd helping. Shouldn't take too long."

I sigh. "You think that until you see the amount of furniture my sister coerced me into buying."

"See, I sort of think you had fun buying all your own things, too."

I squish the air between my thumb and finger. "Maybe a little."

"See you later, girl."

Thankfully, my shift will end in three hours. I can hardly stand the wait. Ever since Lucy called two weeks ago saying the condo is mine starting at the first of the month, I've been running all around spending nearly every dollar to my name. Maya was more than happy to help spend the wad. Even Mom came and helped offer opinions. For a few years, I've felt much like a black sheep in my family, but spending days with the Weber girls, I was reminded that different didn't have to be a negative. We might view the world through opposite lenses, but we can still laugh, tease, and eat with the best of them.

Thirty minutes until shift change, Axel taps the desk, ready to head out into the drizzle that started early this morning. "Hey, I just wanted to check if there was anything you needed me to pick up before I get the cavalry."

"Yes, actually. Can I put you on pizza duty?"

"Do you want a pie eaten by the time it gets to your place? I'm driving with Bass, you realize?"

Rolling my eyes, I lean forward on my elbows. "I have faith that you can protect those supremes."

"I wouldn't," he offers. Clearing his throat, we drift into the familiar tone we've kept since our hard miss in the condo parking lot.

I'm not losing my mind, and clearly Axel didn't miss the tension that brought us close to crossing a line. I didn't tell a soul, and I suspect neither did he, but Brita is sharp. I can't count how many times I've caught her staring at me like she can see the hidden box of secrets. But she's never asked.

"Everyone is a willing participant, right?" I press. "I told you, that was the condition. No one is being forced to help."

He scoffs. "If Bass gets food, he's there. There's no way Jonas can skip out with Brita as his wife, and me—yes, I'm very willing."

"Good," I say. "My family will come, but it will be your secret mission to help me make sure my dad doesn't do any heavy lifting. He's going to try."

Axel salutes with a smirk. "I've got it under control."

"I'm warning you, Maya has enough furniture waiting to be unloaded to fill a mansion."

"Do I look like I can't handle it?"

Axel probably doesn't say it to draw my eyes to his strong arms, but I do on my own volition. And it is worth every second of ogling. I need to flick my wrist with my hair elastic to bring my focus back to reality.

"I think you can handle it," I say, rougher than before. "I'll meet you there. Oh, here are the keys in case you get there first."

Axel wiggles his brows. "You're giving me a key to your place. Don't you think we skipped a few steps?"

"Just go, and don't eat all the pizza."

He waves over his shoulder. Blowing out a shuddering breath, I focus on the notes for the night shift to read over and try to forget the way my heart nosedives at the idea of spending the evening with Axel.

* * *

"BLUE TAPE MEANS KITCHEN. Yellow means bedroom, no . . . that's pink; bathroom," Maya directs when Spence has the audacity to take the color coordinated packing box toward the living room.

I snort and roll my eyes. Spence quickly corrects and bounces toward the full bath while Maya barks orders.

"Coming in," Axel says through a grunt.

Brita bounces away from the front door where she unloads brand new throw pillows and curtains. Jonas struggles through the door first, face red and a bead of sweat over his brow. Axel carries the opposite end of the couch.

"Let me help, guys," Dad says.

"No, no, Dad," Maya intercedes, rather cleverly. As expected, the man has tried to play the macho mover all evening. So far, we've kept him contained by small boxes and blankets and frying pans. "Graham needs help with the bedframe."

Dad pauses and seems to consider his options, but Axel and Jonas are already halfway through the door, so he relents.

"Where does it go?" Axel says, a grimace on his face.

The double-recliner sofa Maya insisted I would love adds to the weight and I feel a pang of guilt. Quickly, I point to the back wall. "Just set it right there."

The twins seem more than thrilled to drop the sofa. Brita moves in without a blink and tosses the new gray and yellow pillows that make the duckling colored wall fit in after all.

"Mattress?" Axel slaps Jonas's chest, both breathing heavily.

"Why don't you guys take a break for a sec," I say, handing each a bottled water. "You've brought in the loveseat, couch, and the chest of drawers. Breathe."

"If you insist," Jonas says, plopping back on the couch and taking a big gulp.

Axel does the same, but shoves Jonas's shoulder. "Wimp."

"I sit behind a desk all day, okay."

"Exactly why we *are* going to start running," Brita stacks books on a shelf and glances at me. "See, I wasn't lying."

"I'm up for a run anytime."

"Elle and I will waste you two, though," Axel says.

"No doubt." Jonas tousles his darker hair as he shoves off the couch and helps Brita with a curtain rod.

I like the way Axel includes us as a pair lately. The sound of it sends a flutter through my stomach.

"Knock, knock."

Stepping through the open door I am surprised to see Axel's parents, each holding white pastry boxes from the market.

"Hey guys." Axel takes a box from his mom.

"Elias, good to see you," my dad calls from the hall. Elias grins, and shakes my dad's hand firmly.

"Haven't seen much of you, Reed. We could use you on the course."

"Been a little under the weather, but before snow hits let's get out there and see what sort of damage we can do."

"We brought a few treats, because moving always goes easier with sugar," Sigrid adds, giving Brita a side squeeze and grinning around the front room. "This is going to look so cute."

I feel content as I take in the place, too. "Thanks. I appreciate the help."

"Are you boys in a competition yet?" asks Sigrid toward her twins.

Brita rolls her eyes. "You should've seen them carrying the TV stand. You'd think it was a test of their entire worth as men."

"Axel wasn't lifting his end," Jonas says, opening his arm so Brita can nestle against his side.

"What? *I* wasn't lifting, are you . . ." Axel groans and shakes his head. "I basically carried the thing in myself."

The brothers shoot witty, snarky remarks back and forth without care for who is in the room. Sigrid sighs, facing me. "Well, glad to see sibling rivalry is in full force. I think you'll enjoy living here, Axel has really liked his place."

"I think I will, too. It feels good to have my own space, that's for sure."

"Oh, I brought you a casserole to put in the freezer."

"You didn't need to do that."

Sigrid waves me away. "It's no problem. You'll be glad to have something when you're exhausted after putting everything in order. Be right back."

Watching her leave there is a tug in my chest. A couple months ago I greeted each day knowing I'd been kicked out of my home, kicked out of my family, and job in North Carolina. Today, though, I know this messy scene is what friends and family ought to be. Even my bossy sister, currently confusing Bastien and Spence once more by her colors and room assignments, is a relief. I can't keep the smile from curling on my face as the condo echoes in laughter and loud voices shouting out questions or direction.

"I think Sigrid likes you almost as much as Axel likes you," Brita whispers. I hadn't even seen her creep away from the couch, but now Jonas and Axel are in a battle on who can hang the straighter shelf.

"Still on that?"

She doesn't respond right away; we need to take time to laugh as Jonas drops his side of the shelf, folding his arms defiantly while Axel struggles with the heavy thing until he apologizes. A subtle insult is buried in his remorse. When the shelf is hung and straight, he flashes me a smile, one I think is meant only for me.

Brita clicks her tongue and elbows my ribs. "Oh, I'm still on that."

CHAPTER 16

I plop down on the couch in a dramatic huff. A bun with wisps of hair falling in all directions top my head by now, and my T-shirt is a little damp.

"I can't move, lift, or organize another thing," I say.

Axel is in my condo—*my very own condo*—and at this point I hardly care that I look like something a cat coughed up. He sits on a chevron accent chair my mother surprised me with this morning, and tugs the chain on my standing lamp.

"I think we did Maya proud."

I laugh, propping my feet. "Do you think she likes to run the show?"

He grins, but closes his eyes. "Just a bit."

The condo feels eerily quiet now that everyone has done their duty, eaten the pizza, all the pastries—most credit going to Bastien—and wished me well in my new chapter. As difficult as moving is, the entire evening brought me to tears from laughing more than once. Spence and Viv are a sarcastic couple, but hilarious together. Abby and her fiancé surprised us by showing up for an hour before heading to finalize their menu plans for the wedding. Brita and Jonas got into a water fight as Jonas tried to fix a spout on the back porch. My family, the Olsens, new friends, created a new confidence in the word home.

"Are you going to survive?" I ask.

Axel cracks his eyes and gives me a thumbs up. "I can't move either, so I think I'll just sleep here tonight."

Tossing a pillow at his face, he jolts up and tosses it back. "Maybe you shouldn't have been so competitive with your brother all night."

"Jonas needs to learn his place."

I'm not ready to see him leave yet. Biting my bottom lip, I think of that brilliant casserole Sigrid supplied. "Are you hungry?"

"You're asking me if I'm hungry after eating tons of pizza and twelve Æbleskivers?"

I nod and head into the kitchen.

Axel smiles. "Good, because yes, I'm starving."

I hold up the casserole dish. "Your mom made this. Should we dig in?"

Axel's mouth opens as he takes the liberty to set the oven presets. "She brought you food? I didn't get food when I moved into my place."

"Of course not. What mother would make her son food? That means you wouldn't come home to eat with them."

He takes the dish from me. "True and manipulative at the same time." With a frown he inspects the food. "She even made my favorite."

"Well, then it's a good thing you're staying."

An hour later only a fourth of casserole is left and my cheeks hurt from laughing so hard.

Axel leans back and groans, patting his stomach. "I think it's time to admit that I ate too much."

I agree, but start gathering the dish and searching for the Tupperware. Maya placed things the way she organizes a kitchen, so I am left to the learning phase. Scooping out the rest of the food into a small plastic square, I turn to wash out the dish with the plan to return it to Sigrid with some sort of thank you in the morning. My breath hitches when I slam the cheesy dish into Axel. He stands in front of me, and his eyes are different. Still playful, but more studious. Slowly, he eases the dish out of my hands and places it in the sink. When did we get so close? I notice the way our T-shirts brushed, and how an electric current pulsed down my spine when my hand accidentally touches his.

Axel's jaw tightens. I'm afraid to meet his eye, unsure what I'll see, what I'll do.

"I feel like I've been saying this a lot, but uh, thank you for helping," I whisper. "You went above and beyond."

"Anytime. I don't mind helping you, Elle."

My head is spinning. Like when the altitude in a plane shifts too rapidly. Finding a sliver of courage, I lift my gaze to his, and see the depth behind the glassy blue of his eyes. We've both had ample opportunity to back away and give space, but I can't move. My legs feel heavy, yet weak. And my resolve to pretend nothing is changing, even weaker.

Something bursts in my chest when he gently curls his fingers around the hem of my T-shirt, and tugs me a few inches closer. My pulse thunders in my head; I forget how to breathe. The same hand rests half on my hip, and half on my back; reserved, as though Axel holds the same nerves as me. No smile on his face, but I'm lost to him all the same. The somber stare belongs to me. I've only observed Axel as playful and carefree with others, but he gifts me with moments of unwavering attention and focus with those piercing eyes. I don't want it to end.

My breaths break through the blockade in my throat and racks my shoulders. Everything is spinning; I'm in control and sort of out of control. I freeze.

"Axel, wait."

He pauses; those perfect lips were about to claim mine. He steps back as though he's been burned. "Sorry," he says gruffly, all connection to my body lost as he steps away.

My throat is gritty; a mix of anger and regret at myself. "No. It's . . . fine."

"I didn't mean to read this wrong or make you uncomfortable."

"You didn't," I say and take a step toward him. "You didn't read it wrong."

He shoves his hands into his pockets, eyes narrowed. The muscles in his arms are tight, and his voice is gentle. "I like you, Elle. I know we're friends, but . . ." He scoffs, shaking his head. "But I shouldn't have let it go anywhere else. I apologize."

I dare a smile. He's a little adorable when he's nervous. I take a step closer. "You're apologizing for telling me the truth?"

"I guess," he says.

"It's not you, it's me . . ."

He laughs bitterly. "The classic it's not you it's me thing? Elle, it's okay, I'm a big boy."

Unafraid of touching him, I trail my fingertips along his arm. "No, it is me. Axel . . ." I practically pierce the inside of my cheek biting so hard. My hands fly into the air. "Can I be totally honest?"

He nods, but there is a second of hesitation. "Yes."

Swallowing my anxiety, I slip my fingers into his. "I'm afraid." Well great. Tears burn behind my eyes. Axel's grip tightens around my palm. "Being married to Rod was great at first. But it didn't last long. He never raised a hand to me, but he trampled me with comments. For two years I had the thought that I couldn't amount to anything without my husband. After so long, you start to believe those things.

"I remember compliments came so rare; on our second Valentine's Day together, he told me a dress I'd picked out looked nice. I cried for an hour, feeling so validated. Looking back, I can see how bizarre that must sound."

Axel glares at me, but I don't feel his anger pointed at me, but at a man he's never met.

"Anyway, he spun the affair as my fault, as you can imagine. I feel ridiculous admitting that words broke me. Even my family noticed I wasn't the same when we were together, and they told me often, but I was desperate to make things work. I should've left him because it was over long before I admitted it." I hang my head, and draw in a shuddering breath. Axel's grip never wavers. "After the divorce, I came back, and promised myself I wouldn't let my guard down—ever. Then, I crashed into you."

"Elle, have I ever said anything that made you feel like he made you feel? Because if I have then—"

Tossing caution to the wind I laugh, shaking my head, and wrapping my arms around his waist. His arms hold me close; safe. "You've made me feel the complete opposite." I rest my cheek against his chest. "But all I have are memories, and . . . back in high school we didn't end much better, if you remember. I shouldn't judge today based on then, but we're being honest, right? And honestly, that is how my mind is working right now."

Axel tenses. Urging me to pull back, my knees buckle when he rests a gentle hand on my cheek. "Elle, I'm not the kid from high school anymore. Can I tell you something now? But you can't laugh. I've only admitted this to Jonas."

I smile, feeling my lashes wet with welling emotion. "I promise I won't laugh. If I do, I'll do your laundry for a month."

Whether he realizes or not, Axel's thumb caresses my cheek. "I've never been serious with anyone. I dated—a lot—through college, therapy school, after. But I never wanted the commitment, until the last year or so. But by the time I was ready it's like anyone I wanted to be with didn't exist. That's why I thought about moving. I couldn't find a connection with anyone here, I guess. Then, as you said, I crashed into you." He doesn't blink, and I don't breathe. "This will make me sound stupid, but you knocked the air out of me when I saw you again."

"That doesn't make you sound stupid," I say through a gurgled sob.

"I knew you were divorced, and I didn't want to make anything harder for you." He drops his hand from my cheek, but keeps close. "I don't know how your ex could say and do those things to someone like you, but I'm not him, Elle."

"I know . . ."

The response is weak at best, but it's all I can muster. I know Axel isn't Rodney, yet the dread that it will all begin again with the same outcome cascades like poison to the sweetest moment I've had in years. There is a gaping precipice, and I stand at the edge. I can continue in doubt with cynicism and chase away the hands touching me now, or take a risk and possibly break my heart for good in the end.

Axel slides away so we aren't touching. Snagging his keys off my counter, he points his gold house key in my direction. "I'm going to take you out. I mean, if you want to, of course."

"Excuse me?"

Axel opens his arms wide. "I want to show you I'm not here to fool around. Forget high school, we've had a decade between then and now. I'd like to ask you out, and start again. If you want."

"Why are you backing away from me, weirdo."

Every step I take forward, he takes one back. Until he stops and pulls my shirt again, so I'm smashed against his chest. The whole T-shirt thing shocks my system a second time as our eyes lock.

"Because," he says, low and raw. "If I don't, I'm going to kiss you, and if I kiss you then I'm not proving my point that I'm different than the punk you dated before."

He leaves me weak when he pulls away; I think I might topple over.

"So, you haven't said if you'll go out with me," he says with a cheeky sort of smirk. "Or am I leaving here with my tail between my legs?"

I lean against the wall and smile, tears drying in my eyes, but my pulse still fires in all directions. "I don't know, I sort of like making you sweat a bit."

"Cold, Elle."

I laugh, and tuck flyaway pieces of hair behind my ears. "Alright, I'd love to. When do you want to go?"

"Do you work Friday?"

"Nope, I'm on Sunday."

"Then Friday."

"Alright." I want to say a thousand things, but my mind can only conjure my brilliant one worded response. This is happening.

"Okay," he says, opening my front door. "Then I'll see you . . . well, I'll see you tomorrow at work, but *then* I'll see you on Friday."

I curl my bottom lip over my teeth. "See you tomorrow."

As if blessed by the heavens, I am given a final glimpse at those white teeth and blue eyes before he leaves me breathless in a clutter of boxes, and bubble wrap.

CHAPTER 17

J hold my cell phone between my ear and shoulder, keeping a lock of hair I plan to curl in my fist, and rush to answer the front door at the same time.

"Hi Mom," I say into the phone. "What's up?"

"Oh, we're about to go to the showing of *Bye, Bye, Birdie* at the new playhouse that just opened. Betty Marks is one of the leading ladies."

"Sounds fun," I say, swinging my front door open and giving Brita a quick grin before she skips inside, practically bursting at the seams. "I'm about to head out, is there something you needed?"

"Oh, where are you going?"

I hesitate. "Um, I'm going to dinner with Axel, actually."

Pause. Realistically, the silence lasts for one blink, but it feels like five minutes.

"Really?"

"Yep." I watch Brita snag a banana and wait patiently with her hangers of clothes in her opposite hand.

My mom clicks her tongue and I'm not positive if it's out of surprise or disapproval. "Well, have a good time. He's a nice guy."

"He is."

"Okay, well . . . talk to you—"

"Mom, did you call for a reason?" I say, helping Brita lay out the tops on my bed. I pick . . . all of them. I want them all.

"I can talk about it later."

"It's okay, what's up?"

"I don't want to spoil your night."

"That's nice of you." I point to a burgundy sweater that has laces crossing over the shoulders in the back. Brita gives me a thumb's up. "I can handle it though."

"Fine," Mom clears her throat. "I keep thinking about that necklace Rod took."

Eeesh . . . maybe I should've taken her offer to wait. "Okay, grandma's necklace?"

"Yes." My mom is nervous; I can hear her manicured nails drumming her counter. "Elle, I think we should get that back."

I appreciate that she says 'we'; somehow it feels more like a team effort rather than sending me to the wolves again. Swallowing the scratch in my throat, I avoid Brita's curious stare. "I agree," I say, because I do agree. He doesn't deserve the necklace. "I can . . . call him tomorrow."

"Are you sure?"

"Yeah, I can do it."

"If he fights you on it, we have the certificate to prove it's ours. If you need your dad, or me to—"

"I can do it, Mom."

She pauses and takes a deep breath. "Okay. Don't let him beat you down, Elle. I hope you know that I truly think you are one hundred times better than that man."

My breath hitches, and a sting of emotion grows in my throat. Good emotion, though. It isn't often my mom talks about the man-who-should-not-be-remembered, but she has my back in her own right.

"Thanks, Mom. That means a lot."

"Alright, have a good night. I won't spoil it anymore. You know I'm going to tell Maya and—"

I laugh. "She'll need a complete update. I know."

Tossing my phone aside after my mom hangs up, I gently handle the sweater and hold it against my chest to inspect the size. Until I rummaged my closet to pick an outfit, I hadn't realized how desperately I needed to buy a new wardrobe. Thankfully, I'm only slightly taller than Brita, although she doesn't quite have the same curves, but she has a slew of cute tops I can't pass up.

"Everything good?" Brita asks.

"Yeah." I offer a nutshell briefing on the necklace and the mistress as I finish curling my hair.

"I want to meet your ex," Brita said through the door once I'm in my closet, trying on her sweaters.

"Why would you want to do that?"

Brita hangs up the reject tops, mouth tight. "So I can slap him silly."

"Get in line, girl." I laugh and step out to model.

"Wow, that looks better on you than me. That color always washes me out," she says.

All at once Rodney is forgotten.

"You think it looks alright? Really?"

She flops onto her stomach over my bed, beaming. "For sure. So . . ." Brita squeaks a little in the back of her throat. "Are you excited?"

"Ask me if I'm petrified. I can answer that one."

Brita rummages through my lipstick. "Don't be nervous. If you two nerds would've listened to me to begin with, the first date could be long over by now."

"I don't know if I can do this," I say, clutching my cheeks and gawking at my reflection.

"Hey, you've got this. I need you to believe me when I say, I haven't seen Axel like this for, well, ever."

"Not even with you," I say, hardly able to say the words without laughing.

Brita pinches the back of my arm. "Tease me all you want, but without my little misguided twin dating, I wouldn't be here pep-talking you and giving you all the insider information. Besides, I can give you a perspective no one else can. Axel loved to play around back then, true. But being his sister-in-law, I've seen a more open side to the guy and I really think he's smitten. Trust me, there were a few years I didn't think I'd ever say those words."

I take a deep breath, feeling a hum of warmth in the center of my stomach. "That helps. I'm still nervous. How do I . . . date?"

"You be you, Elle." Brita hands me a dark rose lipstick. "As cliché as that sounds, do you. Axel asked you out because you weren't trying to impress anyone, right?"

Taking a deep breath, I glide the matte color along my full lips. "I was trying to be as prickly to the idea of dating as possible."

She laughs. "Okay, my last bit of advice, don't think about your ex sleezeball tonight."

"I sort of like how you're giving him nicknames."

"Well, he deserves them. Don't think about him, just have fun and see how you feel at the end of the night. Then you're required to call me and tell me everything."

"I could just text you and give you a play by play all night."

Brita taps her chin. "I'm tempted, but I'd rather you not think of anything but having a good time."

"Did you give Axel this talk, too?"

"No. I wrote it down and put Jonas in charge of that side."

Releasing a breath that trembled too much, I closed my eyes. "Here it goes."

BROTH SPLASHES out of my spoon as I laugh when Axel makes a lunge for the chicken. He catches the piece in his mouth and the table cheers as he shoots his arms in the air.

"Good catch," our Hibachi chef says with a grin.

Covering my mouth with a napkin, I laugh when a man across the tables misses and nearly stumbles off his chair.

"Ah, not so good," says the chef.

Dinner isn't meant to be so entertaining, but I've hardly eaten; I can't stop laughing long enough. Leaning against Axel's shoulder, I snort and chortle, and all unattractive mulelike sounds as the woman sitting next to us hops off her chair, rubs her hands together, ready for a show down. The Hibachi flings vegetables, beef, and I think some shrimp. It's a madhouse as she dives for the morsels, catching all, except the final piece that strikes her in the center of her forehead.

Axel's arm falls around my shoulders. I'd be content to stay this way all night. Over an hour of quips and wit by our talented chef, and I'm stuffed without remembering taking a single bite. As a bonus, we have new friends, even if we'll probably never see each other again.

Axel waves to a quartet of couples who have a few stains on their shirts. I breathe the warmer than usual night, enjoying the scent of caramelized onions and bitter sauces as we trudge to the parking lot. "That was fun."

"It was," he says. He smiles widely enough that a little dimple pits in the corner of his mouth. Axel holds out his hand, fingers wide.

Offering a confident smile, I lace my fingers with his, leaning closer as we walk. Axel pauses at his car, then looks to a nearby park with gilded lamps lining benches and walkways.

"Want to take a walk for a little while? I was thinking of a movie, but if you want . . ."

I smile and urge him toward the sidewalk. "I'd rather walk, for sure. Doesn't mean I don't love a good TV or movie binger, though."

"Candy or popcorn."

"I'm offended you need to ask; I practically bleed popcorn."

He squeezes my hand tighter. "Me too."

We walk through a corridor of trees the city has decorated in fairy lights. The park is quiet, only a soft breeze in the treetops, and the damp grass smells fresh and clean. Axel doesn't say much, but I think he's a little nervous, like me. Still, I love the way his thumb draws gentle circles over mine.

"I've been meaning to ask about your grandpa," I say, breaking the silence. "Everything still doing okay?"

"Yep, up to the same tricks, and trying to run the bakery like he's twenty. With the holidays coming it gets too busy, so it's a joint effort among the families in giving him and Philip jobs to keep them occupied, but not overworked."

Conversation comes easy with Axel. The longer we spend together, the less my nerves control the rate of my heart.

"So, are you glad to be back home, yet?" he asks after a few moments.

"I'd say it's getting easier." I pull him onto a bench that has a perfect view of the twinkling city lights while still being surrounded by trees. "Okay, I'm pretty rusty at this date thing—"

"No, you're not."

I wave him away. "You said there's been a decade between high school and now, so I thought we better get to know each other again. I've got questions, Axel."

He raises his brows, but settles in the bench. "Okay, I'm nervous, but I guess I've got answers. As long as I get to ask questions, too."

I release his hand and dance my fingertips together, chuckling darkly. "Alright then, something has been on my mind—are you ready?"

"I don't know."

"It's a big one. Here it goes: why did you want to be a therapist? Because clearly I've forgotten."

"Whoa." He holds up one hand. "We're getting super personal."

I laugh and shove his shoulder.

"Okay, since you didn't listen to anything I said back then," he goes on, "I'll refresh your memory. Senior year I took that intro to health-care class—with you, by the way."

"I remember that class."

"Yeah, well you should. It was the only class you wouldn't let me make out with you in the back row when the teacher turned around, like you wanted to pay attention or something."

"We were classy."

He laughs, slipping his arm around my shoulders again. "Any-way, I thought therapy sounded cool, so I started doing the peer tutoring with the special education. That started the interest, but then I got a summer job after graduation at a rehab place and it sealed the deal. With the therapists, people would hurt, but after a little while they felt better. For some patients the therapy could be life changing. I liked the idea of helping people, I guess."

"I like that answer," I say. "You do help people, plus you're the only therapist I've seen that can make them laugh while you're torturing them."

He grins shyly, an unfamiliar sight for him. "Thanks. I try to make a tough situation easier for people. Okay, I've got a question, are you still obsessed with breakfast food?"

I love the way Axel pulls me tightly against him. My hand rests on his leg. "How did you remember that?"

"Because, you had that pulled hamstring from sliding into base. You were so upset that you had to sit out for three games. The only thing that made you happy were breakfast burritos from Wayne's Drive-In."

"Ah, yes, but it isn't breakfast food. I am specifically obsessed with breakfast burritos, but they don't only need to come from Wayne's. I've expanded my pallet." I'd forgotten how Axel would tromp up my front steps, me limping to the door only to be greeted with sizzling, sausagey goodness. "That was a sweet thing you did."

He has a faraway look, and doesn't say anything for a second. "You're the only girl I did do that for, actually."

"Wait, other girls don't want breakfast burritos as gifts?"

He responds by urging me closer. "No, I mean something personal. This makes me sound like a jerk now that I'm saying it out loud. I always did such generic things for people I was dating—if you could even call it dating. You know, flowers, chocolate, the same dinners. I didn't try to make a connection."

My smile fades, I trace the lines of his palm. "But you did that for me. I always felt connected to you. That's why it hurt to break up."

He studies my fingers running over his for three breaths before shifting so he can face me. "You were always different, Elle. We were together for six months, that blew my record of three weeks out of the water. I wanted to get to know you, even at seventeen, I did. I don't remember why, but I didn't want to break up with you."

"It's okay, Axel. We were kids."

"No," he says softly, tilting my chin up with his thumb. "I remember convincing myself to do it. We were young, we had college, and . . . life ahead of us. Those were my reasons, but you're . . ." His smile seems to grow as the thought shapes in his mind. "You're the only girl I felt sad about."

My eyes bounce between his. How long we meet each other's eyes, I don't know. Slowly, I rest my forehead against his, and simply absorb the tremble that has become a second part of me whenever we touch.

"You can't say those things," I whisper.

"Why not." His hand traps one side of my face again.

"Because," I say, my voice a rocky rasp. "When you do, I feel like I can't breathe. In the best way."

Our lips drew closer. Axel pulls back for a moment to look me in the eye. I praise him for it. Although heat floods my veins, my heart tries to break free through my ribs. Axel excites a part of me I'd forgotten existed.

His strong palms take my face, and being so close, it's a small thing to pull my mouth to his.

Gently at first, but soon his fingers thread through my hair, deepening the kiss. I'm breathless, and spinning. The stubble on his chin tickles my palm as I slowly draw my hands to the back of his neck. Axel's lips guide mine as though our kiss is designed for each other. Everything is beautifully chaotic. Like the crash of waves, followed by the soothing pull of the tide. One kiss glides to the next, bringing more desire, affection, more meaning; things a kiss should hold, but hasn't for too long in my experience.

When I finally dip my chin and break apart, Axel breathes harder; so do I, but we hold onto each other without a word. One of his safe arms is around my waist, the other hand cups the back of my neck, so my forehead is on his again. I twirl his hair around my fingers, and breathe in his calm that has control of my soul.

"Wow," I say against his skin.

Axel simply nods, and keeps his hold on me, as if I steady him. Hoping that is precisely the reason he holds me, I scoot closer.

"Are you okay?" He's not saying anything, and I've no idea what is going through his head.

Finally, he lifts his heart stopping eyes to mine. "I didn't know it could feel like that."

My cheeks fill with heat. "You're doing it again—saying those things that suffocate me."

He smiles, and kisses me again. Before the night is over, I know I'll be a willing participant in as many kisses as the man wants to give.

CHAPTER 18

*S*taring at my phone, the fluttering euphoria from only hours earlier sinks like cinderblock bricks in the pit of my stomach. Maybe I can pretend I called, and tell my mom he didn't answer—better yet, maybe he won't answer, and I can try again in five months.

No. Sucking in a deep breath through my nose, then releasing the air out of my mouth with a shudder, I dial the number. Deleted from my contact list weeks ago, I still have it memorized. I'm going to vomit. Seriously, sick heaves are ready to rack my body. Three rings in. Confidence that I might be in the clear is brimming. Until . . .

"Hello, Elle."

His voice crushes me, grates down my spine, and draws tears to my eyes all at once.

"Rod," I say sharply—well, I try but it feels a little croaky. "Did I wake you?"

Do I care? Nope.

"We're just waking up."

He says 'we' on purpose.

"What do you need, Elle?"

Just say it. Spit it out and be done. Clearing my throat, I try to live in the peace that has cloaked my body since last night. That park bench is my safe place through this odious phone call.

"I'm calling about my necklace."

He laughs. The arrogant cackle that sends nausea coursing through my insides rears its head once again. "Seriously? You call me over a cheap necklace? It's Saturday, Elle. It's early, and frankly I have better things to do today than listen to you whimper about something you left behind."

"Rodney!" I shout. Whoa—where did that come from? I don't know, but I like it. "I want my grandmother's necklace. And frankly, *I* don't want to listen to you whimper about whether you're going to send it or not. Do it."

Silence. I can picture his face. The salt and pepper on his sideburns starkly contrasting against the red flush building in his sharp features. His bushy, dark brows will furrow in a glare, and his knuckles will get white as they grip his phone.

I close my eyes and imagine how safe it felt next to Axel on the bench. Compared to how stiff I was simply being with Rodney watching a movie or something. A second round first date with a high school flame brings more contentment to my heart than two years of marriage.

"You've got a lot of nerve, Elle." His voice sounds dangerous, ready to fight, and ready to win.

I've had enough. I taste a salty tear that spills over my lips, but I'm not crying because I miss this man, no they come for the lost years I've wasted on him. "You really want to talk about nerve? Here's the deal, Rod: I've got a certificate of authenticity on the pearl in the necklace. It's proof of ownership. If you don't want to go to small claims, then put it in a padded envelope, put a stamp on it, and give it back."

More silence, but I'm not slouched anymore. I sit upright. A blaze is alive in my chest. My jaw tightens with a vicious sort of smile; something wild and free unlocks inside me. I give credit where it's due. I found some personal strength on my own during the last weeks, but having someone find worth in things I say, wanting to know my opinions, is also exceptionally liberating.

Rodney ought to take a few lessons.

"I'll see if I can find it," he finally mutters. "That should be good enough. Don't call me again, Elle."

"Gladly," I say. "But you're not going to *see* if you can find it, you'll find it and send it. I'm not messing around, Rod." I change my tone to chipper sunshine. "Okay, well that about covers it. Be sure and tell Becky to enjoy using another woman's things. Bye-bye now."

* * *

"Yes, that's what I said. Probably not my most mature moment, but it just slipped out," I admit over brownies and apple slices (I'm still a little sluggish from gorging last night).

Brita snickers and gives me a high five.

Maya seems ready to burst into proud, mother hen tears. "It's exactly what you should have said."

Life holds a few perfect things: women who have your back, melted chocolate, and lazily lounging on a couch.

"He deserved it," Brita insists. "But onto happier things. Finish telling us about last night. You stopped right at the good part."

"Elle, I've got to say I'm a little surprised with you," Maya says, reaching for an apple. "I didn't think you'd eat a guy's face whenever you started dating again."

I toss a pillow at my sister. "I didn't eat his face."

"There isn't a thing wrong with it."

"We'll get the truth of it somehow," Brita adds. "A certain guy finally dragged his twin to work out. Apparently Bastien can lift more than Jonas now—that was the final straw. I'll get the goods of the date when Jonas comes back."

"And then you'll tell me," Maya teases, pointing at Brita.

"Maya, you're thirty and sound like a fifteen-year-old girl gossiping," I groan.

She laughs, clutching the pillow over her middle. "I'm sorry, but I've been waiting for something like this for you for a long time. You didn't even light up like this when you dated Rod."

"She is lighting up, isn't she?" Brita chirps. She leans over the arm of the couch, voice low. "Seriously, Elle—how was it. How did you feel?"

"She just told us she kissed him like five times before he dropped her off," Maya teases.

"Pfft, kissing can simply be kissing. How did you feel?"

"This is embarrassing," I say.

"Why? Like you said, we're all grown-ups. Tell us," Brita glances at her watch. "But hurry or Jonas will be here to get me soon because my mom and stepdad are coming into town. We're having a dinner with my dad, too; that means he's probably dating someone."

"Why do you need to have dinner because of that?" Maya asks with a snort.

Brita rolls her eyes. "My parents are awesomely weird. They got into the habit of discussing their relationships with each other right after they divorced. It was this rule that they had to approve since it would affect me or something. I guess they've forgotten I'm a married woman and we don't need a family council every time my dad gets a girlfriend." Brita turns her gaze back to me. "So, you see the need to get all the oozy details before I sit through an awkward dinner. Ready. Go."

"I don't know what to say. We were talking about changes since high school, and the next thing I know we're kissing—a lot."

Maya rests her head back on the cushions. "Did you like it?"

"Uh, easy yes," I say.

"So, you're going to see him again?" Brita says, anxiously.

"Actually . . ." I begin slowly. "Yes. He wants me to go to the therapy fall party next weekend."

Maya coos. "Axel asked you to the work party, huh?"

"What's wrong with that?"

"Nothing," Brita says, pretending to pick at her fingernails. "Just that he doesn't mind if everyone at works sees you together. Next, it'll be a family party, as a couple. Just wait."

"He already invited me to a family party."

"As a couple," she says again.

I twist a lock of hair around my fingers. "Are you going to read into everything?"

Brita and Maya nod together.

A loud knock comes to the door, causing Maya to startle. I stumble on my way to answer it. "Ah, my foot's asleep."

I nearly started crying with laughter as I stumble again, tiny pin pricks shooting through my toes. Flinging the door open while standing on one foot, my heart shoots to my throat. Axel smiles, in workout clothes that require me to scan him from top to bottom twice.

"Hi," I gasp. Forget my dead foot, my hands, tongue, and all ten toes have no feeling.

"Hey," he says in a low voice, then lifts his eyes over my head and he notes the four extra eyes staring at him with expectation.

The tips of his ears redden, until Jonas tromps to his side.

"Do I have a wife in there?"

Brita hops to her feet, gathers her purse, and waves goodbye to my sister. She stops between me and Axel. "Bye, Elle," she says, then pats Axel on his cheek. "Bye, bud. Behave."

Maya, she comes next. Like a typhoon.

"Axel, I have one sister. And I'm very, *very* protective." She tells me to keep wearing lipstick, then follows Jonas and Brita.

I bury my face in my palms. "Sorry. We're having her evaluated."

He laughs and does his thing—the shirt tug, so I flatten against his chest. "Sorry, I'm a little sweaty, but deal with it for a second." Then his arms wrap around my waist like a perfect, missing piece to a puzzle.

"I don't mind." I try not to stare at his lips.

"Why did everyone come over" – He glances at his watch – "at nine thirty in the morning."

"I had to make an uncomfortable phone call. Moral support."

Axel lifts one brow. "What sort of phone call?"

Maybe it is the easy way he pulls out the truth, but for a quick minute I tell him about the effort to get the necklace back. I don't like when Axel looks angry, but I admit he looks rather dashing when his jaw pulses.

"Sorry," he grumbles.

"Why would you be sorry," I say, my smile genuinely in place. Even through the retelling I grin, because . . . Axel is on my front porch. That's all. "They came over for other reasons, too. They wanted to ask a few things about a certain date."

His eyes brighten naturally, and thoughts of Rod are forgotten again. I lock my fingers around his waist.

"And?" he asks, closer to my lips than before. "What were the answers?"

Our lips brush, but we don't finish the job. "What is said at girl talk, stays at girl talk."

"Good, because I really don't want to tell you what Jonas and I talked about."

"No. Guy talk isn't the same."

Axel's slow-moving hand slides the length of my spine, until his fingers play with the ends of my hair. "That doesn't seem fair."

His fingers abandon my hair, brushing the side of my face and leaving delayed sparks of sensation in the wake. Like a reel and a hook, I am snagged and can't keep this close distance without some sort of action. I kiss him; boldly and beautifully. Axel chuckles before kissing me back. The touch is chaste, but has the power to knock the wind out of me.

"Can you eat?" I ask, keeping close, but coming up for air. "Brita brought things."

Axel flicks his eyes into my apartment. "I can, but I was thinking Wayne's for old time's sake."

"Breakfast burritos?"

"Is there anything else worth getting?"

I snort and drag him inside so I can at least slip on some shoes. "Axel Olsen, you get me."

* * *

Wringing my hands in my lap, I watch trees buzz past with an added bounce to my knee. My breath hitches when he takes hold of my busy fingers. Axel links his fingers with mine.

"Are you nervous?"

"That obvious?" I face the window again.

"Why? You pretty much know everyone coming."

"Because," I say through a wispy breath. "This is . . . different. I'm coming as a plus one."

"Yeah . . ."

"It's like . . . you . . . like we're okay with people seeing us together."

He turns the car down a gravel road leading to the lakeside. "You don't want people to see us together?"

"No, it's not that I *don't* want people to see us . . . well, do you?"

The same dimple by his mouth puckers when he smirks and tightens his grip on my hand. Axel doesn't say a word until he parks the car near a row of others in front of a quaint cabin. I didn't even see the house from the road, but the view is beautiful. The setting sun casts orange and gold across the water, and spicy air, free of city grunge, filters through the air vents.

Shutting off the ignition, Axel twists in his seat. Few sensations can top the feeling of his hand against my face.

"Elle," he says with intention. "This is probably weird for you."

"It is," I whisper. "But not in a bad way."

He nudges as close as the console will allow. "I know. I'm good with going as slow as you want, but I want you to know my side. I invited you because outside my family, these people are who I know the best. And I don't mind if they see me with you. I want them to."

I lower my gaze, tracing the stitching along my leather seat. "I don't mean to be weird."

"Look," he says, taking my hand between his. "I know the last few months have . . . well, they've sucked for you, but I'm not here to make anything harder. I want to be here with you tonight. If you don't or aren't ready—"

"No, forget everything I said." My fingers brush the edge of his jaw until his smile fades and that sobering stare meets mine. "I want to be here, with you, I'm just nervous. It's been a bit since I've done all this, and I don't think I'm a pro, and—"

Axel takes my breath away when he kisses me quickly, but proudly.

"Yeah, I think you're better than you give yourself credit for," he says, grinning. "Come on, Viv will be here, so we can hang out by her all night if you want."

I laugh. "If we can keep her attention off Spence long enough."

He waits for me in front of the car, his hand open for the taking. I don't let him wait long before my fingers are curled with his. We're greeted by the boisterous therapy team, a few curious glances from Beth, and the sizzle of the thickest burgers you've ever seen.

Two hours of eating, sharing funny stories from work, and watching Nick, the director of therapy, hand out awards to his team. Axel wins a magic kit designed for five and up, and is named the magical therapist. Meaning he's able to get patients to do exactly what he wants without resistance. He calls it manipulation. I figure it's his alluring smile. We all have theories, but the consensus between the two of us is Agnes will be getting a new magic kit.

"I told you this was great," Viv says, leaning back on a wooden chair, sipping a cup of cocoa.

I stir my cup with candy cane sticks to add the touch of sweetness that puts the drink over the top. Filling my lungs with the aroma of pine, fire, and roasting marshmallows, I sigh and lean back. "It's been so fun. Your Uncle Nick is a goof. I haven't had a chance to get to know him very well."

"Yeah. You know how it goes with the directors of departments. Look how often Ronnie is with administration and not on the floor with us."

It was true. The director of nursing hardly has a chance to take a lunch, he's stuck behind closed door meetings so often.

"It's been fun getting to know them a little more." I stir methodically now, listening to the sounds of the night. The scent of winter is in the air, and this is likely one of the few evenings left where being outside after dark with only a jacket is feasible.

"It's been fun to see you with Axel."

"Stop."

"No, I'm serious," Viv says, flipping her legs over the arm of the chair so she can face me. "Elle, you guys are almost as cute as me and Spence. I've been watching. He keeps looking at you like you make his world go 'round."

"Viv, this is our second date. You make it seem like he's about to drop to one knee."

"No, probably not," she relents. "But I'm saying, he's into you. Are you still dragging your feet because of your breakup?"

I swallow a gulp of cocoa and meet her twinkling eyes. I trust Viv now; she might as well know the truth. "It was a divorce, Viv. Not your average breakup."

"What? You've never said you were married."

"Yep."

"Okay," she slows her tone for half a second before her chipper, bubbly self, breaks through again. "So, are you still dragging your feet because of your divorce."

I snort into my cup. "Don't you think a divorce sort of brings some baggage."

"Sure, but so do a lot of things. Axel knows?"

I nod.

"Then what's the issue?"

"I don't know. I still picture him as this fun-loving guy . . ."

". . . totally is fun-loving . . ."

"And not the one to pick up someone like me, you know?"

Viv cants her head and if she had more of a point to her ear, I would think she came straight from a fairy tale in the glow of lanterns and firelight. "Someone like you? Huh." She settles back against her chair and sips thoughtfully.

"What?"

"Nothing. I'm just trying to see why you think a guy wouldn't want someone like you."

"I didn't say they wouldn't ever." I lower my voice to a whisper. "It's just not the sort of thing I thought Axel would want to take on."

"A babe? A woman who's seen a thing or two? Someone who's been to the trenches in a relationship, and came out with her hands dirty, but head held high?"

"Whoa, easy Oprah."

She giggles. "I have two older sisters, Elle. Both have been divorced, and those are my conclusions I've made about them. Both are now happily married, and I've got the cutest bunch of nieces and nephews I could ever ask for. I'm sorry things fell apart for you. I haven't been through it, but the advice I can give would be take what you've learned, but look at whatever is starting with Axel in a different light. He doesn't seem bothered, so why not enjoy the ride and see where it goes?"

I don't respond right away, and peer over the top of my chair toward the fire. Axel laughs with Mack and Spence as they try to help Beth roast a marshmallow to perfection; the first time we've parted all night. He's held my hand; during dinner, his arm rested around my chair; we've laughed, and I've fallen even more for Axel Olsen.

Against the fire pit, when Axel flicks his eyes to me, they seem to glow like sapphires. He smiles—that quiet, calm grin that only belongs to me. I return the same, before settling back against the chair and sipping my cocoa with more fervor.

"You're right." I say. "I'm going to relax, and just see where this goes. I want to. For the first time in months, I can honestly say I'm open to taking that step."

"Good choice," Viv squeaks. "Be chill and ride the wave. Who knows what will turn out on the other side, but the way you two keep ogling each other—I think good things are coming."

My stomach tightens with an inner thrill when Axel and Spence join us with gooey s'mores. They are followed by Beth and another guy from the administration.

Time is irrelevant, and when we notice the late hour, most of us laugh deliriously at things that likely won't be funny in the morning. My favorite part of the evening is driving home. Lost in the quiet, and the masculine scent of Axel's car, I lean my head on his shoulder and curl my fingers with his. We stay like that, the entire way. Comfortable, and as strange as it sounds, perfectly content.

Who would have thought, I'd find contentment again? Not me. For the first time since signing the end of my marriage, I see what everyone else has been telling me. There is a life to be lived, and I'm giddy at the idea of Axel being a part of it.

CHAPTER 19

"*Y*ou're getting serious."

I stop raking the first fall of leaves, and stare at Maya. "I wouldn't say serious. Are you going to help, or are you supervising?"

She leans on the handle of her rake, one brow raised, studying me like a hawk to a mouse. "I'm thinking."

"Well, think and rake, or Dad is going to get out here and do this all himself."

"I want to know what you're thinking about all this."

I stop scraping damp, smelly leaves with a sigh. "About what? I thought you were on board with me and Axel."

"I am, but you haven't brought him around much. If you're serious, we all want to get to know him better."

"We're dating," I say, taking the pile up to my knees again. "I didn't think we needed to do the whole hang out with the family thing just yet."

"Elle, come on, you know I'm asking because this is the first guy since Rod. Talk to me. What's going on in your head? You think you could end up with him? What makes you like him? Are you being careful?" She says the last bit with a pop to her hip.

"Oh my . . . stop," I say, tossing a handful of crispy leaves at her head. "I'm not eighteen, and one thing I like about him is he *doesn't* expect anything."

Maya lets her rake drop; bursts of red, orange, and brown crunched beneath its weight as she marches toward the stoop. "Come on, give me something. As your older, wiser, more experienced sister, I get to know everything and tell you if you're making a terrible mistake."

"Like last time?"

Maya cocks her head. "Elle, I've never done the whole I told you so thing."

"Not you," I whisper.

Maya takes a deep breath, and shuffles through the leaves. She nudges my shoulder. "Hey, no one here, including mom, would ever want to make you feel bad for what happened. It's a life thing, you know. Stuff happens."

"You told me not to marry him."

"I did," she says with a nod. "But what does that have to do with you talking about what's going on right now?"

Why don't I want an opinion? One might think after surviving the world of divorce, I'd be asking everyone, down to the mailman, if my relationship seemed sound. I swallow the knot bulging like a tennis ball. "I don't want you—" I clear my throat, "I don't want you telling me this one is heading for the ditch."

I think Maya might roll her eyes, think she might laugh and make fun of me. She does none of that. Maya smiles softly and folds her arms. "Because you really like him."

Why am I crying! I swipe at the stubborn, salty drop before it falls, and look to the harvest sun. "I like him. A lot. When I say he doesn't expect anything I mean just that. Axel . . . he takes me as is, you know. I missed a few red flags with Rod, and I see them now. Remember he always tried to dress me up, told me how to style my hair, what clothes to wear? Rod even told me what diet to follow. It's no pressure with Axel. You know?"

Maya grins. "I get it. It's not all physical right?"

I scoff and make sure my sister sees the dramatic eyeroll. "Maya, come on."

She holds up her hands, eyes wide. "I'm just asking."

"There's no pressure all around."

"Okay." We settle into a silence that toes the border of awkward before she flicks my ear. "Want to know what I think about him?"

"I mean you're going to tell me anyway."

"True enough." Maya crosses her arms over her chest, thoughtful, dramatic, as she is. "I don't know if you can understand what it's like watching a light leave your favorite person's eyes. Talking about you, Elle. I know I blurt out what I think a lot, but believe it or not, I've kept a lot back, especially regarding Rod. But these last few weeks—"

"Are you crying?"

She shoves me and sniffles. "You started it. It means a lot to me, alright. As I was saying before you tried to avoid emotion, the last few weeks that . . . light, I guess you can call it, is back. You seem so much like you again. I think you deserve a lot of the credit, finding the guts to leave and all that, but I do think Axel has something to do with it. Any guy who does that for my favorite sister—well, I'm all on board with that."

How to respond? My heart swells in my chest; my gut feels like it rode a tilt-o-whirl. "That means a lot, Maya. Can I tell you something?"

"Always."

My tongue ties for half a breath, but eventually I find the words. "I'm scared."

"What about?"

"Is it too fast? I mean, is there a time frame before dating after getting divorced?"

She shrugs. "I think it's different for everyone. In my opinion, it's important you know that you're good first, but I think you're finding your place here, right?"

"I feel like I am," I admit. "I love my job, my condo."

"You chewed Rod out . . ."

"There's that, too."

"So, I think you're doing things right, Elle. I really do."

"I don't want any repeats, you know?"

"Well, I don't think you're planning to marry Axel tomorrow, but he seems genuine. And we know the Olsens. He's not some random guy." Maya takes my shoulders. "My honest opinion: I think Axel is a good move. I mean it."

I didn't expect hearing that to feel so . . . good. Inside, I believe I don't need my family's approval, but after years of not having it with my choice of men, this feels like bricks lift off my shoulders. A little had to do with the fact that Axel has broken through a bitter, unyielding wall I'd built inside, setting me free in a way.

I've lived a romance that eventually grew loveless. I've survived being broken, tossed aside. My feet found their way under me again, and he was there to help fill the still wounded pieces. I can survive on my own, but truth told, a gargantuan piece of me doesn't want to think of that, doesn't want to think of steps without Axel.

CHAPTER 20

*A*n opened, yellow package is sitting on my desk. I expected the pearl necklace, but only an empty black box came inside. My pulse is hot as it pounds between my ears. The note explains the necklace can't be found, likely lost during the move into his new house. There's also a reminder that Rodney's money was his before we'd ever met, and I shouldn't plan on getting gutsy again with my threats. He uses the word gutsy.

He mailed the empty box to the hospital. I'm not naïve enough not to remember the man knows exactly where I am. Staying within the sister chain of hospitals, with Rodney's position in corporate, there remains a chance we'll cross paths a time or two.

Staring at the empty box, I feel that old tiresome defeat; Rodney always finds a way to win.

Scrubbing my face, I try to chase thoughts of my ex, and lack of sleep away before resorting to caffeine. A smile shoves Rodney worries away as I think of the after-leaf-raking night. The smell of Axel spice is still on my skin. Late nights cause waking up at five in the morning harder. Don't get me wrong, they are oh, so worth it. I stand and stretch to get some blood flow. Patients rouse for the day, or eat breakfast, and I need to get morning medication ready to distribute. Sleeping while measuring pills isn't wise.

The door to the therapy gym opens and I wish the weekend therapist was less woman and more male—blue eyes would help, too. Still, I shoot Beth a smile. We bonded at the dinner, right?

"Good morning," I say, trying not to yawn.

"Hi," she says brightly, tugging her long cinnamon hair into a ponytail. "You look sleepy."

"Yeah, you'd think I'd be more of a morning person with my job, but . . . I'm not. Are you alone today?"

She nods a little hesitantly. "First solo weekend. I'm sure it will be fine, but it's the computer system I'm struggling with. I'll probably need to call Axel to help me over the phone in a bit."

I keep my smile, although I'm in a tug-of-war inside. There's no point in allowing my mind to drift to shaky places, because Axel kissed *me* goodnight last night. He'd texted *me* this morning that he wants us play games at Brita and Jonas's house tonight. I'm desperate to take Viv's advice and not allow the damage done in my previous relationship to sour all the signs pointing to the good coming my way.

"I'm sure you can call him. He's the epitome of a morning person; I bet he's up." I know he's up. My good morning text and all.

"Hey, I actually wanted to talk to you about him," she says as she clips her name tag to her collar. "I feel dumb that I told you I thought he's hot when you liked him, too."

"Oh, no," I wave my hands. "Don't feel dumb at all. He isn't hard to look at." Keeping the mood light is the right move—at least that's what I think.

"It's just, I had no idea that you did like him, and then bam, after I say something, you guys are dating."

"Yeah," I agree, feeling my neck prickle with nervous heat. Although, I don't like the insinuation she made. "It was a little surprising to me, too. I mean, we've known each other for a long time. We went to high school together."

"Ah. He never said anything like that."

"Yeah . . ."

"You guys are pretty new then."

I pretend to scoot papers around, hoping Beth might go back to work. "Um, more like newly rekindled. We dated in high school."

"Well, I guess we'll just wait and see."

I'm not always docile. Even with Rod, I'd spoken my peace a time or two. Heck, Auntie Kathie had to stop me from defacing his property. Flashing my eyes from my pretend work, I meet Beth's eagle gaze. "What do you mean by that?"

"Oh, just that it's early. A lot can change in the beginning. You guys are busy, and Axel seems to have a type."

"Yeah," I grumble. "What kind of type?"

She holds up her hands. "Please don't take anything from this. I'm probably sticking my foot in my mouth, but from what I've been told he likes . . . you know what, never mind. I hope it works out for you guys. We'll just see where it goes."

"Yeah," I say, trying to hold my tongue. I can't. "Seems to be going pretty good right now, if I'm honest."

"Really?"

I nod with a grin. "Yeah."

"That's good. Maybe you'll be the one to tame the player," she says, laughing. "You know Gerald in speech therapy? He might have hinted that Axel plays the field. But don't worry, I'm sure he's smitten."

And there it is: the kryptonite to my insecurities. How she knows where to strike will forever be a mystery.

"Well, I'd better get started or I'll never get out of here," she says with a bit more smugness. As if she knows what she's done. "You said Axel will be up?"

"Should be," I mutter.

"Great. See ya."

Clearly, she hopes Axel and I are a fling, over by next weekend. And what is with the Axel has a type thing? In Beth's eye, I'm not his type, but how in the world would she know that?

He must have known we were talking about him because my phone brightens with another text. A text to wash away the burn of what ifs scorching a trail through my mind; a text to rid me, for even a moment, of the fear that I'll be tossed aside after my heart is completely invested.

Axel: Alright, you know I'm not one for cheesy texts, but I'm sitting here with nothing to do and I've got to admit . . . I can't wait to see you tonight.

* * *

CURLING against Axel's side on my couch, I can't think of a more comfortable place to end an evening.

"You and Jonas are nuts," I say, sleepily.

He laughs and rests his cheek on the top of my head. "That was nothing. I think it's more a game now. The first one to stop competing with the other loses, so we keep getting worse."

"I think it's funny."

"Speaking of competitive," Axel says as he tightens his hold around my shoulders. "You, Elle Weber, have a feisty side."

"I get a little into games. It probably stems from trying to outdo Maya."

"Siblings."

"Siblings," I sigh, hugging his waist. "I'm glad it didn't scare you off."

"Yeah, right. I loved it. And I like that you feel comfortable around my family."

"They're pretty easy to feel comfortable around." My eyes flutter closed as the woodsy aroma of his cologne lulls me into a secure trance.

Axel nudges my shoulders. "I'd better go, you woke up early."

I simply hold him tighter. "Not yet."

He doesn't protest, and hunkers down against my sofa for a longer moment.

"After today," I say. "I can use more of this."

"Bad day at work? You said it was fine."

I shrug. "It was okay. A new surgery ran into some trouble, so you guys will have your work cut out tomorrow. He's in a lot of pain. And then . . . nah, never mind."

"Come on, you can't say never mind. What happened?"

I smirk, wishing I kept my mouth shut. "I don't want anything to be weird."

"Wow, you're really not good at distracting me. Now I want to know even more. What happened?"

"Nothing, I just had a quick conversation with Beth."

"Okay . . ."

Taking a deep breath, I lean back to meet his eye. "Promise you won't be weird around her?"

His brow furrows. "Sure. I think."

"Not long ago she mentioned to me that she might have been attracted to a coworker."

"Can you blame her? Mack is good looking."

I laugh, tracing the toned shape of his arm. "Your attempt to be humble about your sexiness is admirable."

"Keep saying this stuff and I'll keep you talking all night." He presses a kiss to the side of my head.

I smile. "Anyway, she mentioned a bit of surprise that we'd gone to the lake together. I got a vibe she wasn't too happy about it."

Axel isn't playing anymore. "Did she say something to you?"

"Nothing bad." Sort of. "It was a little awkward. She doesn't think I'm your type, that's all. I promise we parted ways with smiles." Fake as they were.

Axel studies my face, clearly assessing for truth. "Okay," he says slowly. "That's weird since I've never talked to her about my dating life . . . ever."

"I just think she likes you."

"Well, there's nothing there, you know that, right?"

"Yes."

Axel urges my lips to his and kisses me slowly, building deeper and with more meaning at the right pace.

Not his type. Girl, please. A man doesn't kiss a woman like it's do or die if she isn't his type. I don't mind Axel taking the time to remind me, either. Not one bit.

CHAPTER 21

$\mathcal{M}$y nose crinkles as I lean over the counter so Agnes can dab a dollop of whipped cream on the tip. The little girl squeals when I do the same to her button nose. Behind the front counter, the bakery opens into a new world. The vast kitchen carries an energy only a few have the pleasure of experiencing. I've now stepped in the back a handful of times, but today is the day I prove if my German blood will hinder my ability to fit into the little Scandinavia surrounding me on every corner.

Axel and Jonas shove each other as they help Bastien roll out sweet dough for the puff pastries. Sigrid rolls her eyes the same as Brita.

"Those two didn't get the baking gene, I'll just say that now."

"Heard that, Mom," says Axel, as he bundles the dough up to roll out again, trying to get the thickness just right.

"Half an inch," Philip Jacobson says, with a tap to Jonas's shoulder, followed by a flick to Axel's ear.

"How bad would it be if we went to three quarters of an inch, though," Bastien asks as he rolls his own dough.

"We wouldn't sell it," Philip insists, his Swedish accent coming thicker the longer he speaks. "Garbage."

Bastien strokes his chin thoughtfully. "So, by garbage you mean we'd get to eat the mistakes."

Philip grins and knocks his cane against Bastien's legs. "Half an inch."

Bastien salutes. "Got it."

Over two months of spending ninety percent of my time with Axel, I'm used to the new love between the Olsen and Jacobson families. Brita told me anyone who takes part in the family needs to fall in love with the bakery—even if they don't work the registers or bake the sweets. The spirit of the place needs to take hold of a heart and never let go. Apparently—and it dumps buckets of butterflies into my gut—everyone feels I am welcome to start piecing bits of the market into my DNA.

I find an ease with Axel's family while he's grown accustomed to the dry humor around the Weber dinner table. Even Graham and Axel get along to the point that Graham loosens up, revealing a side to my brother-in-law I'd never seen before. It's as if Axel is able to put everyone at ease to be their true selves.

"Axel, you'll make sure these get there on time?" Sigrid asks as she folds a few cream-filled pastries into a white box.

Jonas lifts three boxes; Axel doing the same as he laughs. "Elle, is that the first or fiftieth time my mom has asked that question?"

"Whoa, don't bring me into this," I say as Agnes dabs my cheeks.

Sigrid huffs. "It's a big order, Ax."

"I promise, we'll have them at the house tonight, all ready for tomorrow, and our good name will live on."

"Who taught you how to speak?"

"You're glad you did, admit it. Elle, you coming?" he calls.

"Yep." I wink at Agnes, wiping cream off my face and hurry after the twins.

Jonas places the boxes in Axel's backseat; Brita brings more, then Bastien, until a white wall of hundreds of pastries is loaded into the trunk, seat, even on the floor of the car.

"I sort of love that Abby isn't doing a traditional cake," Brita says. "Everyone just gets their own mini cake. Good idea."

"Yeah, but then Jonas wouldn't have been able to smash cake in your face," Axel tells her, closing the back door. "I still think he has some unresolved aggression since he about knocked you off your feet."

Brita laughs and links her arm with Jonas. "We got a little into the cake smashing thing. Did you do a big cake, Elle?"

The whole Elle's-been-married thing is old news with the Olsens. I shake my head. "Uh, no. Basically went to the courthouse then to dinner with fancy sugar-free mousse after."

"Your choice?" Axel asks.

A flush heats my cheeks. Axel asks a few questions about Rod, mostly when he's being protective. I sort of love seeing his defensive side come out. Again, I shake my head. "No, I wouldn't say it was my dream wedding; not by a long stretch."

Axel shoots me with his rare, shy smile before Bastien comes back with a few forgotten boxes and the brothers set to work adjusting to make more room.

"I don't think it's third time's a charm, more like the second time," Brita whispers at my side.

"I'm not sure that was a proposal or anything."

She laughs. "No. Not yet, at least."

"Ready, Elle?" Axel pops open the passenger door. "You'll need to hold a few of the boxes on your lap."

I peck his lips, taking the box out of his hands and slip into the car. "I don't mind."

"Is it wrong that I sort of feel like telling my mom we delivered everything to the wrong place?" he asks when he slips behind the wheel.

"You're mean, sir. And you'd have Brita's grandpa, your mom, and Abby after you; I'm not sure which one is scarier."

"Oh, Abby, for sure."

Deliveries are made to Abby's mother's house twenty miles away. Abby squeals once we pull up; the storm door crashes against the wall as she bounds down the porch, hair half-styled. "You made it!"

"Hors d'oeuvres are officially here," Axel says. "Hey, I like the look, Abs."

She snickers and swats at his hand from flicking one of her misplaced curls. "My sister is doing my hair and wanted to practice. Oh my gosh these smell amazing. Come inside, half the hospital is in there. Ax, I don't think these are going to make it until tomorrow."

"You'll break my mom's heart if you eat them all and don't show any off," he says.

He adjusts a box, so he can hold my hand. There is something sweet about the way he gently threads our fingers together, like an intimate whisper. He always strokes my skin with his thumb, as if checking if I'm solid and real. I never had this heady warmth fill my insides when Rod touched me, more nagging worry over if I pleased him. But Axel's skin, his gentleness, his smile, wraps me in an easy calm no matter how small, or how passionately he touches me.

Abby wasn't lying. Inside, half the hospital has shown up to the mother of the bride's home. Women tie tulle into fancy bows, counters are tossed in glitter, ribbons, lace—everything that will transform display tables, centerpieces, and the aisle come morning. Too many bakery boxes for the stocked kitchen means the guest bedroom soon smells like sweet icing, chocolate filling, and flaky crust.

I drop the final box and brush my palms in a job well done. Axel was wrangled into helping with the wooden archway where Abby and her fiancé Jax will say 'I do' in the morning. I was put on bakery box duty.

"Hey, Elle."

I want to groan, but I don't. I have a little class, after all. My smile holds steady as I turn around. "Hey, Beth, how's it going."

Beth, Beth, Beth—looking all perfect in her tight black top that swoops low enough I catch sight of lace meant to stay under clothing.

"Pretty great. This is so exciting, right? Oh wow, are these from the Olsen bakery?"

I smile genuinely now. "Yep, and take my word for it, don't plan on eating only one. They're addicting."

She peeks in one of the white boxes. "I believe you. So, how are things going?"

"Are we talking about life, or about Axel?" I'm in no mood beating around a bush right now.

Beth grins. "Axel, of course. Juicy talk is my favorite."

Juicy talk? "Things are great."

"Elle," Beth says, her cheeks naturally flushing. "I hope things aren't weird between us. I felt like you took what I said a few weeks ago out of context."

"No, it's all good."

"Woman to woman," she says softly, "I think we need to look out for each other, that's why I brought up how Axel plays the field. You've been through the ringer, and I didn't want you to get hurt again."

Beth might as well have socked me in the gut. "What do you mean the ringer?"

"With your divorce and all."

"How did you know about that? Did Axel say something?"

Beth rests a hand at her neck like a debutante clutching her pearls. "Oh, I'm sorry I didn't know I wasn't supposed to know. Viv let it slip, not in a negative way, she said she was happy you'd found someone after your divorce is all."

My mouth tightens. I should've been upset at Viv's big mouth, but I'm more frustrated at the smug expression on Beth's face. "Right. I'm good, thanks. Good to have my practice marriage over and done with; now I know what to look for. Trust me, Axel is red flag free."

"You're being sarcastic right? Because I think Axel deserves someone who'll commit. Not practice until it sticks."

I feel petty, and truth told, I want it to end. "Beth, I didn't set out to get divorced, alright?" Closing my eyes, I take one cleansing breath and speak a little softer. "Look, I know you were interested in Axel, but I'm not going to apologize for being with him. He means a lot to me, and I mean a lot to him. Honestly, I don't want things to be weird between you and me."

Beth's grin fades. "I'm sorry, Elle." And I believe she is sorry.

"Sometimes I say things without a filter. I didn't mean to be so standoffish."

My attention turns to one of the boxes. I tap the top of the sweets and tuck some hair behind my ear. "Care to start over?"

Beth nods, beaming. "Yes, one hundred percent."

An annoying weight lifts off my back, and I start chatting with her like I do Abby, and Viv. It feels good, and one less thing that ties me up in knots.

"By the way," she says as we go back downstairs. "I think of few people from your old stomping grounds are coming for some big corporate meeting next month. You transferred from Charlotte, right?"

"Yeah, but what corporate thing?"

"Oh, they're expanding the Neurology wing, so there's a lot of remodeling about to happen. I guess some hot-shot corporate people planned a big presentation next month, but hey, we get free lunch."

"Specifically corporate?" My blood feels like ice.

"Yeah, North Carolina is headquarters, so the head honchos are coming to reveal the plans, like we have any say either way. You okay?"

How I hope she can't see the race of my pulse in my neck. I nod. "Yeah, I'm fine. They'll probably be bringing everyone to talk specifics, maybe even marketing, I assume."

Beth shrugs. "Who knows all the job titles, all I know is they drive fancy cars, wear tailored suits while I eat cereal for dinner so I can pay off student loans. I'm not bitter though."

I force a laugh at her irony, but inside a light dims and I taste the sting of bile in the back of my throat. Walking back into the kitchen, the burden temporarily lifts when I hear the relaxing sound of Axel laughing. There he sits at the kitchen table, trying to help Abby, Jax, Viv, and Mack tie little bows around small, white favor boxes.

"Elle," he says, and I swear his face brightened when he sees me. "Abby isn't letting us leave. We're officially wedding preppers. Saved you a seat." He scoots over a bit on his chair as a hint we're to squeeze together.

Abby smacks his arm. "Hey, I spend all my time with you people; you're my work besties and real-life besties. That means you help prep my wedding. Ax, when you give Elle a ring, I promise I'll do the same."

My mouth goes dry, and I fear he'll quickly brush it all away, but Axel studies his little bow and says, "It's a deal."

I slide my arm around his bicep and smile softly when he meets my eye. Maybe with him, I'll survive what's coming.

Without a doubt, I have the sinking feeling Rodney will break my new found peace with his sledgehammer words and manipulative games soon enough. *I've got this.*

Sort of.

CHAPTER 22

"*W*ow, Ellie."

My face feels like firecrackers burst in my cheeks as his pale eyes heat with desire when he scans my figure.

"You like it?" I pop a hip to show off the tight, blue pencil dress a little more.

Axel stares at me, eyes blazing. "I say we ditch the wedding."

One laugh, one tug on his black tie, and soon enough Axel's lips are pressed to mine. A kiss worthy of numbing the mind into delightful oblivion; a kiss he deepens as his arms wrap around my waist, as my fingers rake through his hair. Maybe Axel has a point, no one will miss us, right? Eh, except Abby rage is enough to scare anyone.

"Don't tempt me," I say against his lips.

"But it's my favorite thing."

"Think of next week at work. Think of Abby with all those weights and electrodes in the gym, Axel."

He grimaces. "You're right. We'd better go."

Axel promptly slips his fingers into mine and walks me through the breezeway toward the parking lot.

"Are weddings hard for you?" he asks after we're on the road.

I shake my head. "No, I still love weddings. Jax and Abby are adorable. I'm really happy for them."

"Yeah, I never cared for weddings."

"What about Jonas's?"

"He's my brother; I had to have fun at his by default."

I laugh and twirl a stiff curl around my finger. "Why don't you like weddings? Too sappy?"

He shrugs. "No, I think for a few years I thought sticking with one person was idiotic."

Giving his shoulder a pinch, I furrow my brow. "Wow, what a romantic. Keep talking, please."

He laughs, and I melt a little in my seat, doubtless I'll ever tire of Axel's smile.

"I'm talking past life," he insists.

"Oh, really? You're suddenly into weddings, huh?"

Axel pauses for a breath, his grip tightens around my hand, and he shoots me a glance. "The idea is growing on me lately."

With a deep breath, I lean back in my seat.

"What?" he asks, a touch of caution in his tone.

I lick my lips and smile. "I'm glad weddings grew on you."

He scoffs, but seems nervous like me. Good, we can commiserate in this deeper, stranger ground we've found.

Conversation changes into Bastien's funny stories about making out in cars (the kid just can't stop), but the detour gives me a chance to calm my pulse. Being a week shy of three months together, I can't think such massive future thoughts like being with Axel long term. Originally, I had planned that if I ever get married again, I would date for ten years, insist on a one hundred question survey on likes, dislikes, crazy exes, fidelity, and overbearing mothers, followed by a year of premarital counseling. Too much?

Looking at Axel wipe tears from the corners of his eyes as he relays the way his dad caught Bastien in the latest steamy outing, I have a hard time not forcing him to drive us to the church this instant.

It's a strange, frightening, and wholly delicious thought.

* * *

"TEN SAYS she's going to trip in those heels," Mack mutters as the pastor leads the vows. Mack's wife, Kari, swats his arm.

"Make it twenty and you've got a bet." Axel's expression is totally sincere.

I glare at him, but he slips his arm around the back of my chair and winks.

Hanging willow branches with gold ribbon and twinkling lights burst around the archway, the aisle, and chairs. Abby's ceremony is intimate and lovely with all the soft colors and adorable twin flower girls. I take a deep breath of the burners of cinnamon wafting through the room, and soon realize my wedding more than paled to such an event; frankly the day was rather lame. A peck to the lips after being pronounced man and wife, then Rodney joined the swarms of congratulations by his colleagues, leaving me to huddle with my parents, Maya and Graham. Not exactly the swells of romance a bride hopes for—and you know what, I feel a groom should want such swells, too. My wedding day should've been the first sign of our doomed path, but there isn't much I can do about that now.

"Do you think he'll drop her when he dips her for the kiss?" Mack keeps going.

"For sure," Axel whispers.

"You two are officially uninvited to my wedding," I blurt out before I realize what I've said.

Axel grins, his fingers twist around the ends of my hair gently. "Don't worry, Elle, I won't drop you."

Viv, sitting on my other side, gasps softly, and grins deep enough that I see her dimples when she fans her face, meeting my eyes. Axel doesn't notice her reaction; he's back to betting with Mack, but warmth drips through my stomach, flutters send my heart on a run, and my fingertips tingle as I reach for him.

Nipping my bottom lip, I make sure my mouth skims his ear. Axel's hand resting on my thigh, tightens. "You're saying those things again," I whisper. "Do you want me to pass out?"

He presses a quick kiss to my temple. Perhaps I haven't experienced many men in my life, but one thing I know for certain, I've never felt the sort of fog in my brain brought by Axel. A good fog; a very good fog.

Silence settles over the audience when the pastor steps away from the bride and groom, and Jax kisses Abby hard, without a lick of a stumble. I haven't known Abby long, but I genuinely feel overwhelmingly happy as Jax leads her down the aisle for their first steps as husband and wife.

"Party time," Mack says, clapping Axel on the shoulder.

"A little excited, Mackerel?" Viv asks.

"This is the first kid-less night we've had in . . . I don't know how long; we're planning to enjoy ourselves."

Kari scoffs. "Until we both fall asleep at eight."

"True, babe. True."

In fact, Mack and Kari make it until nine thirty. Viv and Spence dance like no one is watching, enough to give me a stitch in my side from laughing. Beth and her plus-one, a nice enough guy, snuggle close at their table. My favorite part of the night comes when Axel has his arms tight around my waist, his body close, and my fingertips dance along the back of his neck. Moments when the music slows, and I can rest my head against his shoulder, breathe the fresh scent of his skin, and simply be. Those moments are frequent, but always end too soon.

AFTER ONE IN THE MORNING, we make it to my front door. I hug Axel's arm, and yawn against his shoulder. He laughs and unlocks my door for me. I jolt a little more awake when I lean against the door frame, one of his hands on my face, his body making a cage around mine.

"You survived a wedding," I say, voice rough.

His thumb slowly strokes my jaw, my chin; he smiles. "Can't complain about the company at this one." Axel pauses, his eyes turning to the ground. His voice is soft when he goes on. "You know,

Jonas asked me something the other day; I can't stop thinking about it."

"Oh no, is this about to spur some insane twin competition?"

He lifts his eyes. I'll never tire of swimming in those summery blues. "No, Jonas has me beat by being married. He asked me how *we* were doing."

I tilt my head. "Doesn't seem like such an earth-shattering question."

"No, probably not to most people, but it got me thinking."

Oh no. Axel shifts on his feet; he seems nervous. A touch of panic mounts like a lead ball in the center of my chest. He's not freaking himself out, Elle. He wouldn't do that, we're good. Things are fine. Okay, now I'm freaking out!

"Thinking about what?" my voice croaks.

Axel stares at me, one of those heartbreaking, beautiful looks that seals in your mind that only you matter in the moment. My knees buckle—knees really do that—and it takes a solid fight to keep from melting into a puddle.

Without an answer, he kisses me. A new kiss; transformed, I'd say. Axel kisses me in a way that leaves more than a tingle on my lips, more than a rapid heartrate. Slow and pure if a kiss can be called pure. My fingers curl around his suit jacket; his hands hold me safely. This kiss leaves a permanent mark, like a tattoo on my brain with images of future hopes, plans, of future us.

He rests his forehead against mine after he breaks the golden kiss, his hands still on my face. "I realized something after he asked," he whispers. "Before you, I'd probably say fine, or it's nothing serious, but not now. Elle . . . I've never—" He chuckles nervously and shakes his head. "I can't even talk. I've never said . . . but . . ."

Words are funny, sometimes what isn't said draws the loveliest sensations. I think I understand him, and a collision of emotion pummels the line between my head and heart.

I trap his face as he stammers, my mouth dry. I mean every word. "I'm falling in love with you, too."

He releases a shaky breath, smiles that white, head-spinning smile, and crushes his mouth against mine. A golden kiss earlier; this one hits platinum.

"It's too fast, right?" He asks sincerely after a few breathless moments.

I nod; a playful smile draws over my lips. "Definitely, I think we should slow things down."

Axel brushes hair off my forehead, his touch gentle like silk. With a smirk, he smashes me against his chest. "You weren't supposed to agree. Sorry, but not a chance, Ellie."

I peck his lips. "Good answer."

"By the way, I think we should become professional wedding crashers if it puts you in a dress like that, and ends like this."

I scrunch my nose. "Hate to break it to you, Mr. Olsen, but this" – His eyes follow my hand up and down my dress – "is a rare thing. Accept that most days are yoga pants, scrubs, or ponytails."

"I haven't told you ponytails are sexy?"

"Happy to know you feel that way because they're a favorite around here. Don't worry, I promise to add a little eighties flare now and then, and put them high on my head; those will be special for you."

He laughs. "I'm expecting it now."

I start to ease out of his arms, puzzling how I will ever end this moment, but he tightens his arms around my waist, his voice is low and raw. His eyes alive with something brilliant and intoxicating. "Elle Weber."

"What?"

One corner of Axel's mouth curls, and I swear his eyes twinkle a bit like stars. "You should know that I'm not falling, Elle. I'm in love with you."

CHAPTER 23

eet propped on the armrest of my overstuffed chair, I lie on my back on the floor, hair splayed around my head, and a box of chocolate within arm's reach. A favorite, after-awesome-Axel nights position.

Brita sighs, settled the same way, and bites into a caramel. "Sometimes I miss all this stuff."

"What stuff?"

"You know, all the butterflies and firsts. The first kiss, the first I love you, it's always so exciting."

"Oh, come on," I say with a chuckle. "You and Jonas act like newlyweds still."

Brita grins and licks her fingers. "Because he's delicious."

I pop a toffee on my tongue, the chocolate coating oozes down my throat, warm and rich.

Brita rolls onto her stomach and props her chin with her palms. "I've got to be honest; it's blowing my mind imagining Axel saying the big L."

"I'm still reeling, too."

"I don't think you get it, Elle," she says.

I tilt my head so I can meet her eye. "What's to get?"

Brita shifts into sitting, crossing her legs. "Elle, Axel's on the downward slope to thirty and he's never told a woman outside the family he loves her. Never. In three decades."

"Hey, almost three decades," I say, flicking her arm.

Brita rolls her eyes and places the chocolate box lid back in place. "You get what I'm saying, though? You've stolen his heart, girl, and I sort of want to cry and squeeze you to death at the same time."

I bite my bottom lip as I grin at my ceiling. "Firsts do feel amazing, don't they? I never planned for this, Brit, never wanted it, to be honest. But when I told him I was falling for him, I've never meant anything more in my life."

"I'm happy for you, but I'm so happy for Ax. I worried it would be weird being his sister-in-law at the beginning, but I love that guy and he deserves to be happy. Just like you do. I'm just . . ." Brita sighs and leans against the base of the sofa. "I'm just so happy."

"Well, you and me both."

"You excited to come over for Christmas? The holidays are a big deal for our crazy clan."

My stomach squeezes at the idea. "Yeah, it worked out perfect for Christmas Eve, since Maya is going to Graham's parents and my mom and dad were invited to tag along."

Brita leans in, her voice playful and low. "I've got to tell you, Sigrid is probably going to kiss your feet. She keeps going on and on about Axel bringing a girl around for the holidays."

The rim of my cheeks feels as if a match is lit too close as I stand. "It's not a secret we've been seeing each other."

"I know, but she's still excited." Brita pauses and helps gather a few lingering wrappers off the carpet. "Is it strange getting serious with someone new?"

"You mean after a divorce?"

Brita nods.

I gnaw the inside of my cheek for a moment before shrugging. "Sometimes. What's hardest is trying to keep from regretting the past.

There's nothing I can do about marrying Rod, but when I compare him and how our relationship felt to now, with Axel, I want to go back and smack myself straight."

Brita follows me into the kitchen to help clean up our mess from our impromptu lunch. "I'm a believer of things happening for a reason. Think about it, the timing is perfect. A few years ago, Axel wouldn't have been ready for this, and I think you learned a lot being married to that guy. Now, you know what you want and you're going to go after it."

I scrub the plates in the sink with more vigor. "I'm nervous . . . I think Rodney's coming after the new year."

Brita lifts a brow; she stops midturn from the table, water glasses in hand. "What? He's coming? Here?"

"I think so. With the new wing remodel, corporate is visiting, and he's part of corporate. Knowing Rod, even if he didn't need to come, he would just to flaunt his new flavor in my face."

"Well flaunt your guy right back," Brita offers.

I laugh, but can't shake the twist in my gut. "Yeah, I don't know if Axel would want to go on parade in front of my ex. Maybe we'll both call in sick that week."

"Maybe you should. I've said it before, but it seems fitting to say it again, that guy's a sleeze and doesn't deserve one more day of fretting from you, my friend."

I shut off the faucet and face her as I lean against the counter. "Can I ask you something, but I want an honest answer, okay?"

"Okay."

"You don't think this is all too fast, do you?"

Brita smiles softly and shakes her head, so her ponytail whips her cheeks. "No, I don't. Honestly. I didn't realize it, but I'm pretty sure I fell in love with Jonas within a month. We turned out okay. I can't imagine a better woman for Axel. I mean it, Elle."

Down to my soul I agree with Brita, but in reverse. I can't imagine a better man who understands me, the quirks, the broken pieces, like Axel Olsen. Everything is lighter, my heartbeat, my steps. Axel confessed his feelings only four nights earlier, and now I understand the expression of living on cloud nine. Part of my head wants to dissect every syllable, find fault in my feelings, in his feelings. But I haven't. I love him, and I don't doubt he loves me.

* * *

I SNORT hot chocolate out my nose, and Axel seems ready to do the same when he catches sight of me. My dad bursts at the seams from laughing, rare as of late, and such a happy sight. My mom smacks Graham's arm, and Maya wipes a tear from the corner of her eye.

"I'm serious," Graham says. "The office smelled like tuna for a week."

"Well, quit tormenting the guy and maybe he won't hide his food in the vents," Maya tells him.

"Babe, come on, you ladies at the salon play more jokes on each other. Axel, help me out, without office pranks, workdays are soul sucking."

Axel smiles, his hand tightens around mine. "No, we're all work."

I roll my eyes. "That's a lie. Guys, on Tuesday the entire therapy staff had a Nerf gun war for thirty minutes. It hit black ops level, just saying."

Axel laughs as he leans back in the chair. "Completely therapeutic, patients were involved. Good balance work, things like that."

"Yeah, except Mack said you started it. Axel went all commando and hid in the office nook and waited."

"I got him right between the eyes. It went downhill after that. Mack is a sore loser."

"I wish my rehab stint would've been like that," my dad says with a grumble. "The place my insurance shipped me was all work. Seemed like the therapists hated each other and themselves."

"That's too bad," Axel replies. "Therapists love to hurt people, the least we can do is make them smile while we do it."

My dad chuckles. "I like that attitude. Next heart attack, I'm coming to you."

"Yeah, there's not going to be a *next* heart attack, Dad," I say, tossing a marshmallow down the table.

"Not if your mom keeps making me eat the way she does."

My mom swats at his chest and folds her arms as he kisses the side of her head. Dinners are normal with Axel now. Normal enough that the dinners without him feel wrong. He hasn't just added a piece, it's more like he's filled a *missing* piece to our dynamic. My parents even seem more at ease when Axel comes around. And get this—my mom doesn't give a single backhanded compliment all night.

Maya clears her throat after we've downed our hot chocolates and fat-free brownies. She squeezes Graham's hand, and her voice quivers. Not typical Maya fashion. "Hey guys, there's something we wanted to tell you."

My mom grips the edge of the table, her eyes wide. I nearly break Axel's hand, as we all anticipate what we hope.

Maya smiles sadly as if she reads our minds. "We're not expecting."

My shoulders slump. I break for my sister, for Graham. Axel's thumb rubs the back of my hand as it does often; things are better when he does that.

"But," Maya glances at Graham, "we made a decision, not an easy one, but it feels right. We're starting the adoption process."

"Really?" Mom asks, crystal tears welling in her eyes.

Maya swipes at her own and smiles. "Yeah. We feel like it's time to explore other avenues, and the truth is, all we want is to be parents. Doesn't matter to us how it comes."

"No, it doesn't," Graham says, kissing Maya's forehead.

I reach for my sister's hand across the table and offer a sincere smile. "I'm happy for you guys. You'll make amazing parents."

"Thanks, Elle," Maya says.

Dad pulls out a hidden box of sugar cookies after that. Mom doesn't even mind as she blabbers with Maya and Graham about the first steps, the long process, and the potential setbacks.

The house is quiet, and I nestle close to Axel on the porch swing, coats and blankets keeping us warm, the December air icy and clean.

"That's exciting for Maya," he says as he leans his cheek on my head.

I hug my arm around his waist and sigh "It is. I'm surprised she mentioned that in front of you. Maya doesn't like to talk about fertility things outside the family. She's more the pretend everything is okay and smile sort of girl. She must feel comfortable having you around."

"I feel comfortable being around, and believe it or not, that's saying something."

I lift my eyes, smirking. "You really didn't connect with anyone? I have a hard time believing that when you're so . . . connectable."

He snorts. "Maybe to you. I guess a couple of times came close to something, but I always found a way out. Something would get me second guessing, usually something small, and I'd move on. Makes me sound like a real winner, right?"

My stomach takes a plunge to my shoes. I enjoy the honesty between us, but can't deny an itch in the back of my mind often reminds me Axel broke my heart once. It's the sort of reminder that ruins romance, and I don't want it to stay, not for a moment longer. I lift my head and meet his eye. He's so handsome it hurts. But more than that, he's stolen my heart, and I don't want him to let go.

"What's wrong?" he asks when I don't say anything.

I smile and stare at our interlocked fingers. "I eat in bed sometimes when I feel really lazy. Mostly popcorn because I watch shows on my laptop."

Axel chuckles. "What? Okay, random."

"And sometimes I eat dinner for breakfast, because I love leftovers and don't like cold cereal, but who wants to take the time to make eggs or bacon."

"I like leftovers, too. Elle, what's up?"

"The little things that will probably drive you nuts someday. I better get them all out there."

Axel's smile fades, not so it's gone, simply softer. "Elle, things aren't the same with you."

"Well, you don't know all the quirks yet."

"Neither do you." Coy Axel returns, and he challenges me with those eyes. "I've been a chronic bachelor, so you know the toilet seat is never put down. My mom had to teach me how to iron, but I never do. I leave dishes in the sink until I don't have a choice but to do them or it smells."

"Yuck," I say.

"Oh, there's more. My bed is unmade right now, has been for three days; I blast rock music too loud—"

"My hair clogs the drain . . ."

"Expected, you've got to do better than that. Believe it or not I can grow an epic beard; Jonas is jealous, so I shave every other day and sometimes I leave the clippings all over the sink."

"I eat cookie dough before I can even bake the cookies."

"Eighties action movies are my obsession, and you will watch them with me, and tell me you love them."

"I love reality shows, the more drama the better. I'm talking staged outbursts, fake romance, all the insanity."

"I mix whites and colors in the wash because I'm too impatient to do two loads."

Before long we are laughing, out-quirking each other, until Axel has his forehead against mine, breathing me in, and me him.

"Elle," he says softly. "I promise this isn't something I'm going to walk away from, no matter how much your hair clogs the drain."

My eyes clamp into squished slits; slowly I trace his jawline. "Sometimes people do walk away."

He kisses me, softly, perfectly. His hands trap the sides of my face. "I'm not him, Elle."

"I know it's—"

"No, you need to know that," he says. "He didn't treat you right, love you right; he didn't. I'm not perfect. I've been a jerk before, you know as well as anyone, but here, now, I want you. When I told you I loved you, I meant it, Elle. Weird things and all."

I have nothing I can say that can depict how he makes me feel in this moment. I kiss him—kiss him until words blur into sensation, until he understands. A light snow starts to fall, the purple sky deepens, but I don't want to leave our frozen spot.

Eventually I pull away, whisper that I love him, and we watch the night until our toes go numb.

To my recollection there has never been a time when my soul broke so beautifully. Each piece belongs to Axel Olsen, for keeps, forever.

CHAPTER 24

*T*he sky is gray with clouds ready to burst heavy flakes just in time for Christmas. Green, gold, and red lights around windows and railings in the condos brighten the walks more than the stylish lampposts as I help carry gifts into Axel's condo. Brita and Jonas left us a few hours ago to relieve Oscar at the shop, who is home for the holidays; and Bastien so the two friends can hit a concert somewhere around St. Paul. The four of us labeled the day procrastination Christmas shopping day, and vowed to make it a tradition.

Axel exaggerated his slobbishness, unless he tidied up of course, but I always think his condo smells like cologne and leather, and only one old bowl remains in the sink.

He dumps the bags on his couch and sits between the stacks. "We survived."

I start digging through a purple sack, until he snatches it away.

"No peeking. I had one rule." Axel hooks a finger around my belt loop and tugs so I stumble—not gracefully like the movies—half on and half twisted on his lap. He whispers close to my lips. "You'll need to wait until the day, Elle."

"You kill me." I squirm back to my feet. "Need caffeine?"

"Yes, an hour ago."

Like the place belongs to me, I march into his kitchen and take over the brewer, knowing right where to find the mugs. The holidays in my life are the best I've had in years. Thanksgiving came and went with two dinners. Axel joined my family, then I'd been invited to his. Now, Christmas. I came home for Christmas three times after moving to the south. Other years my family had destination holidays. After marrying Rodney, the holidays were made as frivolous and commercial. A complete waste of money, to quote the man. Of course, I never got on board with that mentality, and bought the big grump gifts anyway. I did receive a bracelet one year.

Handing Axel a hot mug a few minutes later, I find a comfortable place next to him on the couch. "So, what did you get your mom? Brita said you and Jonas always try and make her cry."

"Cry in a good way," he explains. "My mom loves thoughtful gifts, but it's getting harder to outdo Jonas. Personally, I think Brita helps him. There's no way he's that sensitive."

"Well, now you've got me. What did you get her?" He shifts on the couch and sips without looking at me. I nudge his ribs with a laugh. "What? Axel, are you being shy?"

"No."

My mouth drops. "You are. You're embarrassed. Now, you need to tell me what you're getting her."

"Nope."

"Excuse me? Why not?"

"Because it's lame."

I rest my chin on his shoulder and tuck my fuzzy-socked feet underneath me. "Please, oh, please tell me."

He laughs and shirks me off. "Okay, fine. I got her a mom birthstone bracelet today. You know, it has mine and Jonas's, Bastien, I put Brita in, too, but there's room for more."

I'll just say that I like the sound of the *room for more* part.

He clears his throat and finishes off his coffee. "Then I thought ahead, and I've written her a letter. That's it."

"You wrote your mom a letter." I offer a tiny pout. "That's sweet; she's going to love it."

"You don't know what it says. Maybe it says, Hey, thanks for birthing me."

"No." I kiss his cheek. "I think you're a softy deep down, and probably told her all the things you loved about her like a perfect son."

"I am a perfect son," he says. "Knowing Jonas, he probably got Brita pregnant or something just to spite me. I can't compete with grandkids. I mean unless . . ." He slithers an arm around my waist.

I squeak as he pinches my side. "Hey, whoa, you cool it."

He kisses the top of my hand, takes my mug, and stands. "So jumpy. I don't know what you were thinking."

"Right. Don't worry, Brita already filled me in on potential grandkid plans. I think you're safe this year, but no guarantees on next year."

"At least it gives me a year to plan."

Silence isn't always uncomfortable. On the contrary, at times moments sitting with Axel in quiet and calm are perfect, and preferable. I rest my head on his lap, and he rolls locks of my hair around his fingers; I trace his palm, simply being close.

Glimpsing at my watch after delightful silence, I sigh. "I should probably go. I've got to get up at five."

Axel stares at his wall, strokes my hair, and nods.

"You okay?"

He glances down and smiles. "Yeah, I'm good."

"What's with the sad look then?" I brush my thumb over his lips.

"I'm not sad," he says. "Just thinking about today."

"Yeah, and it makes you frown?"

I sit up, my hair on the wild side, but I don't care. Axel moves a few giftbags and squares toward me with a touch of impishness in his smile. "I'm not frowning. For the last four years, I've been a third wheel on procrastination shopping day, I liked not being a third wheel today."

"Don't start saying all your sweet things, or I'll never leave."

I try to stand, but he pulls on my hand, so I slam against his chest. His palm cups on side of my face, and I melt like wax.

"Maybe that was my plan," he whispers. "Elle, I love you."

A chaste kiss holds power; power to stir the heart and warm the soul. I kiss him softly, not long, but enough my fingertips tingle. "I love you, too."

And I do. True, deep, and real. I love Axel for his soft touch, his playfulness; I love how he pressures nothing, and walks me to my condo without protest. I love him as he kisses me, and tells me to call him when I get off work. Love him for promising food after the Sunday shift.

I love him. Simple as that.

* * *

"ELLE, sugar plum, it's good to hear your voice," Auntie Kathy says. How I've missed her drawl.

I settle in the front seat of my car, waiting for the heater to chase away the frigid air after my shift.

"How are you Kath? I got your text. Sorry, I sort of fell off the face of the earth."

"No, no, girl, it's fine. How you doing back home?"

The smile comes naturally as I think of blue eyes. "I'm doing great."

Kathy hurries and asks the basics: how do I like the staff, the work. She promises to come see my new condo when the leadership conference is hosted here next summer. Kathy had been the sounding board during the divorce debacle and the backstabbing that came months after. A genuine soul, as my mom called her, with no judgments.

"So, really, you're good?"

"Yeah," I say with a smile. "I'm doing really well, Kath. I've even met someone."

Kathy squeals. I imagine her bouncing up and down, her fists balled and shaking in front of her face. "Don't play with me, Elle. Y'all serious?"

I laugh. "Yes. We dated in high school, and well, things picked up again."

"Oh, baby, I'm so happy for you. He's a good one?"

"Even the parents like him."

"Mmmhmm, a step above the last one."

We can snicker about Rod now; he won't know, and even if he does, what can he do? Kathy is a head honcho, too.

Kathy clears her throat and her voice takes a slower tone. "Listen, Elle, I wanted you to call for a reason. I've been hearing all sorts of things about that hospital of yours."

"I know about the remodel," I say. "And I know corporate is coming in January."

Kathy lets out a long breath. "So, you know, creep will be there?"

My stomach nosedives. "I didn't know for sure; is he really?"

Kathy clicks her tongue. "'Fraid so, sweetie. He made it a point to let me know, figure he still knows we're friendly and chat a time or two. I thought I'd give you fair warning."

"He literally stopped you just to tell you he was coming here?"

"Up to his old shenanigans, the pig."

As unpleasant the topic, I still smile. "Kath, do you have your stress ball with you?"

She chuckles. "You know me, and yes. I'm sure he wants to rub your nose in his glory and manly . . . whatever. Just watch yourself, Elle. And don't let him know about your dream guy. You know the skeez, he'll find a way to make sure you aren't happy."

"He can't do anything to me, Kath. Don't worry."

"Oh, I'm not worried about your sass anymore, you sound like the feisty Elle I used to know; it's his vindictive streak I worry about. The man wants to make sure he always keeps above you, and everyone, to be honest. Ugh, I don't like him, girl. Not one bit. Never did, I can tell you that now."

"What can he do to me, Kath? He's got his girlfriend—"

"A new one now," she says quickly.

"What happened to Becky?"

"Oh, who cares. All I know is there's a new blonde who keeps creeping up at leadership conferences. You know, sometimes I'd like to drop my director tag and just go back to a floor nurse, so I don't have to see the man; I spew in my mouth a little each time."

"Dramatic, but I appreciate the extra touch."

"Yeah, well, it's true. I was worried before we talked, thought he might take advantage of you or something, but you do sound good, Elle. Really. Hold your ground, though, girl. I think he'll want to take the last word as always."

"How about I promise you, I'll do my best to avoid him. Would that help you feel better?"

"Yes. Yes, it would. Just steer clear of him. I think they're working more with your therapy director anyway. There's a few remodels going on up and down the coast, and the only other departments needing changes are therapy gyms—to account for more patients and such."

I groan. "Really? That's not good."

"Why not?"

My mouth is sticky, no matter how many swipes of my tongue, I can't wet my lips. "Axel, the guy I'm seeing, he's a physical therapist here."

"Axel? His name is Axel? He sounds like he'd be soft on the eyes."

I laugh again. "All based on his name, huh?"

"Names say a lot, girl. But bad luck on the side of him being a PT. Bad luck, for sure. You tell him to keep his head down, then. I assume he knows all the dirty details."

I scoff. "He knows about Rod, yes. Don't worry, Kath. Rodney thinks he's got power, but he doesn't. He can't control everything."

"I know, maybe it's the worry wart in me, but I think he'd pitch a hissy fit knowing you aren't on your knees begging him to take you back."

We rant about Rodney for a moment longer before Kathy insists she needs to get ready for a lunch date with her daughter, who is back home from school for the Christmas break. Slowly, I drive away, a twist in my gut. So, remodels moved into therapy gyms. Corporate tycoons will be talking with Nick, hanging around the therapists.

Great. Rodney might stay cooped up in an office doing all kinds of paperwork and might not show his two-timing face. But this is a small floor, a small hospital, in fact.

Rodney can't do anything to Axel, he's done nothing wrong—I've done nothing wrong. One thing I know, if anything comes back around to hurt Axel, that will be the last straw. I won't let it happen, ever.

CHAPTER 25

*C*elebrating Christmas Eve at the bakery, both the Olsens and Jacobsons have more platters with Swedish and Danish breads, meats, and sweets that I won't need to eat for a week. Sigrid makes a cake that melts like butter. Brita's cookies are flaky and lighter than air. I chat with Brita's father, reminiscing about old softball days where Nils Jacobson cheered alongside my parents for his girl. Brita was right about the weird family dinner being for a new woman in her dad's life. Nils is there with Shannon, a paralegal he met a few months ago, and according to Brita she's sweet as a peach. From what I see tonight, I'd agree.

Funny how the formerly feuding families can't celebrate without each other now.

Axel drapes his arm around the back of the couch in Philip Jacobson's living room; his fingers drum my shoulder. A wintry scent of pine and spice soaks the walls, the windows frost naturally, and a soft undertone of Nat King Cole plays from an old stereo. My stomach bulges from the enormous dinner, and even still, floor to ceiling is stacked in appetizers, snacks, and gifts. The family celebrates by passing around family gifts on Christmas Eve, a tradition different than mine, but I love being around to watch the fun. Axel's attention is on Agnes as he hands her a gift bag and his mom swoops next to me.

"Elle, this one is for you." Sigrid hands me a small red box.

"Thank you," I say. "You didn't need to do that."

"It's nothing big, but I found it, and just had to put it together."

I tear into the wrapping paper. Once I open the box, I laugh through my nose. Sigrid beams as I study the framed picture of a moment I'd long forgotten. "Where did you find this?"

"Cleaning closets of all places. I was digging through Axel's old room, and there it was in a box at the top. I mean, how could I not wrap it up?"

"Let me see," Brita insists and hovers over my shoulder. She snort-laughs, too. "Looking good, Elle."

My fingertips brush over the glass, a photo of my seventeen-year-old self, caught mid-laugh, in my muddy softball jersey, ponytail amuck and sweaty, and next to me is Axel; handsome as ever, longer hair, not as delightfully muscular. Younger Axel looks at younger me, laughing, too, his arm around my shoulders.

"This is amazing," I say. "And hideous at the same time. What am I doing?"

"That was the game you won for us," Brita says. "We won by a single run because you slid home and basically tackled the other team's catcher. That's your victory face."

"Oh, I do remember that game. I'm pretty sure I broke my pinkie, toe."

Axel grins. "Mom was about to burst waiting to give that to you. Look how twiggy I was."

I hug his mother, tightly. "Thank you, I love it."

Sigrid snickers and rubs my back like my own mom might do. She whispers against my ear before letting go, "You've always been good for him."

We share a look; a look from a mother who loves her son, but I know she loves me, too. Loves me for him. It's a new experience for me. Rodney's parents both passed before he met me, and his one sister never had a kind word to say. Sigrid though, she accepts me, cares, and wants me around. Knowing she has such a thought for me, not even a member of her family, is more than I could ask for.

Viggo and Philip hand out small gifts of Scandinavian gnomes to all the grandchildren, and the patriarchs of both families gift their children a weekend stay at the Great Lakes. Bastien promptly promises his parents there will be parties while they're gone. I don't think Elias finds it that funny.

Jonas and Brita had an afghan printed with an old photo of Elias and Sigrid when they'd gotten engaged, and score a two-tear gift with the woman as she wraps the blanket around her shoulders. I hold Axel's hand as he finally dares give the letter and bracelet to his mother. Sigrid gawks, and praises the bracelet, but I flash him a smug sort of smile when her chin quivers and she needs a tissue to dab her eyes as she reads his letter, which doubtlessly says more than *thanks for birthing me*.

Since being with Axel, I've gotten used to his and Jonas's proclivity to slug shoulders, so I hardly budge when Jonas punches Axel on the left arm.

"A letter? That was Elle's idea, admit it."

I laugh. "Nope, it was all him."

"A cheap shot, Ax," Jonas grumbles.

"How was that cheap?" Axel asks, gathering the gift wrap into a garbage bag.

"Suck up," Bastien adds.

Axel throws a wadded bunch of tissue paper—hard—and hits the youngest Olsen square in the forehead.

"I'm a simple woman with simple tastes, boys. Thank you, sweetheart," Sigrid squeezes Axel. He winks at his brothers.

"Told you," I say.

"Yeah, but you've got to help me think of something for next year."

How toe-curling exciting is it to talk about next year?

Axel rakes his fingers through his hair. "There might be a little Jonas or something."

I shrug. "I can't stop them, what do you expect me to do? Stand there and throw things at them?"

Axel's cheeks flush a bit, but he laughs. "Not a bad idea, Elle."

I roll my eyes, but quickly stand when I see a battle with cookie plates. "Brita need help?"

Brita balances three trays of cookies, as if we haven't eaten enough. I take one, Axel follows and takes another.

"Mistletoe," Agnes shouts. "You've got to kiss her, Uncle Axel."

Axel and Brita look up, true enough they're stuck under the holly leaves.

"I don't think Jonas would like that, Aggie," Brita says.

Agnes shrugs and turns back to her new jungle animal set. "You said you kissed him before."

Oscar hears his younger sister and lets out a loud whooping sound. "Embarrassing!"

Brita groans and covers her eyes, but Axel simply nudges her shoulder. "True, Brit, might as well own it. Come on for old time's sake."

Jonas comes from the kitchen and shoves between them, carrying a plate of crackers. "We don't need to remember that you used to make out with my wife in your car."

"Okay, that made it worse," Brita says.

Axel says something under his breath that only Jonas can hear, then takes my hand and tugs me back to the couch. I laugh and shake my head. "You're not allowed to get into a competition with Jonas on whose kissing Brita liked better. Don't make it weird."

"What sort of brother-in-law would I be if I didn't make it a little weird."

I peck his lips and nestle against him on the couch when we find our places again. The night transforms into an evening I never want to end. Agnes falls asleep in the window seat, close to eleven, and slowly families fade back to their own homes to ready for the morning.

Axel and I sit in his parents' apartment gathering our coats before dropping me off at my parents' house.

"You know, this is the first Christmas I've ever brought someone home."

"Believe it or not, me, too," I say.

"What? No way."

"Yep, I never came home during the Rodney years. And my parents didn't come to me."

Axel smiles softly. "I kind of like being the first."

"Don't rush tomorrow or anything, just come over whenever you want," I say when he pulls into the driveway. A gold Christmas tree lights the front window and I can see a few shadows inside.

"I'll be rushing." Axel dips into the backseat and returns with the small purple giftbag. "Would you mind if I gave you my gift now?"

"I thought we said tomorrow. I can go grab yours."

"No, it's okay," he says. "I just wanted to give it to you alone, I guess. I'm kind of like my mom; hard to wait."

"You sure?"

He nods, but his hand grips the steering wheel tighter. Slowly, I pull tissue paper from the bag. Axel's jaw ticks. A black box is at the bottom.

"Axel . . ." I gasp when I open the lid.

His shoulders relax a touch when he releases a soft breath. "I saw it, and I had to get it."

Tears blur my eyes as I finger the delicate pearl on the end of the chain; nearly identical to the pearl necklace Rodney never returned. "It's beautiful."

Axel takes the box from me and removes the necklace. "I know how much yours meant, and this can't replace that—"

I wrap my arms around his neck, holding him as tightly as I can without crushing him. My heart triples in size; a sensation both uncomfortable and lovely. Pressing a kiss to his neck, I hardly care that tears drip from my lashes. "I love it."

Axel adjusts a bit and kisses me. And oh, how I kiss him back, wet cheeks and all.

Time didn't matter, but I know a fair amount has gone by once we break apart. I study the intricate swirl of diamond chips that cup the teardrop pearl. "This is almost identical to my grandmother's. Axel, it's beautiful."

"The necklace thing, it never should've happened, you didn't deserve that, and I wanted you to know how much you mean to me."

I brush my hand along the side of his face; the stubble of what he insists is his epic beard, tickles my fingertips. I choke a bit as I laugh, and the sound comes out more like a strangled sob. "I bought you cologne and wallet. I think you win."

He gives me a quick kiss before pulling me against his shoulder. "It wasn't a competition; I just want to be with you tomorrow."

Wiping under my nose, I turn away, the pearl dangling between us. "Will you help me clasp it."

He drops the clasp once, but my skin ripples at the feel of his fingers over the top. He wraps an arm around my shoulders from behind and kisses the crook of my neck. "Looks perfect."

"You know what?" I whisper.

"What?"

I love feeling his lips so close to my skin. Smiling, I lean against him. "I really love you."

CHAPTER 26

"I think this one has the hang of things." Viggo pats my cheek and the old man smiles so his wrinkles bury his lashes.

Bastien holds up a pan with batter that jiggles like Jell-O. "What do you think grandpa? Good?"

"Ack, Bass, it's supposed to look like pudding."

Bastien grumbles and dips his finger in the batter. "Still tastes good."

"Don't worry Bass, your mom beat mine for me, so I cheated."

Bastien smirks. "Well, thanks for waking up to help me make these anyway."

I glance at the clock, surprised a little myself that I'd made it to the bakery kitchen before eight in the morning.

"When are you going to take them over?" Axel asks.

"Not until late tonight. A total knock and ditch thing."

Axel places chocolate pieces on one of the already baked Danish pies, spelling out an asking to a school dance. "What if no one sees them until too late. They need to be refrigerated."

"They'll find them. I'll hang around until someone answers."

"It'd be great if she says no."

"Shut up," Bastien says, giving Axel a shove. "Dude, space it out better. That looks like a six-year-old did it."

Viggo tsks at his youngest grandson and Bastien stops complaining.

"She'll say yes," I say as I dump the batter with Viggo's watchful eye into the springform pan.

"Look at me, of course she will," Bastien insists. He's meatier than Axel was our senior year, and I have a suspicion he might end up being the most chiseled of the three Olsen brothers. I don't tell that to Axel or Jonas though.

"You're a jerk, man," Axel says with a rough pat to Bastien's cheek.

Bastien shakes his head and boxes up a finished cake. "I'd say confident."

Axel licks some of the sweet batter off his thumb and grabs his coat and mine. "Alright we need to go, some of us have jobs, Bass."

Bastien gapes. "What do you call working here?"

"A rite of passage. Ready, Elle?"

"I thought you worked crazy early," Bastien says to me.

I slip my coat on and accept a Swedish tea from Sigrid. "Oh, I'm not working, I need to update my CPR certification."

"Good for you," Viggo says, his grumbly accent delightful. "You can save more geezers like me."

I wave as Axel leads us out of the shop and into the gloomy morning. Something about Christmas taken down, and just gray clouds and snow make January a dreary sort of month. There are a few bright spots—more than half the month has gone by and no sign of Rodney. Heads of full departments, executives, and lawyers come and go, but even with all the corporate faces, the third in command has yet to make an appearance. I consider it a major win.

"Are you sticking around for the meeting at noon?" Axel asks in the elevator. He snaps on his name badge and finishes off the last of his creamy tea.

"My answer entirely depends on yours."

He smiles and kisses the top of my hand he's holding. "Well, I was thinking maybe you could sneak into the gym and come eat with me there. Aggie is coming at twelve thirty, so I planned on ditching the third remodel brag-fest. They talk like we can't live without it. Nick's in meetings all day hearing about how the gym expansion will change his life."

We step off the elevator and walk hand in hand to the gym. "You've been working longer lately, too."

"Yeah, we've had to cover the patients Nick can't see. So, what do you think? Want to come have an epic deli sandwich in the therapy gym?"

"Absolutely."

At the door to the gym, I give him a quick kiss, then squeeze his hand one more time because I can hardly keep myself from touching the man, and finally make my way to the nurses' station. I hope I'm not the only one recertifying; those are always awkward.

"Hey Viv," I say, reaching for the sign-up sheet.

"Elle," she chirps. "You look cute. I like when you curl your hair like that."

"Thanks, I figured I'd knock out one of my four times I do my hair per year, early. How's the morning going?"

"Getting busier, but not crazy. We've got a new part-time nurse starting tomorrow. That'll help."

"Finally," I sigh, and lean forward on my elbows so I can lower my voice. "So, are you ready for this weekend?"

Viv's cheeks shade like a pink rose. "Would you stop, we don't know anything."

I tap my chin. "Hmmm, a beautiful cabin, a fancy dinner at a top-five restaurant. All the extra sweet texts you've been telling me about. What could that mean?"

Viv squeals a bit as she shimmies her shoulders. "Like, do you really think it's going to happen?"

"Oh, I think it's going to happen."

Her shoulders slump. "But what if it doesn't?"

"Well, then you've got a super sweet boyfriend who wanted to spend a romantic weekend with his best girl."

"True, but . . . oh, man I'd flip a gasket if he proposed. And you know I would."

"I know you *will*," I say. "Hey, I've got to get going. I wish you were coming in."

"Sorry, mine doesn't expire until next year."

"Well, I'll see you later."

Viv snaps her fingers. "Oh, wait, I almost forgot. There was a guy —a fancy suit type—asking if you worked today."

It feels like jagged icicles stab into my stomach. I turn slowly. "What guy?"

She shrugs as she types a note. "I don't know, tall, a silver fox. Ring a bell?"

I grip the edge of the counter, my eyes whipping side to side as if he'll jump out from around a corner at any moment.

"Elle, you okay?"

"Viv, I think . . . I think that's my ex."

Her mouth drops. I know something more has gone on when Viv gnaws on her bottom lip like she's preparing to eat her own face. "Really?"

"Yes, he's with corporate. I thought I'd gotten lucky and he hadn't shown up."

"Elle, I . . ."

My stomach cramps as I lean closer. "What?"

"I just said it, not thinking it mattered or anything."

"Said what, Viv?"

She swallows with effort. "I told him you were coming in later with your boyfriend."

"You said boyfriend?"

She nods. "I mean, I didn't think it was a big deal."

"You didn't tell him Axel's name, did you?"

"No, I swear."

Rubbing my head, I lean over the counter on my elbows. "Do you know where he went?"

"Toward the administration offices. I haven't seen him since."

"Okay, if he comes around, just . . . don't tell him anything, okay."

"Elle," Viv says, softly. "He's not dangerous, is he?"

"Manipulative, vindictive, arrogant, yes. Physical, no. Understand, I just don't want him seeing me, or bothering Axel."

"No, I totally understand." She mimes zipping her lips. "Not another word will escape my mouth, and I'll warn you if I see him around."

"Thanks Viv."

"Hey, don't worry, Elle. We've got your back here."

"I know."

And I do know, but it doesn't stop the *thwomp, thwomp* of my heart, or the trembles in my fingers as I hurry toward the office to recertify. It must be Rodney. Who else would ask for me by name? He's come back and I have the feeling—one that makes me want to throw up—that Rodney won't be the one to say a casual hello and ask about the weather.

He always has his game, and he always plays to win.

CHAPTER 27

*S*ix years as a nurse, and two as an aide before that, I feel pretty confident about recertifying. Good thing too, because my mind is a mile away from the dummies on the ground, or chest compressions. By the time the class ends I'm already eight minutes late for my private lunch with Axel. The hallway isn't long, but I take it at a jog anyway. The faster I jump into the safety of the therapy gym, the faster I'll be out of sight from any snooping big wigs.

Part of me feels immature; I should be able to face an ex-husband, but it's difficult to explain. Rodney has this way about him, perhaps I didn't realize it until I stepped away. He's never raised a hand to me, but I'm still afraid of the man. Strange to think, but he convinced me of certain things during our relationship. Convinced me that I needed him, that I was naïve because of my age, convinced me he knew best; even convinced me I forced him into the arms of someone else because I wasn't enough.

So maybe not immature, I simply don't need to have his influence weave its way back in. I smile, straighten my shoulders a bit, and pride myself on recognizing the sleezy antics of the man.

I close the gym door behind me, and peek my head around the cave, as I call the nook of therapist computers. Axel faces a computer, reading something. "Hey. Sorry, I'm late. The class was fuller than I expected."

He turns with a grin. "Not a problem. I haven't even started eating. Did you run?"

"Do I look that winded? Maybe I need to take up running, snow and all."

"I'd go with you, maybe." He winces as he glances at his phone's weather app. "Or, I could cheer you on from the car."

I drag an office chair close to his side and accept a cafeteria sandwich. Before anything I kiss him, maybe with an added touch of desperation, but I like to think it's more gratitude that he is the way he is.

"Don't get me wrong," he says as I pull away. "I love when you kiss me, but you can't kiss me like that here; I'm at work, and I've got to be able to stop at some point."

I laugh and take a potato chip. "I'm not going to apologize."

"No apology needed. I just might need to go home sick or something."

I finger the pearl around my neck, my palms numb since my blood hasn't slowed the race inside, but I can't find the way to spit out the little fact of Rodney making his appearance. Making the excuse that I haven't seen him with my own eyes, I settle that I don't need to bring up something unpleasant when the moment feels too carefree.

Not even ten minutes into eating, a little Agnes giggle fills the gym.

Axel kisses my forehead and stands. "That was the shortest lunch date ever, but I'll cook for you tonight, and by cooking, I mean we'll get take out."

"Sounds amazing."

Agnes rounds the corner, her missing front tooth adding to her adorable face. Inez comes in right behind, scraping snowflakes from her short hair.

Axel lifts his hands and cheers. "Aggie! Ready to race?"

"She's been complaining about the left leg a bit," Inez tells him, taking the girl's coat. "I don't know what could've happened, though."

Axel crouches and gives Agnes a high-five. "Well, let's take a look, okay?"

"I was taking a spelling test at school, so let's go slow."

He laughs. "Don't want to go back, huh?"

Agnes crinkles her nose and shakes her head, but she catches sight of me and beams. "Hi Elle!"

Inez peeks around the corner. "Oh, I didn't even see you in there. How are things?"

"Going well." Oh, except my ex-husband is sniffing around like a bloodhound. "How's she doing?"

"You know it's like Ag is blossoming. Her speech is up to age level, she's starting to mainstream into her classes; it's just the legs. They give her some grief, but this therapy helps. Kind of nice having a connection, I'll be honest."

"Oh, she's for sure his favorite patient."

I enjoy being the wallflower as Axel plays with Agnes. They bounce a balloon back and forth, he sets up an obstacle course, and the little girl never drops her smile. By the time some of the other therapists trickle back into the gym, he settles her onto the padded table, to work out whatever ails her muscles.

"I'd better get going. I'm sure I'll see you soon," I tell Inez.

"See you soon."

"Elle," Axel says. "Just take my car."

"It's okay, I can ride the bus."

He scoffs, and covers Agnes with a blanket. "Take it, but don't forget to come back and get me."

Taking his keys from a top cabinet, I offer my most villainous grin. "Maybe I'll make you take the bus."

"Well, then no take-out, pretty sure they won't make a pit stop."

"Fine, you win. Food always gets me to be nice, Aggie." The girl giggles as I kiss Axel's cheek before waving at Beth and Abby.

Out in the hall, I glance over my shoulder once more—a picturesque setting in my opinion. Axel smiles, teasing Agnes and coworkers. He seems content. For a moment, alone in the hall, I simply feel lucky.

"He seems like a decent guy."

If a voice had the ability to bring back the ice age, his does it to perfection. I shudder, but find the will to glimpse behind me. My jaw clenches, and I have a split-second to worry over the welfare of my teeth cracking.

"Rodney," I whisper.

Rodney in his Italian suit, peppery hair trimmed and styled, a good balance between stubble and clean shaven. A handsome face, with a mean heart. "Hello, Elle. I wondered if we'd see each other."

"Oh, I think you intended to see each other."

I hold my breath as I turn away and stomp in the opposite direction. Rodney chuckles in his arrogant way, and follows.

"Is it so wrong to see someone you were once married to?"

"What's the point, Rod?" I snap, clutching Axel's keys tightly. "Divorce means we don't need to speak, ever again, if we don't want. And I think that's the way I'd like to keep it."

Rodney doesn't care, as expected. Folding his arms over his chest he keeps a close distance as I opt for the stairs instead of waiting for the elevator with the man breathing down my neck. Not that my detour deters him at all.

"Seems like you've found a place here, Elle."

I wheel around when we shove through the door onto the main level. "I have. So whatever you're doing, just don't. I'm not part of your life anymore, Rod. Just . . . please, leave me alone."

Normal humans would take the hint, but Rodney smiles with a touch of venom. "Oh, you don't mean that, Elle. You've got to admit, there's a side of you that's happy to see me. Although, I'm a little disappointed in you; come on, Elle, use the brain I know you've got in there somewhere. Taking up with a coworker again, after being transferred for inappropriate behavior in a relationship, seems a bit risky."

"Stop it, Rod," I say through my teeth. "Just stay out of my life."

"I'd really hate to see anything unfortunate happen to your job, or . . . his."

My mouth drops and I'm positive my heart ceases beating. "Are you trying to threaten Axel's job?"

"Axel?"

Curse you, Elle!

Rodney sneers. "I'm telling you, I'd be careful. I care about you, Elle, and would hate to see any relationship misunderstandings mess up a job because a guy mistreats you, or maybe causes a scene with you—anything perhaps inappropriate in the workplace with a coworker."

My gut twists into noodles and I need the wall to steady me. "Don't you dare make up lies about him."

"I don't lie, Elle. I say things as I see them."

"Stay out of my life, Rod. I don't matter anymore, so why can't you just leave me alone?"

"How about this," Rodney says, stepping closer. "Meet me tonight, and we'll talk about things. You tell me your side of the story, and maybe that's all it is—a solid relationship, nothing inappropriate. We can go out to dinner, like we used to. Maybe I've missed you."

He reaches a hand for me, but I jerk out of reach.

"No."

His smile falters. "That's your choice. Think about it, Elle. I'm giving you the opportunity to explain your side, maybe defend someone you have a silly crush on."

"Rodney I'm—"

"Listen, I'm staying at the Hotel Madison, meet me at eight in the restaurant, and we'll talk then. I've got work to do right now. Really think about things, Elle. You already have a reputation with Jason and Kurt."

He means the CEO and Business manager, and whatever negative reputation I have with the two men can be blamed on Rodney without question. I know he painted me as a woman scorned, a woman who seduced him—as if I could force him to ask me to marry him—and now he's trying to create a pattern of the same thing with Axel.

I stand stiff, unable to move as Rodney walks away. The cheeky smile on his face tells me he's started his game, and I'm expected to play.

* * *

I ONLY MAKE it to the front lobby. I sit in the chair nearest the gift shop, my body sinking into the cushion from the weight crushing me. Axel needs to know, but the thought of causing him such an upset in his life sends panic to my head.

My phone buzzes a little after five.

"Hi," I say softly.

"Hey," Axel says. "I'm finished so—"

"I'm already here." My voice sounds flat, but I can't hide this; imagining Rodney and all his power hurting Axel in any way, it is too much to cover with false smiles.

"Oh, cool. You're good."

"I'm just in the front lobby."

"Be down in a bit."

I hug my middle as tension fills my gut again. Axel hardly seems fazed by anything, but what about someone threatening him and his livelihood. I know how much he enjoys his job, and I am proof Rodney has pull. I'm confident Rodney can put a golden spin on anything and the board will eat it up.

I jump when Axel kisses my cheek from behind. Meeting his smile soothes the storm inside. "You scared me."

He holds out his hand and I link my fingers with his. "Are the roads bad? It's been snowing all day."

I squeeze his hand tighter; the inside of my cheek bleeds from gnawing on it all day. "I actually never left."

Axel furrows his brow. "You've been sitting here all this time?"

I nod, then we head out, bracing ourselves against the cutting night. The cold has a way of slicing through my coat into the marrow of my bones. We both must've been saving our breath and don't talk until we're inside the car, waiting for the heat to melt the thin layer of ice on the windshield buried beneath snow layers.

Axel blows onto his hands after ice scraping as long as he can stand it. "Why didn't you go home?"

My fingers coil in my lap, tangled like my heart. "I need to talk to you."

Axel stops warming up his own fingers, clearly unsettled by my mousy voice. "What's wrong?"

"Do you think we could talk at home?"

Axel turns in his seat. "Elle, you're freaking me out, what happened?"

Blasted tears. I stare at my lap, desperate to steady my voice. "Rodney is here."

Axel doesn't answer right away. He taps the steering wheel, his jaw set. I want to see his smile, the playful one, the one that says things don't matter. But this does matter—in the worst way.

"What did he do? Elle, did he hurt you?"

I shake my head. "No. We ran into each other in the hall. I just . . . I need to talk to you, but I don't want to be here anymore."

Axel doesn't nod, he simply puts the car in gear. His face like a stone. For the first time, I don't know how Axel will respond to something. Rodney obviously doesn't sit well with him, and perhaps Axel enjoys pretending this part of my life doesn't exist. I breathe a little easier when Axel takes my hand once we're on the road, still he doesn't say anything. I close my eyes and constantly repeat things will be fine, but truth told, things don't feel fine. Not at all.

CHAPTER 28

*A*xel leans against the wall, his arms folded, and he focuses on the coffee table in my front room. Salt from dried tears sticks to my cheeks, and my head swirls in a haze of exhaustion and frustration. He's been quiet through the explanation, but bit by bit his face hardened, and his smile faded.

"Ax," I whisper. "I don't want him to do anything to you."

"Elle," he says, direct and intense. "He's not going to do anything to me."

"Look what he did with me! He manipulated things so I was forced to transfer."

"We've done nothing wrong," Axel shoves off the wall and sits by me on the couch. "There's no hospital rule about coworkers dating, there's nothing we've done wrong."

"But he'll lie."

"He might, but we can stand up for ourselves. Nick will have my back; Viv and the nurses have yours. What makes me angry is how upset he's got you. Elle, the guy doesn't matter."

"You don't know him."

"I don't need to know him," Axel says, taking my hand. "He's not a man for making you feel this way all the time. I can't even think of what it was like when you were still married to the guy if he's like this now."

I dab my sleeve under my wet nose, a little gross, but I don't want to let go of Axel's hand. "It's not me that I'm worried about. When he even hinted of coming after you . . ."

With the knuckle of one finger under my chin, he tilts my face toward him. "Elle, I can handle myself."

"Maybe we should—"

"No."

"You don't know what I'm going to say."

He smiles, and a calm relief replaces my distress. "You're going to make a decision based on him, right?"

My cheeks burn. I rest my head on his shoulder. "Maybe."

"Well, we're not going to do that. If you're okay with it, I'm going to fill Nick in on what's going on. I think the only thing we can do is get ahead of something."

I nod, agreeing, with a tinge of shame the therapy staff will likely be pulled into my life's soap opera. "You should." My chin quivers, as I wrap my arms around his neck. "I'm sorry, I never wanted any of this to fall back on you."

Axel traps my face in his palms, urging me to meet his eye. "Hey, there are no regrets here."

"Just promise you'll keep your head low."

Axel rolls his eyes. "Come on, Elle . . ."

"I'm serious," I say. "Please."

Axel doesn't answer, but kisses me for too brief a moment. "Fine, I'll keep my nose clean. It's going to be fine, Elle. They're leaving at the end of the week anyway. When do you work next?"

"Not tomorrow, but the next day."

He nods. "Okay. You've got to promise me if he makes you feel uncomfortable again, you'll report it."

It's my turn to scoff and roll my eyes.

Axel squeezes my hand. "I don't care how high up he is; as an employee no one gets to intimidate you, Elle."

We stare at each other, tongue tied, or unsure how to go on maybe.

"I'm waiting," he said softly.

"Waiting for what?"

"For you to promise that you'll report it if he does anything."

"You know you're cute when you get all defensive," I snuggle closer, but Axel releases my hand.

Our lips hover near enough that skin touches, but still at a distance that spins the head. He speaks low, his fingers tangle in my hair. "I'm still waiting."

"I'll take care of things." He cocks his head, drawing a weak laugh from my throat. "I will, now may I please kiss you."

Another half a breath, and I forget the worries for a moment.

* * *

THERE IS a sense of relief as I step into the quiet hospital, that at least for two or three hours there'll be no corporate faces roaming the halls. A velvet sky shades in deep blue over the horizon as the sun decides whether to rise or not. A great day, everything will be great. I keep repeating the same thing in my mind as I climb the levels to my floor. Waving to Viv, I settle into the day. Soon enough, I almost forget I should keep on the lookout for ex-husbands.

Keeping busy works nicely, too. The rooms are filled with metal knees, hips, and a few shoulders and plated collar bones. And seeing Axel when he makes his way into work. He comes to work later the days I work, so we typically get off about the same time. He stops at the nurses' desk, hands me a tea, and kisses me quickly. Life can carry on normally. I really believe it can.

One hour left, one more round of medication, and I'll be home free. Axel let me know he finished his case load, and will be charting until I finish. A smooth day, cautious, but smooth. I caught a glimpse of Rodney once; he hadn't seen me since he'd been buried in conversation with a group of busy bodies, probably planning logistics and budgets and marketing on the new wing. I couldn't care less what they talked about if he keeps his distance.

"Have fun this weekend, Viv," I say with a wink.

Viv stops gathering her purse, off an hour early to head to what we all anticipate as her big proposal weekend. "I intend to, but I'm so nervous."

"Don't be. You and Spence are what dreams are made of."

She laughs. "I'd like to think so."

Viv's smile fades a second later, and her cheeks pale. I don't have a chance to turn around before a man's hand grips around my bicep.

"I need to speak with you. Now," Rodney hisses close to my ear.

My body tenses as he pulls me toward the elevators. As if an instinct kicks in, I say nothing and follow, though I have enough guff to rip my arm out of his hold when he stops next to a pair of vending machines and glares at me, a look that shreds through skin.

"Away from security cameras, huh Rod?"

He shoves his face inches from mine. "What are you trying to pull?"

My mouth drops. "Excuse me? What am I trying to pull? Look in a mirror; you came here threatening me."

"No threat, Elle," he says, dark and dangerous. "Concern. Concern that your behavior is truly starting to diverge with the company values."

I straighten my shoulders, but hope he can't see how my hands shake. "Give me a break."

Rodney speaks through his teeth. "I told you to meet me the other night, we'd talk like civilized adults, but you refused, like an immature, ungrateful girl."

I suspect it isn't wise to laugh, but red anger takes hold of my brain and I do, like a cackling hen. "Oh, you're upset that I stood you up? Get used to it, Rodney. We're divorced last time I checked."

His hand clamps on my shoulder, close to my neck. I wish I slapped him down the hall, but I am surprised enough I simply gasp as he slowly backs me against the wall. "You think you're something now, Elle. Hate to tell you, sweetheart, you opened this can of worms by demanding things from me, *threatening me*. We'd settled, you had what you needed, I had everything else. Then you wanted more; couldn't leave it alone, so here it is. Maybe you need to remember who helped you get to this place and take a step off that high horse."

I balk. "The necklace; you're angry because I asked for my necklace? You're pathetic."

His grip tightens and I wince, but shirk him away. I narrow my eyes, mad enough I could scream.

He doesn't seem intimidated in the least. "Watch it, Elle. I'm not a man you want as your enemy."

"Stay out of my business, and stay away from the people in my life."

He chuckles, darkly, and it sends the hair on my neck on end. "I will when my point is made. You brought this on yourself, Elle."

I lower my own voice. "Because I found something to be happy about and your side girls weren't cutting it, huh?"

His hand is back on my shoulder. "You just keep going, Elle. Keep going, let's see what happens."

I open my mouth to retort, as foolish as it might've been, but stop when a throat clears.

Rodney releases me, but my heart drops when Axel steps to my side, flawlessly finding a place between Rod and me without being too obvious.

"Hi, there. I'm Axel." He holds out his hand, and Rod seems stunned enough he shakes it. Briefly. "Listen some of the nurses are getting a little upset over this whole thing."

He glances at me, and I feel my eyes bugging out of my head. What is he doing?

Rodney folds his arms, his face turning purple as if he's holding his breath too long. "This is a private conversation."

Axel smiles, but it isn't kind. "Maybe that was the intent, the problem is that most employees are seeing a man bothering one of our own. Now, it doesn't look great when corporate starts putting hands on nurses, does it?" Axel takes a step closer to Rod, his smile never wavering, but I see the clench in his arms as he shoves his hands in his pockets. "And on a personal note, I'd really appreciate you stepping away from Elle. Now."

Rodney clears his throat and adjusts his suit coat. I can't move, can't think, really. Axel came in like a white knight, but he doesn't understand the danger in Rodney's expression as he takes a step back.

"We'll be in touch, Elle." With a seething glance at Axel, Rodney smirks. "You can count on it."

He stalks away, and I collapse against the wall, my palm pressed against my forehead. Axel whips around, his hands on me, soft, gentle. "Are you alright?"

"I'm fine," I say, but I'm not so sure.

"Come on, we're leaving after you talk to HR."

"No," I say, shaking my head. "Not right now."

"Elle . . ."

"Not right now." My voice cracks when I look at him and rush toward the nurses' desk.

Viv is still there, thumbnail between her teeth as she waited. "Elle, oh my gosh, are you okay?"

"I'm fine, but I need to leave."

"Of course, I already called Spence, it's fine."

"Thank you," I say giving her a quick hug. "I owe you one."

"No, go. We're good here."

I hug my middle and hurry toward the elevators, Axel at my side, but we don't say anything. A flurry collides in my mind and heart like a whirlwind. Anger, bitterness, fear, confusion; all bump and ping against the others until silence becomes simply the only thing I can do.

Axel opens my car door for me. I start the ignition without a word, knowing—hoping—he'll follow. He must recognize my processing stone face because Axel never tries to get me to talk, though he doesn't look happy. In fact, Axel Olsen seems madder than a hornet.

My heart races as I drive. Rodney isn't going to let it go, the man being incapable of being beaten. I saw the daggers he shot at Axel. With a slap to my steering wheel I curse like Auntie Kathy and battle with my gratitude and frustration until I pull into my parking stall.

I trudge to my front door, leaving it cracked for Axel to walk in— he does not one minute later—and I hug a pillow on my couch.

Axel stays standing, but he paces. I've only seen Axel pace when he thought Viggo wasn't going to make it. Now he takes my living room, back and forth. I've always loved those moments of silence, now the silence channels pure misery. I hate not talking, but I don't know what to say.

After at least five minutes of pacing, and me staring out the window, Axel sits on the edge of my coffee table. "Elle, you need to tell someone what happened."

The center of my chest feels like thick tar; it sticks and globs around my ribs and heart. I narrow my gaze when I look his way. "I don't need to do anything."

Axel shakes his head; his jaw pulses. "Why won't you do it?"

"Because you, my parents, my sister, or Rodney can't keep telling me what I need to do."

"Whoa, Elle," he says, taking my hand. "I think you need to tell HR so you can get ahead of whatever he's going to say. You're an employee, and what he did freaked out other employees. It was classic harassment."

"Why did you step in?" I snap, blinking to relieve the burn of tears in my eyes.

Axel releases my hand and chuckles bitterly. "Why? Because Viv came and got me; she was terrified. Because some guy had my girlfriend backed against the wall. Next time would you prefer I just stand there?"

I roll my eyes and close him off, tucking my knees against my chest.

Axel takes a slow, deep breath and leans onto his elbows over his knees. "I'm sorry, I don't mean to come at you. Elle. But seeing him like that, trapping you, I about lost it."

"I was fine," I say.

Axel scratches his chin and studies his fingers. "Are you really mad that I stepped between you?"

I shoot to my feet, Axel's beautiful eyes following me as I take up his nervous pacing. "Yes! I am mad. Ax, I told you—*warned* you—what Rodney is like. Now, he's got you on his radar. This isn't a game where macho guys face off and then it's done. It's never done with him."

"Elle, stop it." Axel is on his feet, too. He's never taken such a curt tone before. "I'm serious, quit giving the guy so much power over you."

"Easy for you to say," I say.

"No, it's not, because I care about you, but you can't let go of something—something you deserve to let go."

I don't answer at first and twirl the ends of my hair around my fingers, grumbling in the back of my throat. He has no idea what it was like to live with Rodney, with his condescension, his threats. Axel's only serious relationship is here, me, and he has the guts to preach to me?

"Well everyone knows best, but me," I say under my breath.

"Really?"

I close my eyes and try to calm the heat in my veins. "Axel, I asked you to keep your head down. I never wanted any of this to fall onto your shoulders, now it's going to be worse, for both of us."

Axel leans against the wall, his hands in his pockets again. "What do you want, Elle?"

"What do you mean?"

He sighs and stares out the window. "What do you want? Do you want to be happy, or only when Rodney says you can be?"

"That isn't—"

Axel stops my protests by stepping closer. "I'm not going to apologize for today. I love you, Elle. I love you so much." His hand covers his heart as if it hurts. "But I can't . . . fight this . . . *shadow* of a guy who never deserved you. I want you for myself. I want you to see everything I see in you; I want you to be happy, no matter what you do, be happy." His palms gently cup my face. "I want all that, but what do you want?"

Tears, both broken and angry—though at whom, I didn't know—soak my cheeks. I tell myself I'm protecting him. "I think . . . I think I need some time."

Axel hangs his head, and his hands slowly drop from my face.

"Don't say that, Elle, please."

My voice sounds like a frog. "I just think maybe time to let things blow over, then we'll see how things go from there."

Axel takes three steps back as if I've scalded him. His blue eyes grow darker as his brows pull in the center. "See how this . . . see how it goes? This isn't a *see how this goes* sort of thing for me, Elle. Not even close."

"That's not what I meant."

"Are you telling me to leave, to step back, or—what was my favorite line—oh, yeah, I think it's time to take a break, right?"

"Axel, I just don't want my problems to be yours."

He turns away, and a piece of me breaks, even more when he opens my front door. He pauses and looks at me from the cold doorframe. "Make that decision for us if you want, Elle. But I'm ready to take your problems because I want you. I thought you knew that."

"This is different."

"No, it isn't."

"He'll make life hard for you."

"I knew that, Elle. And I didn't care." Axel's voice softens and he taps the molding around the door. "I wish . . ." He pauses and looks at the ground. "If I could have one thing, it would be for you to know you are miles above him; he doesn't deserve the air you breathe. Report it, Elle. Not for me, but because you are worth more than how he treats you."

"Axel," I say through a sob. "Don't go."

He shakes his head. "I can't . . ." His voice catches, and a second part of me breaks. "I need you to know what you want; I need to . . . think."

"Axel . . ."

But Axel doesn't turn around, he leaves. I pushed him out, truer being I forced him out. Rodney won, in the slimiest way he could've won. I drop to my knees, cover my face with my hands, and cry.

He won and Axel left, hurt and angry. But the worst part of it all remains that I let him win, and let the man take everything all over again.

CHAPTER 29

$\mathcal{T}$wo days. Two loathsome days since I've spoken to Axel. Day one, I convinced myself we both needed a cool down time. At the end of day two, I am spooning mint chocolate chip like it is the last tub on earth. In the back of my head, I have a terrible suspicion this is more than a cool down time. I started to call at least a hundred times, and started even more texts, but never found the right words.

"Why didn't you tell us what happened?" Maya shrieks through the phone after I confess through my tears the disaster of the orthopedic floor. "I absolutely agree with Axel!"

The conversation drifts to a lot of scolding, a few choice words, and I still feel the sting.

A few hours later, a text comes from Viv with a photo of a pretty diamond ring on her finger. I cry selfishly, but also because I am happy for her, and find the good friend side of me to send her a congratulations. I feel dead inside.

At one in the morning on day three, I'm wide awake on my couch, a half-finished book at my side, as I flip through movies on the TV. My phone rings. For half a moment I hope, but my stomach falls when I see the name. I need to face him sooner or later. Clearing my throat, I answer. "Were you hoping to wake me up and ruin my night, because you didn't."

Rodney scoffs. "I planned on leaving a voicemail. I've been in meetings, and I've got to say, this little incident has caused more trouble than I would've liked. It's completely upset my focus on this new addition and doesn't bode well for you, Elle, since the board transferred you because of your explosive behavior toward me."

Oh, the man is good. I bite my bottom lip and swallow my sarcastic remark. "Rodney, I'd like to ask you a question."

He pauses for a long moment. "What?"

"What do you want? We don't have kids, we didn't have joint assets, what do you want from me? Why can't we go our separate ways?"

Again, he's quiet. Longer than typical; perhaps I stumped the guy. When he speaks again, I feel the ice in his tone. "Take it as a lesson not to let anyone disrespect you, Elle."

"But it's exhausting, Rod. Just live your life, and let me live mine. Don't we both deserve that? I feel like I'm willing to let everything go, harbor no ill will, and just live. Can't you respect me enough to do the same? You married me; I suspect you must've loved me a little bit. So, if you did, please let's just leave each other alone."

White noise hangs between the phone lines, and Rodney's voice is a bit softer. "I've worked my way to my position, worked hard. Since the day we met, you've been a distraction. It was exciting at first—your youth, your zeal. But I quickly realized what a mistake marriage was."

The words bite. Bad. "You can't blame me for everything. You created *this* distraction, Rod, and I'm not going to let you keep cutting me at the knees. You don't have a place in my life anymore."

"Hear me, Elle; I refuse to let a past mistake ruin my reputation, understand? Be careful what you say about me." The chill in his voice doesn't hurt as bad this time.

Enough is enough. "What have you said? What lies have you spread? Let's start there. I'd never lie to hurt someone else, not even you."

He clears his throat, his next words pretentious. "You'd be surprised what you'd do to protect what you've earned. Well, maybe not you. You give everything away for a fling."

"I love him," I blurt out. "Axel is far from a fling, and be honest, that's what bothers you most because you see it, too."

The next silence is thrilling because I think he is dumfounded. I think the firmness in my voice takes him off guard, and it's a powerful feeling that draws a smile to my face.

"I'd expect a call from Jason and your human resources soon enough," he finally says. "And I wouldn't get used to working with your boyfriend."

I close my eyes, beyond done. "Bye, Rod."

I hang up, finally tired of everything. His simple, yet callous, response flips a small switch. I've been a prize to my ex-husband, and a prize he'll play with until the next shiny object takes its place. I pushed away a man who loves me to my soul because of Rodney, for what? So, I can keep being his plaything to torment?

As I said, enough is enough.

WHEN MY ALARM GOES OFF, the morning seems more like velvet night. I stay tangled in a blanket on my couch, and scrub sleep from my eyes. The skin underneath my lashes is squishy from crying, and an ache throbs between my eyes, but my mind whirs like a spinning top.

Calling at five thirty in the morning isn't a problem nurse to nurse, and the sleeping city keeps me calm as I wait.

"Sugar plum," Kathy says, cheery as ever. "I saw your text."

"Oh, good. I sent it at one, so I figured you'd see it this morning."

"No, I was awake, and I planned to call you later today. I've already put a few things in motion."

"Wow, you're quick. Thank you."

"Girl, it's no problem. Gave me something to plot in my dreams. I've already got one response with interest. Seems we aren't the only ones wide awake when we shouldn't be."

"Really?"

"Looks like it, sweetie. You holding up okay?"

I rub the bridge of my nose. "I don't know."

"Well, keep your chin up, I'm sure it'll work out."

"Kath, I really appreciate your help."

"Girl," she says and sips something loudly on her side. "Don't even worry. I knew Mr. Scum would be up to his tricks, knew it. Listen, you keep me updated, okay."

"Thanks, Kath. I will."

"You've got friends, sugar. We might not be in high places like him, but you've got us all the same."

Personally, I think my friends are higher than any fancy office, BMW, or business trip to Manhattan or L.A.

There remains one major problem. Axel. He's hurt. Frankly, I think a part of me wanted him to walk out, to prove the cynic in me right and all; a cynic that says no one can have the one true love fairytale. With a clear head, all I see now is my unwillingness to accept what is right in front of me. Now, I don't know how to get it back.

Five hours later, the sun has hardly warmed the day, and the bench in the park is soaked with snow, but a few blankets from my trunk keep me semi-dry. I watch people strolling in all their layers, some with dogs on leashes, or kids with mittens. Before I moved away, I complained about the snow every year. The cold, ice storms, everything. Don't get me wrong, I adore the ocean and heat, but the arctic breeze is a part of me, and I feel at home.

"Hey, Elle."

I flip around and smile. "Hi, Brit. Thanks for meeting me."

Brita hands me a to-go cup from the bakery. Cinnamon and cream steams under my nose. "How are you?"

"A mess," I admit.

She smiles, and props her elbow on the back of the bench, resting her head on her hand. "I heard all about your ex."

"I bet Axel said a lot of things."

Brita clicks her tongue. "I haven't talked to Axel. The only person he'll talk to is Jonas."

We look at each other, both with smirks, and say, "Twins" at the same time.

She takes a sip of her own cup. "I know he's worried about you."

"I made him think that I didn't want to be with him unless Rod gave me the green light. I saw it on his face."

Brita watches a group of teenagers laughing and tossing snowballs at each other as they walk by. "Well, do you?"

"Do I want to be with him?"

"Well, yeah. Or do you want a break? Sometimes a break is a good thing. Jonas and I almost broke up, too, I never thought our families would get along. It wasn't long, but the idea of being apart from him made me die a little inside. It's how I knew he was my guy."

"I already know that, though," I whisper.

Brita offers a small smile. "Then what's the problem?"

I sip the tea a few times; Axel's frustrated, hurt expression bleeds through my thoughts. "He hasn't talked to me. Maybe he needs some time, now."

Brita sighs. "Elle, do you love Axel?"

I nod, clamping my eyes shut. "Crazy love him, Brit. I'm borderline obsessed, I think."

She laughs and slithers her arm around mine. "I know he feels the same."

"I don't know."

"Well, that's the problem then. You need to know that. Axel isn't one to open to just anybody. As fun loving as he is, giving his heart to someone else—we were all starting to think it wouldn't happen. Jonas thinks that's what really hurt Ax so much. He put himself out there, and maybe you didn't believe how much he cares about you."

"I believe him." I say firmly. "But I handled everything wrong, said everything wrong. I freaked out because I was afraid Rodney would come after Axel, you know, maybe even hurt his career or something, but it came out like it didn't matter how Axel felt, only how Rodney felt."

Brita nods. "I don't think you need to worry about his job, but ask

Axel. I understand where your head was, really. But I still think you need to decide what you need right now."

"I want him," I say, softly. "He's your brother-in-law, how do you think I fix it?"

Brita grins. "Well, I'm a big old-fashioned fan of the truth. Talking, listening, those things."

"You think he'll listen?"

Brita snorts. "Elle, I think if you told Axel to jump into that snowbank naked, he'd do it without a second thought. Yes, he'll listen. Doesn't mean he's not a little flustered, maybe you are, too, but one spat isn't enough to toss away the crazy sort of love, is it?"

"No, not with him."

Brita shifts on her seat, one leg tucked beneath her other. "I've got to be honest, Elle. These last few months, I feel like you've become one of my best friends, truly. But I also love Axel, and I want to make sure you're ready for this, for both your sakes. There's no shame after what you've been through if you need more time."

I swipe at my eyes before the cold air freezes tears to my face, and smile through a hiccup. "Brit, the second Axel left my condo, I knew I needed to go right after him. I've been letting Rodney control me, even though we've been split up for nearly a year now, and I don't want to let him anymore. I'm sure he's not finished with me, but I don't even care. Right now, I can hardly breathe thinking of losing Axel."

Brita grins, her eyes glassy like mine. "Then you better go tell him that, right this second."

I blow out a long breath. "I feel like I'm going to throw up."

"Yeah," she says with a smile. "That's a good thing, in my opinion."

We laugh; a weight eases off my shoulders. Brita hugs me before I get into my car, where I sit for another ten minutes.

Turning the key, I carefully back out of the park. "Well," I say out loud, a little pep talk for myself. "Go get your guy, Elle Weber."

CHAPTER 30

J turn around after raising my fist to knock. "He's probably eating, or something."

Quickly, I spin on my heel and start to walk away. With a groan, I force myself to stop. "Come on, Elle." During this time there are many out loud speeches, because sometimes you need to pump yourself up. Holding my breath, I face the door, the anticipation of leather scent causes my mouth to water.

My fist hovers over of the door again. What am I so afraid of? This is Axel; how many times has he professed love for me? And true enough, I believe him. We can talk, it's not like we've been silent that long. Three days. Three measly . . . terrible days.

"Okay," I say under my breath, and knock. Fast and rapid, like my heart.

Now the wait. My insides turn to soup as I clasp my hands in front, but that doesn't feel natural, so they go behind me. Again, not right. Pockets? When the lock clicks on the door, and swings open faster than I'm prepared for, one hand rests on my own cheek, the other awkwardly out to one side. Great opener.

Axel's eyes widen. He's dressed in gray basketball shorts that look amazing, and his T-shirt is damp and sweaty in an ultra-sexy way.

Could've been the three days apart making me think such things, of course. Nope, he is just that easy on my eyes.

He pops earbuds out and I hear the beat of his music.

"Elle?" His voice is husky. "What . . . hi."

My tongue is sticky, half because of nerves, half because I can't take my eyes off his beautiful face. "Hi," I say as I remember how to breathe. Time to just spit it out. "Axel, I love you."

His brow furrows, but I don't give him time to respond.

"As in I love you so much, I can't sleep after what I said; I want you every day. You're the first person I think of in the morning, and the last at night, and then all in between. I love you, and I don't care who knows, or who threatens me for it. I'm a mess, but there's one thing I've never doubted since coming back home, and that's loving you."

Axel hasn't budged. One hand is still on the doorknob, the other rests against the door frame. I blurt everything in two breaths, and now mentally recount what I've said in case I might have offended him in some way. We stand there, staring. My heart feels ready to burst through my skull.

Clearing my throat, I swing my hands at my sides and take a step back. "So, if you want to say anything, that would be great."

Axel opens his mouth, but stumbles a bit on his words. His forehead crinkles and he glances over his shoulder. He holds up a finger, at least I think so, but then he closes the door! Yes, he turns around and closes the door.

Stunned isn't the right word; I'd use shredded. Three days, that's all it took to have Axel Olsen change his mind. I suck in clipped breaths, stupidly standing on his welcome mat. Clutching my throat to slow my pulse, I turn away and stagger down the breezeway toward my building.

My mind goes black. I don't want to think, can't think, or my heart might shrivel into nothing. Being that Axel's building is built on a slope, I climb a few steps to the sidewalk, feet unsteady.

"Elle, wait." I stop on the top step, my heart leaping back into my head as I turn over my shoulder. Axel doesn't bother with a coat, and he'll be blue in a second, but he jogs to the bottom step, sweaty and perfect. "Where are you going?"

I choke on my tears boiling beneath the surface. "Um, you closed the door in my face."

One side of his mouth curls up and my knees threaten to give out. "I told you to hang on for a second."

My mouth parts. "No, you didn't."

He holds up his finger again. "I did that."

"And left me outside."

He chuckles. "Sorry, I'm nervous and had to get something."

"Okay, well it's freezing, want to go back inside? We can talk."

He shakes his head; my hands go numb (not from the cold), but he smiles and climbs the steps until he stands one below me. "No, I don't want to move until I do this. But just so you know, this is not how it played out in my head."

My mitten covered hand catches my gasp when Axel lowers to one knee—right there on the cement steps.

"Elle, I had a really negative way of looking at relationships and love until you." Axel reaches into the pocket of his shorts, and pulls out a blue box. "You came back and knocked me off my feet. From that first date, I knew I wanted to be with you always—"

"What are you doing?" I interrupt.

Axel smirks. "What does it look like?"

I swallow the grit in my throat. "Well, it looks like you're proposing. If your neighbors come out, then they'll think you're proposing, and that's . . . I mean you can't be doing that because we haven't spoken in three days, and you told me you needed to think. Now, you're holding a ring box. Oh, my gosh, are you proposing? Out here, on the stairs? In shorts? It's fifteen degrees."

"Are you finished being weird?" he asks with a grin, unmoved and still holding his little box.

I nod vigorously, hugging my middle. "I think so."

He laughs. "Okay, as I was saying. This week has flipped us upside down a bit, but not once did I question how I feel about you. I planned on waiting until we'd dated for a year or so since everyone says that's the best way to do this, but you know what, I don't care what other people say. So, Elle Weber, yes, I'm asking you to marry me."

Behind my gloves I suck in a sharp breath. It's a little embarrassing, but I can't find the will to stop breathing weird. He keeps his eyes on me, down on one knee, a beautiful ring gleaming in the winter sun.

"Axel . . ." I sniffle and finally lower my hand. "You want to marry me?"

"I've wanted to marry you for a few months," he says. "But I'm sitting here now, freezing, hoping you'll answer my question."

"Yes! *Yes*, I'll marry you tomorrow if you want."

I don't wait for him to slip the ring on before I have my lips on his. I kiss him, and kiss him, and yes, kiss him some more.

"When did you get this?" I ask, between kisses.

He smiles against my lips, his arms tight around my waist. "When I bought your necklace."

I trap his face between my hands. "I love you."

Axel rests his forehead against my own. "I love you, too. But mind if we go inside? I can't feel my legs."

Inside, I kiss him a million times more, we drink hot chocolate, he kisses me. He takes a shower, I stare at the ring. I taste his lips a bit more, before we make our way to announce the good news to family and friends—but that basically means family.

My dad shakes Axel's hand, my mom squeezes him to death. The sneaks have known he planned to ask me since Christmas. Maya squeals and Graham seems relieved to have another brother-in-law he actually gets along with.

The Olsens and, yes, the Jacobsons were a different story. We are passed around like cake, laughing, hugging, eating. I breathe in all the smells of flour, sugar, sweet flaky crusts. Closing my eyes, I know this is all going to be part of my life, and I can't imagine it any other way.

"I told you it was a good idea to go talk with him," Brita whispers.

"You knew he had this?"

She scoffs. "Are you kidding, I directed him to the best jeweler in Minneapolis."

"Brit, I've been married before, but I didn't know it could feel like this," I say.

Tears brim in her eyes. "Well, I'd say that means you're off to a pretty great start."

Axel pulls me close when the excitement dies down later that night. He kisses my head, and twirls the ring around my finger, simply grinning.

"I never thought I'd be here," he admits.

I nuzzle my head against his neck. "I'm glad you picked me."

With a nudge to my chin, he tilts my mouth to his. The man has a way of cutting off my brain function with a single glance. "Same, Elle. Thank you for picking me."

I wish life went on without a blip from that night forward, but there is still the matter of dealing with threats at work. The next Monday, the hospital human resources calls a meeting with Jason, the CEO, Roonie the director of nursing, and of course Rodney saw to it that Axel and Nick were asked to be in the room.

Axel holds my hand as we walk toward the conference room.

"Ax, what if he made up terrible things."

He kisses the top of my hand and grins. "We'll be fine. I mean it, Elle. There's no evidence that we did anything wrong besides what he might've said."

I squeeze his hand tighter, until I let go to walk into the room.

"Good morning," Jason says. He stands and buttons the center button of his suit. Jason is a young CEO, and has a pleasant smile. I don't know Jason well, he'd stepped into the position a month before my marriage crumbled, and at that point Rodney wasn't bringing me to the executive company parties.

Mr. Gregory, the hospital director, and the human resource lady, Patty, sit in the back; she keeps a three ringed binder open on her lap.

"Have a seat," Jason says, still smiling. A smile is good, I hope.

We all take the invitation. My pulse is in my stomach, and my hands feel so sweaty I need to wipe them on my scrubs.

Jason settles back in his seat and crosses a leg. The longer he talks the more southern he sounds. "Well, from what I've been told y'all have had a bit of an upset around here. Care to tell me your side of things. Let's start with you, Miss Weber."

I swallow; Axel flashes me a small grin. "Yes. I'm sure this is regarding Mr. Mitchell and myself. You likely know, I was married to Mr. Mitchell, and we didn't have an amicable divorce. I transferred here on his request and I thought that would be the end of it. However, during the visits for the remodel, Mr. Mitchell found out I was seeing Mr. Olsen, and then proceeded to threaten us both with our jobs."

Jason keeps reading a piece of paper, he nods, looks up sometimes, then back down again. After I finish, he steeples his fingers in front of his mouth. "You understand, Rod gave a different account." Jason squints at a sheet Patty hands him. "He states you defaced his office in Charlotte and physically assaulted him after your divorce at his house. He said Kathy Higgins needed to escort you off the property at the hospital down south."

"That isn't true—"

Jason smiles, and holds up his hand. "He goes on to explain meeting here, and you—and I quote—caused a hysterical confrontation amid patients who then feared for their safety. He offered to provide witnesses upon request. He also goes on to describe inappropriate behavior in the offices between you and Mr. Olsen, but we don't need to go into that."

"Sir, with all due respect," Axel says, "none of that's true. Elle has never been unprofessional, and I saw that confrontation. He had his hands on her and pressed her against the wall, forcefully. It wasn't her, at all."

Jason nods, and leans over the table after a moment. "Oh, I believe you." The room goes dead quiet for several breaths until Jason laughs. "I do. Mr. Olsen, you've never been at risk of losing your position, as much as Rod would've liked. As you well know our therapy staff is contracted and not actually employees of the hospital, but employees of Therapeutix, our contracting company."

Axel nods.

I narrow my eyes. "What? You never said that."

"Jonas got all lawyerly for me and Nick after I told him what happened, and he checked it out to be sure. Sorry I forgot to say anything," he whispers.

Jason leans back in his chair. "Besides, I value the input of our directors more than a supposed list of witnesses in the form of interns too afraid to speak out against the boss, and Nick here only speaks highly of you."

Nick claps Axel on the back. "He's one of our best."

Jason takes a pen and rolls it between his thumb and index finger. "Now, Miss Weber, regarding your situation. I want you to know that I was unaware of what happened in Charlotte. It all happened, I'm afraid, when I was home with my wife and newborn daughter."

Patty taps the table. "Congratulations."

"Thank you," he acknowledges. "The point is I suspect the transfer was kept from me or, not to theorize, but possibly misdirected from my notice. I've spoken with Kathy Higgins, and she has since presented me with many reports given by several department heads in Charlotte, all speaking in your favor. She also provided a very convincing pattern of behaviors, complete with a timeline, that showed Mr. Mitchell's inappropriate treatment of you, even after your divorce."

I smile. "The sounds like Kathy. She's very thorough."

Jason folds his arms with a grin. "Your coworkers here in Lindström have nothing but positive compliments of you, as well." Jason looks to the hospital director who nods importantly. Then he reads from a piece of paper. "A Miss Vivian Pompeo also stated she witnessed Mr. Mitchell use physical force against you, along with corroboration by two nursing assistants and a member of the housekeeping crew, who said, quote, 'the man dragged the nurse by the arm and shoved her into a corner.'"

Jason leans forward, and I clutch Axel's hand, unable to breathe.

"Elle, do you mind if I call you, Elle?"

"No, sir."

"I take mistreatment and abuse of power very seriously. I started with this company as a nursing aide, did you know that?"

I shake my head. "No, I didn't know you had a nursing degree."

He chuckles. "Oh, I don't. I switched to business, but I was always treated well, no matter what level I was at, and I have no patience for the leadership of this company using that status against anyone else. Before I head back to Charlotte, I felt it important to call you in here, so I might personally tell both of you that this won't be a problem any longer."

I release a shaky breath and dare a smile. "Really? We get to keep our jobs?"

"I hope you stay until you retire. I've also placed Mr. Mitchell on administrative leave, pending an investigation on his behavior. Given that you were forced to transfer under questionable circumstances, I'd like to offer you the opportunity to return to Charlotte, and have your old job. If you'd like."

My cheeks heat as I glance at Axel. I shake my head. "Thank you, sir, but I'm going to stay in Lindström. I'm exactly where I belong."

EPILOGUE

Summer carries magic. I've always loved the scent of fresh cut grass and warm breezes. Even the sky has an aroma in the summer, like I can smell the bright blue. With the window cracked just so, I breathe deeply the scents of summer. Each breath brings a calm to my upset stomach and fiery heartbeat.

A knock comes to the door; a door tall enough a ten-foot man can slip inside. My dad pokes his head in, smiling ear to ear. "Elle, it's time."

My grin flashes, but soon green queasiness forces me to close my eyes and gasp in the fresh afternoon air.

"You okay, kiddo?" Dad closes the door and crosses the room in ten steps.

Tears! Really, right now? Makeup will run, then where will I be? I offer my dad a watery grin. "I'm fine."

He tilts his head and quickly has me against his chest. "Come on kid, what's up?"

I sniff, masterfully focused on keeping the tears from spilling onto my freshly mascaraed eyelashes. "It feels so different this time, but I don't ever want to do that again."

He pulls my shoulders back, and stares at me. "What are you talking about?"

"I don't want a repeat of what happened with Rod."

Dad smiles and brushes a wisp of hair off my forehead. "Elle, sweetheart, no one knows what the future is going to bring, but that shouldn't keep you from living."

"I know, I really do, it's just a thought that's there sometimes."

"Tell it to leave," he says softly.

I roll my eyes.

"I'm serious." My dad takes my hand between his. "I want you to hear me, Elle. There isn't a comparison to this day and the day we flew to Charlotte to watch you get married in a smelly room, with a bald, grumpy judge. That day, I felt like throwing up."

"Pleasant," I try to laugh.

"I'm serious. You forced your smile that day, forced your optimism. It wasn't what you wanted, and I knew it, your mom knew it, so did Maya. I was heartbroken when we left because I'd watched my daughter settle. *You* just didn't know it yet. But," he says, squeezing my hand. "Today, my heart is soaring. I see light in your eyes, Elle. You hope again, laugh. And even more important to me, as your father, I see a guy that looks at you like he'd go to the ends of the earth to make you happy. That's the look I've waited for you since you started noticing guys. I've no worries about your future kid, and if it matters, I think you're making one heck of a choice. That's not so easy for a dad to say, you know."

Forget the dripping tears, I let one fall as I fling my arms around my dad's neck. "Thanks, Dad."

He pats my back gently, and clears his throat, his own eyes a little wet. "Alright then, are you ready?"

"I'm so ready."

The marble halls seem to glow in gold as the sun starts to set in the distance, and the bits of glitter on my white dress sparkle like stars. My dad kisses my cheek as the two ushers open the doors and I embrace my new beginning—my true new beginning. I see my mom first, wrangling my new nephew. The cutest little guy I've ever seen, but Maya and Graham have their hands full starting parenthood at age one, instead of newborn. Mom tries to direct his attention toward Dad and me, but he simply giggles as my mom blows raspberries in his chubby little neck.

Viv and Spence, Jax and Abby, Mack and Kari all sit near the back. Viv dabs at her eyes when I take the first step forward. Jonas, Bastien and Graham stand at the front, dapper and pressed in suits. Maya and Brita are opposite the guys, smiling ear to ear. It isn't that noticeable in Brita's flowy dress, but I can see the tiny bump. June hit, and the little guy or gal popped, and Brita couldn't hide it anymore. Of course, Axel and I knew early on, the twin shared thoughts thing—it's real. Everyone I love is in one place. My smile can't be helped, nor the tears of bliss. That's the word I'd use—bliss.

There are moments in life you wish you could capture as mental pictures to keep forever. The way pale flowers in glass vases line the aisle might be one. Rows of family, friends, coworkers, perhaps another. But my eyes find the sight I never wish to forget. Axel's smile fades when he sees me, his hand splays over his chest as if his heart thunders the same as mine. His gaze falls to the white runner at his feet, and I am certain the pulse in his jaw means his own tears spring to his eyes—relentless little pests, mine drip shamelessly down my cheeks.

That moment, when he lifts his eyes to me again, I'll cherish forever. When my hand passes to his, and he presses my fingers to his lips, I feel beautifully calm, beautifully right. And when Axel kisses me, when he becomes mine forever, well some instances are impressed on a mind in one breathtaking image until a heart stops beating; never lost.

How strange it is, not long ago I made little fuss about love and romance. Such things caused agony, and heartbreak. But looking back, the speedbumps along the way led me to this moment. A moment where I hand my heart to Axel Olsen, and he promises to keep it safe forever.

And without question, I keep his.

ACKNOWLEDGMENTS

There have been a great many people who have helped this series come about. Sara and Larissa for your feedback, my mom who loves sweet romance, my sisters who like a little saucier love stories and help me find the balance, and my husband and kids. Thank you for always supporting me on this wild ride.

Thank you to Jennifer Murgia for your fabulous edits and smoothing out the rough spots. And of course thank you to the readers of this book and my others. I am so grateful for your support and hope to send you many more sweet stories.

Made in the USA
Las Vegas, NV
19 June 2022

50428299R00125